D0044201

DYING
ON THE
Vine

ALSO BY MARLA COOPER

Terror in Taffeta

DYING
ON THE
Vine

MARLA COOPER

MINOTAUR BOOKS

A THOMAS DUNNE BOOK

A THOMAS DUNNE BOOK FOR MINOTAUR BOOKS.
An imprint of St. Martin's Press.

DYING ON THE VINE. Copyright © 2017 by Marla Cooper. All rights reserved.
Printed in the United States of America. For information, address
St. Martin's Press, 175 Fifth Avenue, New York, N.Y. 10010.

www.thomasdunnebooks.com
www.minotaurbooks.com

Library of Congress Cataloging-in-Publication Data

Names: Cooper, Marla, author.
Title: Dying on the vine : a mystery / Marla Cooper.
Description: First edition. | New York : Minotaur Books, 2017. | Series: Kelsey
  Mckenna destination wedding mysteries ; 2
Identifiers: LCCN 2016047071| ISBN 9781250072559 (hardcover) |
  ISBN 9781466884373 (ebook)
Subjects: LCSH: Wedding supplies and services industry—Fiction. |
  Weddings—Planning—Fiction. | Murder—Fiction. | BISAC: FICTION /
  Mystery & Detective / Women Sleuths. | GSAFD: Mystery fiction. |
  Humorous fiction.
Classification: LCC PS3603.O582696 D95 2017 | DDC 813/.6—dc23
LC record available at https://lccn.loc.gov/2016047071

Our books may be purchased in bulk for promotional, educational,
or business use. Please contact your local bookseller or the Macmillan
Corporate and Premium Sales Department at 1-800-221-7945, extension 5442,
or by e-mail at MacmillanSpecialMarkets@macmillan.com.

First Edition: April 2017

10 9 8 7 6 5 4 3 2 1

For my mom, Maribelle, who taught me how to laugh

ACKNOWLEDGMENTS

Thanks to my agent, Jill Marsal, and my original editor, Anne Brewer, for getting this series out into the world, and to Melanie Fried and Alicia Clancy, for shepherding this book along. Another big thanks to Shailyn Tavella and Alison Ziegler, for helping get the word out and for their general awesomeness.

Thanks to my amazing writing group—namely Daisy Bateman, Madeleine Butler, Sharon Johnson, Kirsten Saxton, Karen Catalona, and Cornelia Read—for giving me such thoughtful feedback on my entire manuscript even though it was only my second meeting. And to Diana Orgain and Laura-Kate Rurka, who were there from the start as the story took shape.

Thanks to the amazing community of mystery writers I've met along the way, including Sisters in Crime, the Guppies, and my fellow bloggers at Chicks on the Case: Lisa Q. Mathews, Kellye Garrett, and Ellen Byron.

And, finally, thanks to my family and friends who cheered me along. Your support and enthusiasm have meant the world to me.

DYING ON THE Vine

CHAPTER 1

There was an air of excitement as brides-to-be and their entourages streamed through the front entrance of the Wine Country Wedding Faire. Some of them were hoping to find a venue that was somehow both rustic and modern. Some were looking for a baker who could make their wedding cake look like the one they found on Pinterest. Some were searching for a magical bridesmaid dress that would flatter both their childhood best friend *and* their supermodel-tall college roommate.

I just wanted to find a parking space.

I'd promised my friend Brody Marx that I'd hang out with him at his booth during the midday crush at the biggest bridal event in Northern California.

"Join me," he'd said. "It'll be fun," he'd said.

I'm sleeping in, is what I should have said.

It was going to be hard work. It was going to involve hours of standing. It was going to mean smiling until my cheeks hurt. But I had to admit, it was a good place to network, and, hey, free cupcakes. Maybe while I was there, I could even get to the bottom of why it was a "faire" instead of a "fair"—like the extra *e* makes it extra classy or something.

After circling the parking lot for several minutes, I was finally able to squeeze between two huge SUVs wedged into spots that were clearly labeled "Compact Only." I grabbed the box of brochures Brody had asked me to bring and balanced them on my right hip for the hike to the entrance.

I smiled to myself as I thought of all the reasons I love my job as a wedding planner. I got to be there for the happiest day in someone's life about twenty times a year. I got to travel to destinations all over the world and rack up thousands of frequent-flier miles. And now I was about to spend the day with one of my favorite people. Life wasn't all bad.

"Kelsey, where have you been?" Brody hissed the second I got to his booth. "Did you get my text?"

"Well, hello to you, too," I said, foisting the box of brochures into his arms.

"I'm up to my ears in happy people," he whispered, jerking his head toward the mob surrounding his table. "They're nuts!"

"Sorry I'm late," I said. "There was a—"

"Yeah, yeah, yeah." He thrust the box back into my hands. "Go put these out on the table for me while I run to the bathroom, okay? I don't want to be known as the wedding photographer who wet his pants."

"I don't know, I think it has a certain panache." I set the box on the floor as he sprinted toward the back hall.

A pretty brunette and her fiancé were thumbing through one of Brody's albums, oohing and aahing over his editorial-style engagement photos. "Where were these taken?" the bride asked me. "I want this same backdrop!"

I craned my neck to look at the shots, but I didn't recognize the setting. "I'm not sure, but Brody will be back in a second. He's the photographer."

"How much does he charge?" asked the brunette's fiancé.

"Let me find you a rate card," I said, searching the printed materials Brody had laid out on the table. Why hadn't he given me an orientation before he'd bolted for the men's room?

"Is he available the first weekend in November?" asked an eager-looking redhead.

Now, where had he put his calendar? I smiled and held up a finger. "Um, if you could just give me one second. . . ."

Before I could explain, the girl looked at her friend and whispered, "He needs to get a new assistant."

You got that right, lady.

I took a deep breath, did a quick assessment of who was serious and who was just window-shopping, and got busy answering questions. I found his appointment book, scheduled him two consults, and was fairly sure I'd even managed to sell one couple his most expensive photography package. He so owed me for this.

I saw Brody down the row, snagging a stuffed mushroom from a caterer who was offering samples. This was no time for snacks. I darted over to Brody and grabbed him by the arm, pulling him back toward his booth. "Break time's over. Sorry, but they're like a pack of rabid wolves over there!"

"Now you see what I've been dealing with all morning."

"Well, don't worry," I said reassuringly. "I'm here now."

He slowed down long enough to give me a quick squeeze. "Thanks, Kelsey. This'll go a lot easier with you here."

"Don't mention it." I stopped in my tracks as I noticed a booth down the row that rented out special-occasion kilts for betrothed Scots. "Ooh! Can I talk in a Scottish accent if I get bored?"

"If you must."

I nodded. "I think I must. We should both do it!"

"Aye, then. *Haud your wheesht,* lassie."

I stopped and looked at Brody. "*Haud* my what now?"

"I was speaking Scottish."

"That's not Scottish. That's, like, pirate or something."

"Fine," he said, ducking back behind the table. "We'll work on it later."

The next few hours passed quickly as Brody and I hit our stride. By midafternoon, I'd become an expert on every detail of his photography business and I was kind of enjoying working the crowd.

"Hey, Kelsey," Brody said, wiggling his finger at me. "Come here for a second."

I pretend-scowled at him, then turned to the couple I'd been talking to. "Excuse me, I'm being summoned."

"This is Haley Bennett and Christopher Riegert," he said, motioning to a couple in their late twenties. Haley was a cute blonde with a pixie cut and bright red lipstick, and Christopher had faux-nerdy glasses and a bushy beard. Together, they looked like an indie rock band from Brooklyn.

"Nice to meet you," I replied with a smile. "Whatever he told you, it's not true."

"I told them you were awesome," he said, "but you're right, I take it back."

"Oh, well, in that case, you should listen to everything Brody says."

Haley giggled as she shook my hand. "You guys are such a cute couple."

"Oh, no," I said. "We're not—"

Brody laughed and put one arm around my shoulder. "Oh, come on, darling, don't be that way."

I wriggled out of his grasp, laughing, and punched him in the arm. "Cut it out! That's how rumors get started."

"She's just mad because I hog the blankets," Brody said, a twinkle in his eye.

I blushed a little, despite myself. I was always surprised when people thought Brody and I were dating. I mean, sure, he was good-looking, but it was so obvious that I wasn't his type. In fact, I was off by a whole Y chromosome. No reason to let that stand in the way of a beautiful friendship, though.

"These two are getting married in Napa and they need a wedding planner," Brody said. "And Kelsey here *is* a wedding planner, and a fabulous one, at that. What a coincidence! Talk amongst yourselves."

"So, any chance you're free on the eighteenth?" Haley asked hopefully.

"What month?" I asked.

"Next month. In four weeks."

"Four weeks? That's *soon*."

"I know. I'm sorry." The bride-to-be looked chagrined. "Most of the planning is already taken care of, so all we need is a day-of wedding coordinator. Do you do that sort of thing?"

"I do offer a day-of package, but I'd have to check my calendar." I thought about my assistant Laurel and how she'd been dying to take on more duties. We could probably divide and conquer. "I'll tell you what, why don't you call my office tomorrow? I'm sure I can figure out a way to make it work."

"That would be amazing!" Haley said, her face beaming a radiant smile.

I liked her. And I had to admit, these quick little meet-and-greets were a great way to prescreen clients, kind of like speed dating. We made an appointment for the very next day.

The afternoon flew by and the crowds finally started to thin out a little. Brody even let me take a break, after extracting a promise that I'd bring him back one of the signature cocktails they were serving at the bar.

"One lavender lemonade with vodka, coming up!" I said as I darted away.

The line was long but seemed to be moving quickly. As I joined the queue, I recognized a Silicon Valley couple I'd met earlier at Brody's table. They'd spent quite a while flipping through Brody's sample albums, and if I remembered correctly, they'd let out quite a few appreciative murmurs.

"Hi," I said. "You having fun?"

"It's fun, but the crowds are kind of getting to us," the bride-to-be said. "I had to promise Raj a beer to keep him from abandoning me."

"It's enough to make you want to elope," her fiancé said.

"Well, hang in there. The drinks should help."

The bride looked at me and tilted her head. "You were at the photography booth, right? Great work."

"Thanks!" I said. "I mean, it's not my work, but I'm glad you liked it. Did you get a business card?"

"I think so," she said, lifting up her official Wine Country Wedding Faire tote bag. "Although who knows if I'll ever be able to find it in all this."

"Maybe we should get his number just to be sure," said Raj.

I whipped out my iPhone, eager to help Brody land the gig. "Here, I can give it to you." I read off the numbers as Raj punched them into his phone.

"Well, well, well. What have we here?" said a man's voice from behind me. I turned around to find myself facing Stefan Pierce, an assistant to one of the most prominent wedding planners in Northern California, giving me a look that could have wilted a bridal bouquet.

Dang it. If I'd only seen him coming, I could have avoided him. Over the years, I'd run into him occasionally at industry events like this one, and it was never a pleasant experience. He'd always been fairly obnoxious, but even more so since he'd landed a gig working for Babs Norton, the self-proclaimed Queen of Wine Country Weddings.

"Hello, Stefan," I said. "I was just—"

"Trying to steal a client?" he said. He tried to sound light-hearted, but there was a definite edge to his voice.

"No! Not at all. I'm here helping Brody and they were interested in using him."

"Mmm-hmm," he said as he looked me up and down. "These two have already signed a contract with Babs, so they won't be needing your help."

Did he really think I was trying to woo a client away from him and Babs? "Seriously, Stefan, I was just giving them Brody's number."

"It's true," Raj said, holding up his phone as proof.

Stefan pressed his lips together in his best imitation of a smile. "Babs and I will make sure they connect. Thanks, anyway." And with that, he steered the couple off toward a display of place settings, as the bride gave me an apologetic look over her shoulder and the groom looked longingly toward the bar.

I took a deep breath and counted to ten. No way was I going to let Stefan get under my skin. Why would he consider me competition, anyway? Babs wasn't threatened by me. She threw absolutely amazing weddings for anyone who could afford them. I mean, it's not exactly like we attracted the same clientele.

I blew out a deep breath. *Shake it off.*

I returned to Brody's booth, drinks in hand, to finish out my shift.

"Guess who I just ran into?" I asked. "Stefan Pierce."

"Ewww," Brody said. "The 'Ankle Biter'? I'm sorry."

I laughed. I'd forgotten about the secret nickname Stefan had earned among many of the local wedding vendors because of his frequent tendency to behave like an irate Chihuahua. Why Babs had hired the petty, temperamental Stefan I'd never know, but they seemed to get along fine. She told me once that she appreciated what she kindly referred to as his "tenacity."

Thank God I had time to slurp down my spiked lemonade, because twenty minutes later who should appear but Babs Norton herself, followed by Stefan and the couple I'd talked to at the bar.

"Hello, Kelsey," Babs said, air-kissing me once on each cheek. "These two wanted to speak to your photographer friend again before they left." She arched one eyebrow at me. "Stefan tells me you met them, as well?"

"I did, yes."

Babs pulled me aside as the couple chatted with Brody at the end of the table and Stefan hovered nearby. "Well, I can't blame you for trying," she said, whispering theatrically. "They're *loaded.*"

I shot Stefan a look. "I promise you, Babs, I was only trying to give them Brody's phone number when we got interrupted."

Stefan crossed his arms in front of his chest. "Just in the nick of time, or so it appeared."

"No harm," Babs said, gesturing to her attack dog to stand down. "There's no way you could have known they were working with us."

Stefan snorted, then said under his breath, "Besides, they were looking for something a little more . . . *refined* than what you typically do."

"Now, Stefan, Kelsey does perfectly lovely weddings," Babs said before I could protest. "We have different styles, that's all."

"Thanks, Babs," I said. *I think.*

"If you say so," Stefan muttered. He looked dejected that she hadn't commanded him to chomp on my Achilles tendon.

I thought it was time for a good old-fashioned change of subject. "So, where's your booth?"

Babs laughed merrily. "Oh, I'm not an exhibitor. *Heavens.*"

"Hardly," said Stefan, puffing out his chest. "We have *plenty* of business as it is."

"I only came by because I'm a featured sponsor," Babs said, waving her hand in a flourish. "Didn't you see the grand prize? It's a wedding planned by me, and it's going to be absolutely fabulous!"

Of course. Heaven forbid Babs Norton should have to do anything so pedestrian as peddle her services at a bridal-fair booth.

"That's terrific," I said, trying hard to sound enthusiastic. "I'm sure you'll make some couple very happy."

Babs turned back to the couple. "Okay, kids, I have Brody's information. We have a lot we need to accomplish today, so let's not dillydally."

Stefan lingered behind long enough to get in the last word. "Good luck finding some new clients." His sarcastic tone told me he didn't really mean it. "But in the meantime, stay away from *ours.*"

CHAPTER 2

The next morning, I got to the office early. Well, early for me, considering my long-standing grudge against mornings in general. My assistant Laurel, on the other hand? Total morning person. She'd probably already been out for a six-mile run and volunteered at a soup kitchen on her way in.

"Laurel?" I called out as I walked up the stairs to our sunny office space on the second floor of a restored Victorian. There was no answer, so I dropped my bag in my office before yelling down the hall. "Laurel? Don't tell me I got here before you!"

"Kelsey? Is that you?" She popped her head out from the kitchen. "Have you had coffee? Because I just made myself a cappuccino and I can make you one, too!"

"Oooh, fancy," I said. "It's like having my very own barista." Laurel had set us up with an impressive brewing station that whipped up lattes in mere seconds. She said it was for clients, but I suspected it was meant to help keep us at our enthusiastic best.

She pressed some buttons on the bulky, overpriced machine and grabbed my favorite mug from the cabinet. "So how was the wedding fair? Oh, we got a call from a couple you met there.

Haley and Christopher? They're coming in later this afternoon. You had an opening at three."

"Oh, good," I said. "They're adorable. They're getting married in Napa on the eighteenth. But you probably know that already."

"You had me at 'They're getting married.' Count me in." I knew Laurel wanted to take on more responsibilities, and with wedding season approaching, I was excited for her to get her chance.

Laurel handed me the steaming mug topped with frothy foam. "Here you go. I was thinking if you had time, we could go over the notes for the Catalina Island wedding, and then I had some ideas for our website. I was also thinking we should start a blog."

I laughed. "Okay, slacker. Too bad I can't get you more interested in the business." Even though it was going to take about three more grandes to catch up with her, I loved her enthusiasm. When I first hired her, I thought she was trying to impress me with her initiative, but it turned out that that's just her personality.

We settled in for our Monday morning meeting and divvied up our task list. It turned out to be a pretty easy day—a few calls for me, a few invoices for Laurel, a longish lunch where we talked about work just long enough to make our salads tax-deductible—and it was three o'clock before I knew it.

When the buzzer rang, I ran down to let Haley and Christopher in, then escorted them to our meeting room, a cozy space I'd furnished with an orange love seat, two chairs, and a coffee table. They took the love seat, of course. Couples always do.

"I looked at your website last night after we got home," Haley began. "You're a destination wedding planner, right? Does Napa still count as a destination?"

"Believe me," I said, "it counts. Actually, the wine country is one of the most popular places for a destination wedding in the United States, so it's kind of a no-brainer for me. I'm just lucky to be geographically advantaged that way."

"That's perfect, then," said Haley. "It should be a piece of cake."

"Any chance you can help with the rehearsal dinner, too?" Christopher asked. "I have a huge family coming in from all over the country, so it's going to be a little nuts."

"Yeah," said Haley, "they think we're throwing them a family reunion!"

"That's not unusual," I said, laughing. "Are they wine lovers?"

"Oh, yeah," Christopher said, "my parents *love* wine. That's why they buy the extra-large boxes of it."

Haley giggled at Christopher's joke, then added: "I wouldn't say anyone's really a wine aficionado, but they all love a good party."

No wine snobs on the guest list? *Awesome.* Don't get me wrong; I can work with even the pickiest of palates, and I can talk *terroir* with the best of them, but Haley and Christopher's families sounded fun and low maintenance. "That sounds great. I'm happy to help with both." I poised my pen to write. "So what's the venue?"

"Higgins Estate," Haley said. "Out on Silverado Trail?"

"Yes, of course. It's a gorgeous place." I tried not to let my surprise show. Higgins was one of the most elegant wineries in all of Napa, with a huge château perched above rolling hills. It was a popular spot for high-end weddings, and it fetched an exorbitant rental fee. Not that there's anything wrong with that. I just wouldn't have chosen it for them myself.

Haley chewed her lip anxiously. "But? I'm sensing a 'but.'"

"No, no buts," I reassured her. "It's lovely. They're sticklers for the rules, but I can work with that. Sounds like they may have even lightened up a little. A couple of years ago, they wouldn't have even let you book it without going through one of their approved wedding planners."

Haley's eyes widened with surprise. "Really!? I didn't realize you *had* to have one."

"Well, I mean, clearly they've relaxed the rules if they let you book it."

"They didn't," said Haley. "I mean, they did let us book it, but—"

"But it was through that other lady," Christopher said.

I was confused. "Wait, what other lady?" *And why do you both look so sheepish?*

"I guess I should have mentioned it before," Haley said. "We did have a wedding planner, but she was kinda pushy. In fact, she's the one who insisted we go to Higgins in the first place."

I was getting a bad feeling. Pushy? Insisting? Surely it wasn't . . .

"Babs Norton," Haley said. "Do you know her?"

I let out the breath I didn't know I'd been holding. *Babs.* And here things had been going so well.

"I do know her." I tried to keep my expression neutral. "So what happened?"

Christopher and Haley looked at each other. "Well, she was great," said Haley, "but she was kind of bossy. She kept telling us who we *must* hire and what we *must* do."

I wasn't surprised. Babs threw impeccable weddings, but she could be a bit opinionated. Most people just considered it part of her special charm. After all, you don't get to be the Queen of Wine Country Weddings by leaving things to chance.

"So you parted ways?"

"Not because of that. My dad thought she was being too extravagant, so he set up a meeting with her. I don't know what happened, but they got into an argument. And, well, I guess he sort of fired her."

Whoa. Someone had actually fired Babs? That was news.

"It was kind of a heat-of-the-moment thing," Haley continued. "Once Dad cooled down, he wanted to just forget about it and move on, but the damage was already done. Now she won't return our calls!"

I blew out a breath. Was this going to be weird, me taking on Babs' former clients? I could see how it might look, especially after the scene Stefan had caused at the wedding fair. Then again, I was sure Babs had collected a hefty cancellation fee from them, and it's not like her Pomeranians were going to go hungry. *Ah, screw it.* Surely Babs would understand, and she was the only one whose opinion I really cared about.

"What the heck," I said. "I'll do it. I'm going to have my assistant Laurel help out, and I promise we'll make it awesome."

"Oh, thank you!" said Haley. "You won't regret it."

I excused myself for a moment and walked down the hall to Laurel's office. "Laurel?" I said, rapping on her door. "Have you got a second? I'd like to introduce you to our newest clients."

Laurel's eyes lit up. "I'd love to!" she squealed. She leapt from her chair and checked the large, gilt-frame mirror that hung on the wall of her office, fingercombed her blond bangs and checked her teeth for leafy green bits, and then followed me back down the hall into the meeting room.

"Haley, Christopher, I'd like you to meet my assistant Laurel. I'm going to have her get you guys started, if that's okay. I have a couple things I need to take care of."

"Thanks, Kelsey," said Haley, hugging me impulsively. "I'm thrilled we're going to be working together."

"Me too. We'll talk soon," I promised, waving as I pulled the door shut behind me.

I thought about Babs. Would she really be okay with me taking on her clients? I mean, it's not like I sought them out. Normally I wouldn't have given it a second thought, but after the incident at the bridal fair I had no doubt Stefan was going to cause a stink.

Only one way to find out. I went back to my office and dialed her number. She answered on the third ring, and after a few pleasantries I launched right in. "I had a meeting today with a couple I met at the wedding fair yesterday. Haley Bennett and Christopher Riegert?"

"Oh. Yes." Her tone wasn't betraying much, but I could imagine that she was pursing her lips. "I trust they're well?"

"They are. The thing is, they came to me looking for a wedding planner. . . ."

"Did they, now?" I could almost hear an eyebrow arching.

"I met them yesterday, but I didn't realize they'd already been working with you."

"So this is my courtesy call?"

"I'm sorry, Babs. I just wanted you to hear it from me." *And not from Stefan.* I didn't need him causing any more friction between me and Babs.

She paused for a moment, then blew out a breath. "It's fine. Water under the bridge."

"So you don't mind if I take them on as clients?"

"Now, Kelsey, it's not like you need my permission. We're all adults here."

Well, two of us are. "I know, it's just—after everything with Stefan yesterday . . ."

"Oh, don't worry about him. Look, these things happen. And business is business, right?"

"All right, as long as you're okay, that's all that matters. Thanks for understanding."

"Of course! Someone's got to do it, right? And if it's not going to be me, I'm glad it's going to be you."

Whew. Weirdness averted.

"In fact, why don't you come by first thing tomorrow morning and I'll give you all their files."

I hesitated. "Any chance I could send a courier over for them?"

"Stefan has an appointment and won't be in until ten, if that's what you're worried about."

I laughed. "In that case, I'll see you at nine."

The next morning, I stopped by a pastry shop near Babs' office to stock up on baked goods. I was so relieved that this wasn't going to be an issue between us, and I wanted to express my appreciation in my favorite way: with food. I'd pick up the files, we'd eat mini scones, we'd laugh and chat, and everything would be fine.

When I got to the ornate building in Pacific Heights where Babs' office was located, I circled the block until I found a spot, then I grabbed the box and trudged up the hill to her front door.

I buzzed and waited for someone to let me in. Why didn't I have a jacket? The morning fog hadn't burned off yet and it was still chilly outside. I buzzed again, feeling impatient. If she didn't let me in soon, I was going to have to eat all the pastries and she'd have no one to blame but herself.

I pulled out my phone to call up, but before I had a chance to dial, the door opened and a young man in his twenties came through, winding a scarf around his neck. I ducked past him and darted into the marble hallway, relieved to be out of the cold air.

An old-fashioned brass dial showed that the elevator was already in use, so I climbed to the second floor. I knocked, but no one answered. Had I really beaten her to the office? Dang it, she must have forgotten about our appointment. On a whim, I turned the doorknob and was surprised to find it unlocked. Maybe I'd just leave the box on her desk with a note to call me.

"Hello? Babs?" I called, in case she was there but had been ignoring all my buzzing, phoning, and knocking. I stepped inside her gorgeously furnished front office and had the urge to take off my shoes so I didn't sully the hand-tufted silk rug under my feet.

"Anyone here?" No answer. I tiptoed across the room toward her office but found it empty. I paused. This was creepy. I mean, right? My intentions were good, but I shouldn't have been there.

Right behind me, a loud, jangly noise caused me to jump so fast that I actually threw the pastry box into the air, causing fresh baked goods to rain down around me. It was her phone. *Who still uses landlines?* I wondered, trying to quell the pounding in my chest.

I dropped to my knees and started gathering pastries up off the carpet. Oh, why had I included croissants? It would take me half an hour to remove evidence of their flaky goodness. I crawled across the carpet to chase down a cruller that had rolled under a high-legged couch that sat a few feet in front of a wall of bookcases. I bent my head toward the floor to see where the cruller had gone, but let out a yelp when I saw a pair of eyes staring back at me.

"Babs! I'm so sorry!" I said, shooting up off the floor. "I knocked, but no one answered."

I waited a beat, but she said nothing in response. What was she doing back there?

"Babs?" I popped back down to the floor again, prepared to launch into a lengthy apology for breaking and entering. But when I saw her vacant stare, I could tell no apology would be necessary.

Babs Norton was dead.

CHAPTER 3

Scrambling backwards across the rug, I bumped into Babs' coffee table and knocked over a silver vase full of roses.

Maybe I was wrong. Maybe I was jumping to conclusions. Maybe she was . . . napping?

I rushed around to the back of the couch, careful not to disturb anything, and let out a gasp as I noticed a halo of blood surrounding her head.

She definitely wasn't napping.

I clutched at my stomach, feeling a wave of nausea. 911. I had to call 911.

Determined not to touch anything else in the office, I fumbled for my cell phone and frantically dialed.

"911. What's your emergency?"

That was an easy one: "It's Babs Norton! She's behind the couch," I stammered out.

"Someone's behind a couch?" the operator repeated serenely.

How could she be so calm at a moment like this? Oh, yeah. That was her job.

I tried again, this time explaining what I had discovered in Babs' office. Namely Babs. And I would have liked to have thought I was pretty calm, too, but the operator's repeated requests that I please stop hyperventilating told me otherwise.

"Can you tell if she's breathing?" asked the operator.

"I don't know," I admitted. "When I saw the blood, I called you immediately."

"Okay," said the operator. "I'm going to ask you to go ahead and step outside, in case there's an intruder and he's still there."

"An intruder?" I spun around and quickly surveyed the room, looking around for something I could use as a weapon in case I had to defend myself. If someone was still there, maybe I could heave a laser printer at him.

"Ma'am, are you still with me?" the operator asked. "I need you to vacate the premises."

"Sorry," I said, "I'm going. I was looking for something I could use to protect myself."

"No, please don't touch anything," she said with a little more urgency in her voice. "I need you not to disturb anything."

"What? Why?"

"In case it's a crime scene."

Crime scene? Damn, she was right. I might actually be standing in the middle of a crime scene, and I'd already disturbed it when I flung a box of pastries at it.

I didn't want to leave Babs there, but the 911 operator was right: it was time to go. I raced down the stairs as the operator waited patiently. When I got to the ground floor, I burst through the front doors, pausing there on the sidewalk to catch my breath. The sound of the lead-glass door swinging shut behind me caused me to let out a loud *"Eeep!"*

"You okay?" said the operator.

"Yeah," I said, "just a little jumpy, that's all." Not only had I vacated the premises, I'd locked myself out of them.

"So what now?" I asked the operator.

"I'd like for you to stay on the line with me until someone arrives."

"Ummmm, okay." An awkward pause ensued. "So, what do you want to talk about?"

A squad car came screeching to a stop on the street in front of me, lights flashing, and two uniformed officers emerged. *Thank God.* I hung up the phone and slid it into my back pocket. *Oops. Sorry, 911 lady.*

"You Kelly McKenna?" asked the older of the two.

"It's Kelsey, but close enough," I said. I pointed toward the door of Babs' building. "She's right up there. Hurry!"

"The ambulance is two minutes out," he said. "Can you let us into the building?"

"No," I said. "I don't have a key. Someone would need to buzz us in, but we could probably—"

The officer took the butt of his pistol and broke a pane of glass, reached in, and unlocked the door all in one fluid movement.

"Oh, okay," I said. "That'll work."

We stepped over the shattered glass and into the lobby just as the wail of the ambulance's siren came to a stop outside. The paramedics had caught up to us by the time we reached the stairs.

"Second floor," I yelled, pointing up as they raced past me.

"Wait here," said the older cop as he followed the others up the stairs.

I sank down onto the stairs and leaned against the banister.

How could this be happening? Babs was kind of a legend in the wedding-planning community, and even though I didn't know her very well, I'd always respected her. She'd even sent a couple of clients my way back when I was just a fledgling wedding planner with big dreams and few credentials.

I shook my head. What was happening up there? I crept up to the second-floor landing, but they'd closed the door behind them. After pacing for several minutes, I couldn't take the waiting anymore. Air. I needed air. I also needed to hear a friendly voice, so I went back outside and dialed Brody.

Pick up, pick up, pick up.

"What's up, Kels? You must've read my mind. I was just thinking about breakfast and, look, here you are!"

"Brody, thank God you picked up," I said. My eyes had actually teared up a little at the sound of his voice.

"What's wrong?" he said. "You sound weird."

"It's Babs. I'm at her office."

"Uh-oh. What did you do?"

"No, no, it's not like that. I found her on the floor of her office. The paramedics are with her now."

"What?! Where are you? Do you need me to come get you?"

"I'm waiting outside for the police. I'm okay." I was glad he couldn't see my hands shaking.

"Are you sure?" he asked.

"Yeah, positive. Just keep me company until they come back, yeah?"

"Of course," he said. "So what happened?"

"Well, I stopped by to talk to her about a client and—" The sound of a siren interrupted my thought, and a second squad car pulled up as the two officers from before emerged from the building. The older one spotted me and waved me over. "Brody, I'm going to have to call you back."

"Dang it! You can't leave me hanging like that!" he said.

"Sorry, I gotta go." I hung up and rushed toward the officer, who was pointing the two new arrivals toward Babs' office.

"How is she?"

He tightened his lips and shook his head.

"You mean, she really is . . . dead?"

He nodded grimly. I felt like I'd been punched in the gut. "But what—how?"

He gestured toward his cruiser. "I'm going to need you to come down to the station so we can get your statement."

Before I could answer, a loud screech came from over my shoulder. I instinctively ducked, thinking someone's pet monkey was on the loose, or perhaps an out-of-control velociraptor.

I wasn't far off. It was Stefan Pierce.

"What are you doing here?" He was practically yelling, his eyes darting wildly from me to the policeman and back to me again. Was he talking to me, or to the cops? I couldn't blame him for panicking. Seeing me in front of his office talking to a policeman must have tipped him off that something was seriously wrong.

"Stefan, I'm so sorry!" I blurted, not sure what to say. I was still processing the news myself.

"What's happened? Where's Babs?" His voice became more shrill with each passing question.

"Sir," said the cop, "I need you to calm down. Are you a friend of Ms. Norton's?"

"Friend? I'm her partner," he said, indignant that the cop didn't know who he was. He was inflating his credentials quite a bit, but I didn't dare correct him. Stefan put his hands on his hips. "Now tell me what's going on *right now!*"

The cop eyeballed Stefan for a second and said, "Are you just now arriving at the office, Mr . . . ?"

"It's Pierce. Stefan Pierce, and I was with a client. What is this? Was there a robbery?"

"Something terrible has happened," I blurted. "It's Babs!"

The cop looked irritated at me. Was I not supposed to say anything? The police officer pulled a notepad and pen from his shirt pocket. "We're going to need to know the name and contact info of Ms. Norton's next of kin."

"What happened?" Stefan's eyes darted back and forth between the officer and me. "Tell me right now!"

I laid what was meant to be a reassuring hand on Stefan's arm. "Stefan, if you can just calm down for one—"

"Don't you tell me to calm down!" He practically shrieked the words at me as he yanked his arm away.

The older cop gestured to the younger one, who came trotting over to join us. "Ms. McKenna, I'm going to ask you to go with Inspector Ryan here."

"My pleasure," I said, but what I meant was "Abso-freakin-lutely!" I don't know why I'd felt the need to get in the middle of things—always the helper—but I was clearly making it worse.

"Right this way," Inspector Ryan said, taking me by the elbow and leading me toward his squad car.

"Why is she here?" Stefan yelled toward our backs. "Is she under arrest?"

"Miss McKenna isn't under arrest," Inspector Ryan called out over his shoulder.

The detective opened the car door for me, his expression inscrutable. I climbed in and buckled up—this was certainly no

time to be a scofflaw—sinking down into the seat as Ryan circled around to the driver's side.

"So . . . Babs," I began, as we pulled away from the curb.
"What happened to her?"

The detective gave me a sideways look and tightened his lips
in a grim smile. "That's what we need to find out."

CHAPTER 4

*T*ell me again what you were doing in Ms. Norton's
office."

"I was there to get some files for a new client."

"But who let you in?"

"Nobody. The door was open."

"What about the front door? According to the building manager it stays locked at all times. Did someone buzz you up?"

"No, I tried calling, but she didn't answer, and—"

"And you let yourself in?" I'm no detective, but I could tell there was a hint of judgment in Detective Ryan's question.

"Someone came through the door, so I came on in." Ryan gave me a long hard look as if he was trying to decide whether to believe me. "What?" I said. "It was cold outside."

For someone who wasn't under arrest, I sure felt like I was getting the third degree. I'd been sitting in the tiny room for over an hour, patiently answering the detective's questions and wishing like crazy I hadn't skipped breakfast in anticipation of eating one of the scones that were probably being bagged as evidence. My stomach was grumbling angrily at my deferred maintenance, and my phone had gotten so many text alerts I had to turn it off.

But that was nothing compared to the sober realization of why I was sitting here. Babs was dead. It just didn't make any sense. I wanted so badly for it not to be true. But there was no denying it, especially while I was in the presence of Detective Ryan.

"So when you got up to Ms. Norton's office, was the door open?"

My cheeks flushed. "No. When I said it was open, I meant that it was unlocked."

"So you just let yourself in?" Again. Judgment.

Once more, I explained what would have been completely insignificant had I been visiting a professional peer and not stumbling into a crime scene.

Had I moved the body? How did I know Babs? Who might have wanted to hurt her? The questions went on and on. Funny how things take on heightened significance when you're in an interview room.

Ryan excused himself, leaving me alone in the interrogation room. I scanned the ceiling for cameras, wondering if I was being filmed. Probably. A minute later, he returned. "Okay, just one more question. Did you touch anything at the crime scene?" Ryan asked.

The crime scene. I hated thinking of Babs' office that way. "The door. The phone. I guess I touched her couch when I stood up."

"What about the floor?" he prompted. "Did you pick anything up off it?"

I scanned my memory and shook my head. "Just the pastries."

"You didn't see anything behind the couch?"

What was he getting at? The murder weapon? Must be. What else would have been behind the couch that I could have picked up that would have mattered? Nothing I could think of. I shook my head. "No, as soon as I saw Babs, I called 911, and then I came downstairs until you arrived."

Finally, the detective flipped his notebook closed. "Okay, Ms. McKenna. That's all for now."

Walking out into the midday sun, I gallantly resisted the urge to throw up on the sidewalk. Actually, maybe it was for the best that I hadn't had breakfast.

I hailed a passing cab, hopped in, and shut the door behind me.

"Where to?" The cabby peered at me suspiciously in his rear-view mirror. Maybe it was my imagination; a lot of cabbies have that look.

For a moment, I just stared back at him, the mirror acting as our go-between. I wasn't sure what to do next. The competing needs of eating something, returning to the office, collecting my car, and going straight home and crawling under the covers were duking it out inside my overtaxed brain. Finally, the prospect of adding a parking ticket to my day's tally won out, and I directed him to the intersection near Babs' office where I'd parked.

We rode in silence until he turned onto Babs' street. "Whoa," he said as he spotted the police cars and TV crews outside of her building. "Wonder what happened there?"

Knowing it was a rhetorical question, I kept my mouth shut. I scanned the crowd that had gathered to see if I could spot Stefan, but it seemed to be nothing but gawkers and the officers keeping them at bay. Stefan was probably at the police station like I had just been.

"You can let me out at the corner," I said, fishing through my wallet for the correct change. I passed the money up to him with a quick thanks, jumped out, and darted over to my car. If Stefan was still around, I didn't want to see him without a police escort.

I dialed Brody from the car, and he picked up immediately.

"Kelsey! What happened? Are you okay?"

"Yeah, I'm okay." I took a breath. "But Babs isn't."

"Oh my God, so it's true. It's all over the news, but nobody knows anything yet. What happened?"

Still in a daze, I told him everything I knew—which, granted, wasn't much. "There was blood on the floor. I don't know what happened."

"They said something on the news about blunt force trauma. Could she have hit her head or something? Like maybe she fainted?"

"I don't know. She fell onto a carpeted area behind a couch, and there was nothing for her to have hit her head on."

The other end of the line was silent for a moment as Brody considered my words. "So you think maybe . . . ?"

"It wasn't an accident? Based on my conversation with the police, I don't think so."

After I filled him in on everything that had happened at the police station, we agreed that an accident seemed unlikely, but then again, someone wanting to hurt Babs didn't make any more sense.

As I pulled up to the office, we made plans to talk later. I briefly considered taking the rest of the day off, but I had too much work to do. Besides, I really wanted to check on Laurel.

"Laurel?" I called out as I climbed the stairs. "You here?"

"Hey," she yelled from the general direction of her office. She came bouncing out of the room right about the time I reached the landing. "Where've you been? I tried calling you a bunch of times."

"Sorry. I—" I was about to tell her that I'd been at the police station, but something about her tone said she hadn't heard yet.

"How did it go with Babs?" she asked, her tone breezy. "Were you able to work your magic with her?"

Oh, no. She hadn't heard yet. "Yeah, um, that's what I wanted to talk to you about. It didn't exactly go the way I'd hoped." Her brow furrowed as I struggled to find the words. "In fact—well, here, maybe we should go sit down."

"What happened?" Her expression changed from curious to concerned as she followed me into my office and sat in the chair across from me. "Was she mad? Wow, that's weird. I really didn't think she'd care."

"I didn't get to talk to Babs."

Laurel laughed a twinkly laugh. "Oh, that's all? You had me worried there for a minute."

"Wait. Listen. I didn't get to talk to her because when I got there, she was—well, there's no easy way to say this." I took a deep breath. "She was dead."

Laurel searched my eyes, not fully comprehending the words I had said. "What? I mean, how?"

Laurel stared at me in shock as I told her everything that happened that morning.

"Poor Babs," she said, her eyes welling up with tears.

"I know." I grabbed the Kleenex box from my desk and sat down beside her, offering her a tissue. "I just hope the police catch whoever did it."

Laurel's eyebrows shot up in alarm. "Did it? You think someone did it on purpose?"

"I keep trying to come up with some scenario where it's an accident, but the more I think about it, the less plausible that sounds."

"You think she was attacked?" Laurel's voice rose in alarm. "Did you tell the police?"

"That's just it. They asked a lot of questions that sure didn't sound like they thought it was an accident. Plus, when I was up in her office the 911 operator told me to wait outside in case there was an intruder."

"An intruder?" Laurel's eyes flew open wide. "Kelsey, you didn't tell me you were in danger!"

"I wasn't. At least, I don't think I was."

"How do you know?" she demanded.

"Well—I guess I don't. But it doesn't matter, because I'm here, and I'm okay."

"Thank God," she said as she grabbed me and hugged me hard.

"Thanks, Laurel," I said, trying hard to breathe. If she didn't stop squeezing soon, I was going to lose oxygen.

"I don't know what I would do if you . . ."

I smiled, trying to put on a brave face. "I know. Now go get your files. We've got a lot of work to do."

Okay, so maybe I was deflecting, but I wasn't ready to admit how shaken up I was. I hadn't really allowed myself to think about it, but I had to admit: the thought that I might have been in the same room with Babs' assailant freaked me out more than a little. And I still hadn't fully processed the fact that Babs Norton was dead.

I was just glad Laurel was there to help keep my mind off things.

For the rest of the afternoon, we threw ourselves into our work. I needed the distraction, and crossing things off our to-do list proved to be very therapeutic. Plane tickets for next month's site visit in Fiji? *Booked.* Call from a potential client who wanted to get married in Tuscany? *Returned.* Group rate with the hotel in Chicago? *Negotiated.*

Done, done, and done.

I'd almost managed to forget about the situation altogether—
almost—but when I heard the front-door buzzer, my heart did a
little flip-flop. It was Haley, who had called earlier to say she was
going to swing by and drop off her contract.

"Laurel?" I yelled down the hall. "Can you get that?"

"I'm on it!" she yelled back.

I took a deep breath to prepare myself as Laurel escorted
Haley into my office.

"Hi," Haley said as she took off her cardigan. She dropped
her handbag onto my guest chair. "Did you hear about Babs? It's
all over the news."

"I know," I said. "I'm still kind of in shock."

She sank down into the chair and we sat in silence for a moment. "It's so weird. I was in that very office just a couple of weeks
ago. I wonder if Stefan found her?"

I froze. As awkward as it was, I didn't want her to find out
later from someone else. I got up from my chair and walked
around my desk, sitting next to Haley in the chair next to her.
"Haley, listen. I have to tell you something, and I don't want it
to freak you out."

Her eyes grew big. Just my saying those words seemed to have
freaked her out already. "Okay . . . ?"

"I went to Babs' office this morning to pick up the files for
your wedding."

Haley looked alarmed, and her voice rose an octave. "You
were there?"

"Yes." I tried to keep my voice calm and steady. "I'm the one
who found her."

"Oh my God." There was a pregnant pause as the news sank
in. "Oh my God!"

"I know. It was awful. The police came and, well, it was awful."

After peppering me with questions—and who could blame her?—Haley stared at me for a moment, and I realized she was trying to decide what to make of my story. What would I think if someone told me they'd found a body? I'd be shocked. I'd be concerned. And depending on how well I knew them, I'd probably wonder if they knew more than they were telling me.

"Holy cow," she said at last. "The cops probably think you did it!"

"I don't think—"

"Did they question you?"

"No!" I said. "I mean yes, but as a witness, not a suspect."

"They probably suspect you. It's always the person who found the body. Or the husband. Was she married?"

"What? No. I don't—it wasn't me!" What kind of common criminal did she take me for?

"No, yeah. I know that. But they don't know that. And then with me seeing her, and then me seeing you . . . You have to admit it's a weird coincidence."

Tell me about it. If Haley hadn't visited Brody's booth, I never would have gone to Babs' office. I'd be hearing about Babs' death like everyone else instead of thrown into the middle of it. Of course, if I hadn't been intent on being what my dad had always called a dad-gum do-gooder, I never would have gone to Babs' office in the first place. I would have just signed the client and maybe sent an e-mail as a professional courtesy. Or if I hadn't found a parking space, maybe I would have waited until the next day and someone else would have found her instead of me.

A million little things could have changed the outcome of the last twenty-four hours, but here I was.

Me and my stupid pastries.

CHAPTER 5

$\mathcal{C}$oordinating Haley's wedding wasn't going to be as easy as she thought. Because being a day-of coordinator involves more than just the *day of.* Sure, it would seem like all I had to do was just show up the day of the wedding, drink champagne, and tell people where to stand, but there's actually a lot of preparation that goes into it. You have to be in close contact with the vendors, go over the contracts so you know what's expected of everyone, oversee the rehearsal itself, and put together a schedule to keep everything on track. In other words, we only make it *look* easy.

The next morning, Haley, Laurel, and I gathered in the conference room, ready to get to work. I was sure Babs had done a great job on the planning stage; I just needed to know what she'd planned. I grabbed a new-client questionnaire and readied myself to write. "Okay," I said, "first things first. How many people are you expecting?"

"Right now the RSVPs are at eighty-three," Haley said.

"Okay, and is Higgins Estate the venue for both the service and the reception?"

"Yes," she confirmed.

"All right. Next question, what caterer are you using?"

"Um . . ." She looked up and to the left. "Oh, gosh, I can't remember their name. We went for a tasting, but it was like six months ago."

"Was it Tartine Catering?" I asked. "I know Babs uses them a lot."

"No, it was 'Wine' something."

About 70 percent of the businesses in Napa were called Wine something or another, but I noted it anyway. "That's okay. What about the florist?"

Haley grimaced and shook her head. "Babs basically told me what I wanted and assured me she knew 'just the person,'" she said, using air quotes to drive home the point.

"Okay. Hmmm. What about alcohol? I assume the wine would have to be from Higgins, right?"

"That sounds right!" Haley said, happy to have finally had an answer.

"Do you know if they were going to supply the other beverages?" asked Laurel.

Haley slumped in her chair. "I don't. I'm sorry. I guess I'm not being much help. I've been crazy busy with my job and I was leaving it to Babs to keep us organized."

"That's okay. I mean, that's what we're here for, right? We'll just have to—" *Huh.* I wasn't sure. Usually brides hire a day-of coordinator because they've done all the planning themselves. I'd never been in a position like this one before, where someone else had done all the planning but wasn't available to give me the answers.

I chewed on the end of my pen for a second. "You don't happen to have files at home or receipts or anything, do you?"

"Well, we paid Babs and she paid the vendors, so she had all the receipts." A hint of regret tinged her voice.

"That's okay," I said. "Lots of people do it that way." It wasn't uncommon—although it sure would have been easier for me if she hadn't. Don't get me wrong, I love a low-maintenance bride, but in this particular scenario it would have helped me out a lot if she'd been a little more of a control freak. Not that Babs would have tolerated that. Her motto may as well have been, *Leave everything to me—or else!*

I looked at the next item on my list. "Anything you can tell me about the cake?"

"Oh, it's gorgeous. Three tiers, kind of looks like it's covered in lace." She paused. "That's not what you meant, is it?"

I laughed. "Well, I was hoping you could be more specific. . . ."

"It does sound really pretty, though," Laurel added encouragingly.

Haley smiled. "I don't remember the name of the bakery off the top of my head, but I think it was in Yountville, if that helps."

"Yes! Actually, that does help. I remember one time hearing Babs rave about Renee at The Sweet Spot. Is that it?"

Haley nodded. "I'm pretty sure that's right. Oh, Kelsey, this is so embarrassing. I'll ask Christopher if he can remember anything, but I doubt he can. Maybe I can look up Napa caterers on the Internet and see if anything rings a bell."

"You do have your dress, though?"

"Yes, I definitely have the dress."

"That's good," I said, looking at my mostly blank list. "We have a bride, a groom, a venue, and a dress. I can work with that."

After getting what information I could out of her, I sent Haley on her way and promised to see what I could do. After all, being resourceful is part of my job description.

That said, I was stuck. Without the files, there was no way to confirm with the vendors. And without confirming with the vendors, I had no idea who would show up—or even if they *would* show up.

As much as I didn't want to, there was only one thing I could do: call Stefan and ask him for the files. *Ugh.* The timing couldn't be worse, and he especially wasn't going to like it coming from me. I briefly considered my options. And I do mean "briefly" because there were really only two options—one of which involved breaking into Babs' office.

It was time to deploy my secret weapon.

"Hey, Laurel?" I said in my sweetest, most persuasive voice.

She tilted her head at me. "Yeah?"

"You want to do me a favor?"

"Sure, boss," she said. "What is it?"

"You know how you wanted to be more involved in the planning side of things?"

"Yeah?" she answered, her tone suspicious.

"Since you and Stefan have never met, I was hoping you could call and ask for his files on Haley and Christopher's wedding. Pretty please?"

Laurel gave me a look of reproach. "Dude! We can't call him *now*."

"Why not?"

"Hello? Babs? It's too soon. Give the guy a chance to grieve."

"I know. You're right." I pinched the bridge of my nose. It was definitely too soon, but the clock was ticking. "I hate to bother him, but this wedding's only a couple weeks away and I don't even know where to start!"

"Can't we at least wait until after the funeral?"

I thought about it. In reality, "never" was the only time that it was going to feel right, but we didn't have until then.

"I wish we could, but I don't think we have the luxury of waiting until an appropriate amount of time has passed."

She sighed. "Oh, okay, fine. I'll call him."

"Don't even mention my name. As far as he knows, you're just some random wedding planner, okay?"

"Random, check." She headed off down the hall.

"Where are you going?"

"I'm not going to call with you watching!"

"Why not?" Just because I didn't want to call him didn't mean I didn't want to listen in.

"Because you'll start waving your arms around, trying to get my attention so you can tell me what to say. No thanks."

She had a point there. While she was off calling the Ankle Biter, I looked up the number for Higgins Estate, the winery where Haley and Christopher were scheduled to have their wedding, and punched it into my phone. Divide and conquer. Maybe someone there would know something about something.

After pressing 1, then pressing 5, then pressing 1 again, I was connected with a real, live, and very bubbly female. "Good afternoon, Higgins Estate, how may I direct your call?"

"Hi, may I speak to your events coordinator?"

"Um . . . we don't really have one specific person. Were you wanting to throw an event?"

"Yes. I need to talk to whoever handles your weddings."

"Oh, weddings! We do *beautiful* weddings here, but they book up pretty far in advance. What month were you and your fiancé thinking?" Her enthusiasm for the topic was evident from the tone of her voice.

"Oh, no, it's not for me. I'm a wedding planner. I just wanted to know who I should talk to about a wedding happening there in a few weeks, like maybe if you have an events coordinator?" I hoped my tone didn't say, *Can you put your mommy on the line?*

"Hmmm, I guess you would want to talk to Lucas Higgins. He's the business manager."

"Okay, great," I said. "Can you connect me?"

"Oh, he's not in the office. He's out of town for a couple of days on business."

"All right, then. Can I leave a message?"

"Oh, sure!" She sounded really pleased to be able to help at long last. "Let me put you through."

I left a message begging Lucas to call me back and hung up the phone. How long would it take him to get back to me? And would he even know anything? Luckily, Laurel was probably fixing everything, right at that very—

Interrupting my thought, she poked her head in my office, phone to her ear.

"Mmm-hmm," she said calmly while pointing frantically at the phone.

"What's happening?" I mouthed.

She held up one finger. "I understand."

Another pause. "Okay, hold on. I'll put her on."

She tossed the phone to me. "Sorry," she whispered. "Caller ID. He recognized the number."

I picked up the phone. I tried not to sound sheepish, although I was totally busted. "Hi, Stefan. How are you holding up?"

"So I take it you're planning the Riegert/Bennett wedding now?"

Okay, straight to the point. I got it. "I'm sorry, Stefan. I feel horrible about calling you now with all you've been through. But they don't have any records and I can't help them without knowing who the vendors are."

"What did I tell you about staying away from my clients?"

"Stefan, I didn't seek them out. They came to me."

"Well, how *lucky* that you were around to accommodate them." The sarcasm practically dripped from his tongue.

"I didn't call to cause a fight, Stefan. Haley's father fired Babs and now she needs someone to oversee her wedding."

"Whatever problems he had with Babs are irrelevant now. You can send them back to me and I'll take care of them."

"C'mon, Stefan, you're being ridiculous. I have plenty of clients and so do you. It's just not going to work out with you guys, okay?"

There was a long silence on the other end of the line.

"Look, it's nothing personal. They just wanted to start fresh with someone new." It wasn't exactly the truth, but what was I going to say? "So can you just help me out and give me the files? You'll still get paid for everything you and Babs did up till now. In fact, send me an invoice and I'll make sure it gets paid right away. Please, help me out here."

"Drop dead," he said. And then he was gone.

CHAPTER 6

The memorial service was held at Grace Cathedral—a fitting venue for a woman of Babs' stature. Sitting at the top of a steep hill across from the Fairmont hotel, with cable cars passing by right outside, the grand, hundred-year-old church was a San Francisco icon.

I'd been to Grace Cathedral before. I'd even planned a wedding there once. But I'd never seen such a glut of flowers surrounding the altar. The place was crammed with supersized bouquets, colorful wreathes, and elaborate sprays, and the bottom half of the casket was draped in a blanket of roses that would look right at home on a Kentucky Derby winner.

Babs looked impeccable, as usual. She was wearing a vintage Chanel suit along with her signature leopard-print glasses that showcased her expertly applied makeup. No way that was done by the mortuary. Someone must have hired one of the professional makeup artists she worked with. Probably Thierry Beland. He was a pro with a mascara wand.

As the guests filed in and took their seats, a string quartet that was usually impossible to book during the busy summer season played Pachelbel's Canon. Sure, it's known more for weddings than funerals, but if it was good enough for Princess Diana's funeral, it was good enough for Babs'.

I smiled to myself. This event had Babs' touch all over it, and I wouldn't have been surprised if she'd planned the whole thing herself, leaving explicit instructions for someone else to carry out in the event of her death. Babs had always liked to make sure everything was perfect, and today was no exception.

Laurel nudged me in the side, then leaned over and whispered, "Don't look. Stefan's here."

I nodded discreetly to let her know I'd heard, and I locked eyes on Babs' portrait. *Don't look at him. Just focus on Babs.* But, in my peripheral vision, I could still see him glowering at me.

Just then, Brody slid into the seat next to me. "Sorry it took so long. The lot where I usually park was full."

"I take it you found a spot?" I said, my eyes still focused on the front of the church.

"I'm here, aren't I?" he said, sounding a tad defensive. He waved a hand in front of my face. "Hello? What are you doing?"

"What do you mean?" I asked, not daring to shift my gaze.

"Why won't you look at me?"

"She's avoiding Stefan," Laurel offered.

"Well, stop it," Brody said. "It's creepy."

"Sorry," I said. "Is he looking?"

"No," Brody said, "he's whispering to someone and he has kind of a pissy look on his—oh, wait. Yeah, he's looking."

"Great," I said.

"And pointing," Laurel added helpfully.

"At me?" Against my will, my voice went up an octave.

"At us," Laurel said.

"The pointing is definitely at you," Brody said.

"Thanks for the clarification," I said, sinking down lower in the pew and wishing I'd worn a hat with a black veil. Perfect for funerals and avoiding people you don't want to see.

I pretended to be immersed in the program while the Ankle Biter took his seat, and soon enough the service began.

The room was packed with people, and I wasn't surprised. Babs was well known, both in San Francisco and up in the wine country, and it seemed like every caterer, photographer, and florist in a hundred-mile radius had come to pay their respects. I couldn't help but think Babs would be proud, not only of the turnout but also of the production values.

After the minister led us in prayer, a stylishly dressed woman of a certain age approached the front of the church.

"Who's that?" Brody whispered.

I shrugged. "Beats me."

"And now," said the officiant, "we'll hear a few words from Babs' sister, Margot."

"Oh. It's Babs' sister, Margot," Brody said, the tiniest trace of a smile tugging at his lips.

I shot him a look as he gave an innocent shrug.

Margot was dressed in an emerald-green suit, dark hair swept up into a tidy updo. I could see the resemblance now. Partly the way she looked, but more the way she carried herself. Confident. Bold. Efficient.

"My sister was a force of nature," Margot began, kicking off a twenty-minute-long eulogy that had half the crowd in tears—myself included. I didn't know how Babs' sister managed to keep her composure. As stunned as we all were by the loss, I couldn't imagine how she must feel.

"As most of you know, my sister loved a party. Please join us for a final celebration of Babs' life at my house immediately following the interment. It's what she would have wanted."

As Margot folded up her notes and made her way back down the steps to the front pew, the string quartet started playing once more. "My Way." Yep, Babs had definitely planned her own funeral.

We filed out of the church, stopping to offer our condolences to Margot. "I'm Kelsey McKenna," I said, taking Margot's hand in mine. "I'm also a wedding planner and I've known Babs for years. I'm so sorry for your loss."

"Thank you," she said. If she knew I was the one who'd found Babs' body, she didn't let on.

I gestured to my friends. "This is Brody. He's a wedding photographer."

"My condolences," Brody said.

"And this is Laurel; she and I work together."

"I hope you'll all join us afterward," Margot said as she took Laurel's hand. "Babs told me once she'd come back and haunt me if I didn't make sure there was a good turnout at her after-party."

I laughed and shook my head. "That sounds like Babs."

Laurel looked at me, eyebrows raised. "I think we can stop by, right, Kelsey?"

"Of course. We'd be honored."

"Great," Margot said. "The address is in your program."

We stepped outside into the bright morning sun.

Brody pointed down a steep hill. "I'm parked down Taylor Street. Want me to go get the car and pick you two up?"

"Oh, Brody, you're amazing. These heels are meant for flat surfaces. I'm not sure I could make it."

"Okay, wait here," he said before disappearing over the crest.

Laurel and I leaned against the wall, nodding to people as they filed out of the church and greeting old friends.

I noticed a man approaching, but I didn't immediately recognize him. I groped around my memory for a name. Expensive suit. Expensive haircut. Tall, blondish, tan. I couldn't place him, but he seemed to know who I was.

"Kelsey McKenna?"

I held up my hand to shield my eyes from the sun as I looked up at him. "Yes?"

"Lucas Higgins, from Higgins Estate Winery."

"Oh! Hi," I said, taking his outstretched hand. "So nice to meet you."

"Likewise. I've heard a lot of good things about you."

"You have? I mean, thank you."

"Sorry I haven't had a chance to return your phone call," Lucas said. "You're taking over one of Babs' weddings, right?"

Over Lucas' shoulder, I noticed Stefan walking out of the church. He spotted us immediately, but I quickly looked away, determined to ignore Stefan's stare. "That's right. I'm coordinating a wedding that's scheduled at your winery on the eighteenth. Haley Bennett and Christopher Riegert. Can we set up a time to talk?"

"Sure. Why don't you come up next week and we'll meet in person? I could give you a tour and answer whatever questions you might have."

"That would be great. The sooner, the better."

Lucas lowered his voice to a more confidential level. "I'd also like to talk to you some about your availability over the next couple of months."

I was taken aback but tried not to show it. "My availability?"

"Sorry, I hope this doesn't come across as insensitive, but Babs did a lot of weddings for us, and with her gone . . . well, let's just say we're going to need to fill some gaps."

I glanced over my shoulder to see Stefan, arms crossed in front of his chest. He was glaring at me with all his might, barely listening to the woman standing next to him.

Laurel nudged me in the side with her elbow. She probably would have kicked me in the shin if she thought Lucas wouldn't have noticed.

"Sorry," I said, snapping out of it. The whole reason I'd had to call Lucas in the first place was because Stefan had refused to talk to me, so Stefan was just going to have to deal. "Of course. I'll call you tomorrow and we'll set something up."

"That would be great," he said. "I'll look forward to hearing from you."

I grabbed Laurel's arm and dragged her in the opposite direction, keeping my head down as I went. "C'mon, let's go wait by the curb."

She stopped and put her hands on her hips. "Okay, weirdo, what was that about?"

"I'm sorry, okay? Did you not notice Stefan standing ten feet away that whole time?"

"So what? You didn't do anything wrong."

"I know that. But you know how it is. He's going to assume Lucas and I were talking business."

"Weren't you?"

"Well, yeah, but there's no reason to antagonize him."

She rolled her eyes. "Well, Stefan's going to have to put on his big-boy pants."

She was right, of course. There was just one problem: I wasn't sure if Stefan owned any big-boy pants.

Half an hour later, we pulled up in front of a brick Tudor that sat high atop a hill in Pacific Heights. It was modest by Pacific Heights standards, but in the real world it would have fully qualified as a mansion.

A tuxedoed cater waiter greeted us at the door, and I gladly plucked a flute of champagne from his extended tray as he gestured down the hall to where the party was. *Nice touch, Babs.* I made a mental note to leave some instructions to be opened in the case of my death and to make sure they included champagne.

As we paused in the foyer—itself large enough to house a family of four—Brody let out a low whistle. "Nice place."

"I'll say." I took a moment to let my eyes adjust to the opulent setting. "What do you think something like this would go for?"

"More than either of us have," Brody said.

"Maybe if we all chipped in?" Laurel said. "I could sell my Prius. It's worth at least eight thousand dollars."

"Nice," Brody said. "I bet that would at least cover one of these light fixtures, maybe even a doorknob."

"C'mon," Laurel said, leading the way toward the back of the house. "I bet it's got a great view."

The sounds of piano music mingled with forks clinking against expensive china got louder as we approached, and as the hallway spilled out into the parlor, we were greeted with floor-to-ceiling windows with a view that extended all the way from Coit Tower to the Golden Gate Bridge.

There was a flurry of greetings as I saw several faces I recognized. Like the funeral, it was a veritable Who's Who of the wedding community.

"Kelsey, *comment ça va?*" said Thierry Beland, the makeup artist I assumed had given Babs her final powder.

"I thought I might see you here," I said.

"It's been way too long, darling," he said, kissing each cheek.

"Babs looked fabulous," I said. "Were you behind that?"

He leaned in conspiratorially. "I've begged her to let me do a makeover on her for years, and I finally got my chance. I'm just destroyed that this is what it took to get my way."

"Well, she looked amazing," I said, squeezing his arm.

"It was my honor," he replied. He took me by the shoulders and held me at arm's length. "Speaking of makeovers, I would love to get my hands on those cheekbones of yours. Have you ever considered contouring?"

I blushed a little and touched my face. "I didn't have time to do my full makeup routine this morning."

He smiled slyly. "Don't be silly. You always look marvelous. Not that I couldn't work *wonders* on you, but if everyone could do what I do, I'd be out of a job."

Right after we made a pact to have lunch one of these days—I knew it probably wouldn't happen with our busy schedules, but it was nice to pretend it was a possibility—I spotted Margot sipping a martini and made my way over to say hello.

"Margot, thank you so much for having us. Your house is gorgeous."

"Thank you," she said, slurring ever so slightly. This clearly wasn't her first trip to the bar. "And thank you for coming."

"The service was lovely. Exactly what Babs would have wanted."

"You've got that right," she said, sloshing a bit of her drink as she waved her glass in a gesture of agreement. "Let's just say I had some help."

"Doesn't surprise me in the least," I said. "We wedding planners can be control freaks."

"Don't I know it," she said. "If only Babs had been as good at managing her own life as she was at micromanaging other people's. I can't remember the last time I ordered my own wine without Babs 'suggesting' a better vintage. Or a better vineyard. Or that maybe I shouldn't be drinking at all."

I was surprised by Margot's blunt assessment, and she must have been, too, because she quickly switched topics to something about the caterers. I didn't catch most of it, though, because right at that moment Stefan walked in the door, his eyes narrowing to tiny slits when he saw me talking to the hostess.

What was his problem with me, anyway? Surely this wasn't just about one measly little wedding contract. I mean, I didn't ask Haley and Christopher to sign on as my clients. They'd sought me out. Still, I didn't want there to be a scene in the middle of Babs' meticulously planned reception.

"Say, Margot, I'm so sorry, but can you point me to the ladies' room?"

"Of course. Down that hall, third door on the left."

"Thanks so much." I reiterated my condolences and retreated toward the back of the house. I couldn't make Stefan like me, but at least I could avoid him for the next little bit, and with any luck, it would be a long, long time before I bumped into him again.

That was the plan, anyway.

CHAPTER 7

*H*aving removed myself from Stefan's general vicinity, I set off to look for Brody and Laurel. Where had they gotten off to, anyway? I decided to check the bar, and okay, yes, it was partly so I could grab a drink, but I was thirsty, and besides, if Stefan decided to throw a cocktail in my face, I didn't want to find myself unarmed.

In addition to an excellent wine selection, the bartenders were serving signature cocktails created just for the occasion. I ordered a Babs Bellini in her honor, then scanned the room for my friends.

"Kelsey!" said a voice from over my shoulder.

I turned around to find Danielle Turpin, a fellow wedding planner I knew from around town. She specialized in local weddings, and over the years she'd graciously thrown a couple of out-of-town referrals my way.

"Hi, Danielle," I said as she leaned in for a hug. "Good to see you."

"You too," she said, "although I wish it were under different circumstances."

"I know." I shook my head. "I still can't believe she's gone."

"I just saw her last week, and she looked healthy as a horse." Danielle leaned in, her voice dropping an octave. "I heard the police suspect foul play."

Although I had suspected foul play myself, Danielle was known as a world-class gossip. Maybe she could fill in some pieces of the puzzle for me. "You mean murder?" I dropped my voice to a whisper. "Why would they think that?"

"I heard they found her on the floor of her office."

They. Should I just fess up that it was me? Danielle would probably find out anyway. Then again, if I did tell her, she'd just pepper me with questions.

Instead of answering, I continued my tack of turning the questions back on her. "Who do they think could have done it?"

"I don't know. It doesn't make any sense. She was beloved by most of the wedding community." She glanced around the room. "I heard Stefan is a suspect."

"Really?" I asked, surprised. Despite my firsthand knowledge of his personality deficiencies, I couldn't imagine him wanting Babs dead. He seemed much too ambitious for that. "That seems like it would be kind of shortsighted of him. She was kind of the goose that laid the golden egg."

"True, but I'm sure she must have been one tough goose to work for." Danielle looked around the room, munching thoughtfully on a carrot stick. "I hope it's not true. I'd hate to think someone we know could have had something to do with it."

"Tell me about it," I said, glancing around at the sea of faces.

"I feel so bad for her sister," Danielle said.

"Oh, I know," I said. "I'm sure it must have been such a shock."

"And being questioned in your own sister's death"—she shook her head—"I can't even imagine."

"Wait, what?" This was definitely a tantalizing tidbit.

"Well, I heard from a friend of mine whose husband is with the San Francisco Police Department that they—" She stopped herself and waved her hand, as if to make her sentence fragment vanish from where it hung in the air between us. "Well, I probably shouldn't spread rumors."

I couldn't believe she was going to make me drag it out of her when it seemed fairly obvious that she was dying to dish.

I glanced furtively over at Margot, who was leaning against the grand piano, belting out "Those Were the Days." Surely Babs hadn't left a tipsy serenade as one of her final requests. On the plus side, though, there was no way Margot was going to overhear us talking.

"C'mon," I said, "you've gotta tell me what you heard."

"I'm sure it's nothing," Danielle said, shoveling quinoa salad into her mouth.

"They think Margot might have had something to do with it?" I whispered.

Danielle swallowed, then jerked her head toward a far corner of the room, away from the crowds. I followed her, scanning the room to see if anyone had noticed us talking.

"It's probably nothing," Danielle said, once we were out of earshot of the other guests. "So don't repeat this, because I don't even think she's really a suspect. It's just that she sort of had a motive."

"Motive? To kill her own sister? But why?"

"Look around you," she said.

I surveyed the dining room. Stained-glass windows. Enormous oak table. Antique chandelier. But no motives for murder that I could see. "I'm not sure I understand. Something in this room?"

"No, look *around* you. All around. As in, this whole house."

"It's beautiful," I said, puzzled. "So what?" For someone who loved to gossip, Danielle was certainly making me work for it.

"This house belonged to their parents, and Margot and Babs inherited it," she said. "Not just the house, but a couple of other buildings in San Francisco. Babs didn't have any heirs, so if she died—I mean, since she died—it all goes to the sister."

"Whoa," I said, looking around the room and through the door to the living room with its multimillion-dollar views. "Okay, so Babs' death is going to make Margot a very rich woman, but surely she wouldn't murder her own sister? If they owned several buildings together, she's already pretty stinking rich."

"No, you're totally right," Danielle said, setting her empty plate on an antique sideboard and dabbing at her mouth with a cocktail napkin. "I'm sure it's nothing."

I hoped it was nothing. Surely Margot wouldn't be so heartless as to kill her own sister and then still go out and buy an ice sculpture.

"Anyway," Danielle said, "forget I said anything. Shall we?" she asked, gesturing in the direction of the party. We reentered the living room, and I made my way over to Brody and Laurel, who were lurking in a corner.

"There you are!" said Laurel. "We were about to send out a search party."

"Yeah, you're missing all the fun," said Brody, gesturing across the room to where Margot was sitting in some man's lap while she sipped her martini.

"Sammy, can I get some more olives?" Margot shouted to a passing waiter.

My eyes grew big as she slapped the waiter's butt for punctuation. "Oh, my. Someone's going to regret this in the morning."

"Not me," said Brody, snapping a picture with his phone. "I love a good spectacle."

"Maybe we should get a keg," Margot said to some nearby guests. "You know? I mean, life is short."

Just past Margot, I could see Stefan in a huddle with Thierry and a couple of wine reps I knew. They were whispering excitedly about something. No doubt gossiping about our hostess' condition. Okay, so sobriety wasn't one of her strong suits, I thought. Leave the lady alone. She's not hurting anyone.

Stefan looked up and our eyes met, his mouth twisting into a cruel smile. He turned back to the group to say something, then looked back at me, and I realized with horror that I was the topic of conversation.

"Hey, guys?" I said, nudging Brody and making my "this is important" face at Laurel. "I think we should go get a drink." I tried sending them both a psychic message as I cut my eyes in Stefan's direction, but they didn't notice the angry little man.

"But I already have a drink," Laurel said.

"I know, but you know how you hate conflict?"

"Yeah?"

"Well, there's about to be one," I said, jerking my chin toward Stefan, who was now officially walking toward us.

"And me without my Mace," Brody said.

"C'mon, Kelsey," said Laurel, "he's not going to make a scene here."

"Don't be so sure," said Brody, setting down his champagne glass. "He looks pissy."

"Yeah, let's just go," I said as I turned toward the front door. I wasn't in the mood, and I certainly didn't want to have it out with him here, in front of the entire wedding-planning community.

"Oh, sure," Stefan yelled after us. "Just run away."

Too late.

"Stefan," I said, pretending I was just noticing him. "We were just leaving."

"You know, Babs trusted you," he spat.

"Excuse me?" I didn't know where he was going with this, but things were about to turn ugly.

"I told her that you were out to steal her clients, but she vouched for you—and look where it got her."

I edged toward the door, ready to make a break for it.

"Don't you try to leave when I'm talking to you!" he bellowed.

"We have to go," I said. "Weddings to plan. You know how it is."

"Oh, I know *exactly* how it is," he said, his tone downright venomous.

I glanced anxiously around the room. People were starting to notice the hubbub, and I saw Danielle actually shushing the person she'd been talking to so she wouldn't miss a word. *Great.* "Maybe we could talk outside."

"You'd like that, wouldn't you?" Stefan sneered.

"Yes?" I said, confused as to why that was even a question.

"Stefan," Brody cut in, placing himself between me and Stefan while Laurel cowered a few feet away. "If you have some sort of issue, maybe we could go discuss it privately."

"Look at you, defending her. How sweet."

"Look, Stefan—" Brody said.

"Don't you 'look' me," replied Stefan. He whirled to face me again, jabbing a finger in my face. "Babs always defended you, too, and how did you repay her? By stabbing her in the back!"

"Don't be ridiculous," I said. "I didn't stab anyone in the back."

"You've always been jealous of Babs, and now she's gone." He crossed his arms in front of him. "This all seems to have worked out exactly how you wanted it."

What? I counted to ten while I fumed silently. "I did not want this," I said. "How can you even say such a thing?"

"Did you hand out plenty of business cards at the funeral?" Stefan asked, his voice mocking. "Should I just go ahead and hand over my client list?"

I could feel my exasperation coming to a head. This was absurd. "Don't you mean *Babs'* client list?"

Stefan's expression turned dark with rage, and he got right up in my face. "You know what I think?" His eyes locked on mine as his voice grew slow and deliberate. "I think it was no coincidence that you were the one who found Babs' body."

Several people around us gasped, me included. "Is that true?" said Danielle, who hadn't missed a word. "You were there that night?"

"Oh, it's true," said Stefan. "And I'm starting to wonder if maybe she knows more than she's telling."

My face flushed in a mixture of embarrassment and anger. I was acutely aware of the attention our conversation was getting from the rest of the crowd. A couple of people were even holding their cell phones in the air. Were they videotaping us?

"What happened?" he asked. "Did you want to rub it in her face that you'd stolen our client?"

"No, that's not what happened!" I could feel everyone's eyes on me. "I've never stolen a client in my—"

"Did you get into a fight? Did she threaten to tell everybody?" His voice was getting louder and higher by the second. Soon he would be speaking in a pitch that only dogs could hear.

"Okay, buddy, you need to bring it down a notch," Brody said, taking Stefan by the shoulder.

Stefan yanked away from Brody. "Why? What are you going to do? Shut me up, like she did to Babs?"

My heart started pounding and I could feel adrenaline flooding my body. I opened my mouth to reply, but no sound came out. Before I could form a thought that didn't involve me unleashing a string of expletives, Margot stumbled into the room. She took a gulp from her cocktail and swiped at her chin with her hand. "What's going on in here? I could hear you all the way down the hall."

"I'm sorry if I caused a disruption, Margot." Stefan paused for dramatic effect as the room grew silent. "But I was just telling everyone how this woman"—and with that he lifted his hand and pointed directly at me—"killed Babs Norton."

CHAPTER 8

*N*othing brings a party to a screeching halt like a murder accusation. Well, at least for the person being accused. For everyone else, the drama is like a really juicy party favor, something to take with them when they leave.

After his big pronouncement, Stefan turned on his heel and stalked into the other room. A moment later, conversation resumed, but mostly at a whisper and punctuated with words like "Babs" and "murder."

I closed my eyes and willed myself to be invisible. I took a deep breath and turned to our host. "Margot, I hope you don't think—"

"Nonsense," she slurred as she made a dismissive gesture with her hand. "Stefan's always had a flair for the dramatic." And with that she wandered off into the other room to refill her glass.

It was nice of her to let me off the hook, but I couldn't tell if she meant it or if she just really wanted to get away from me. With any luck, she wouldn't even remember what had happened.

Brody squeezed my arm. "You okay?"

"Not really," I said, my hand trembling as I set down my glass on a mahogany side table.

"C'mon," said Laurel, grabbing my arm. "Let's say our good-byes and get out of here."

I followed her, noticing the pointed lack of eye contact from the other guests. Surely they hadn't put any stock in the crazy things Stefan had said?

I smiled and gave a little wave as I passed Danielle. "Good to see you again."

She gave me a tight-lipped smile in return and nodded curtly.

"Just keep walking," Brody murmured, pulling me along after him.

I blew out a long breath. Leave it to Stefan to ruin a perfectly lovely reception.

I'd intended to go back to the office afterward, but Brody and Laurel outvoted me, suggesting instead that we'd all had enough for one day. Who was I to argue? I said goodbye, went up to my apartment, and immediately put on my favorite pair of pajamas while I boiled water for tea.

Earl Grey or Jasmine Green? No, I was already wired enough. I grabbed a chamomile and ripped open the bag, then leaned against the granite counter and sighed. Did they still make Calgon? Because I was sure ready to have it take me away.

I settled in with a book, but I couldn't focus on it. How could Stefan really think that I could hurt anyone, much less Babs? I clicked on the TV and halfheartedly channel surfed for a while, catching the last half of a movie that would probably have been a whole lot better if I'd watched the first half.

I must have dozed off at some point, because I awakened with a start when I heard the pounding on my front door. I tiptoed to the foyer and looked through the peephole.

Cops. I peeked again and saw that it was the two police officers I'd met outside of Babs' apartment: the one who'd taken me down to the station, Detective Ryan, and the older one, who had too many consonants in his name for me to remember. What were they doing here? And why hadn't they called first?

"Just a second!" I said as I frantically tried to smooth my mop of chestnut-brown bed head. I wanted to ask them to come back in twenty minutes, but I was pretty sure I already knew how that would go over.

I swung the door open. "Hello, officers." I tried to sound friendly, but there was no disguising the question mark in my tone: *What are you doing here?*

The older policeman smirked as his eyes flicked down at my pajama pants. "Are we catching you at a bad time?"

Oh, why had I picked the pink and purple ones with the cute cartoon owls? Were they adorable? Yes. Were they appropriate for meeting with the SFPD? Hardly.

I could feel myself blush. "No, Detective"—I checked his nameplate on his uniform, which was little help: *Blaszczyk. Darn it.* I decided to go for it. Surely he'd appreciate it, like when you're in a foreign country and you make an effort to speak the language. "Detective Blas . . . zec . . ."

"I'm a homicide inspector, and it's pronounced 'Blay-chek.' " Okay, he didn't look like he appreciated the effort.

"Really? You don't pronounce the *z*?"

"No, ma'am," he said with the kind of patience you usually reserve for a small child. "The *z*'s are silent."

"Wait, there are *two z*'s in there?" I squinted and read the nameplate again. "Wow, you don't see that very often."

"Miss McKenna . . . ," began Detective Ryan, doubtlessly trying to save me from embarrassing myself further. It was a good call.

I glanced up and caught him staring at me. "Please, call me Kelsey."

"Okay, Kelsey," he said, a smile creeping across his lips.

Wait, was he *flirting*? No, he was probably just embarrassed for me because of my owl pajamas and my inability to pronounce last names. "Can I get you some tea? Coffee?"

Blaszczyk shook his head. "This isn't a social visit, Ms. McKenna. We're here on official business. We need to ask you a few questions."

I groaned silently. At least I hoped it was silent. I'm not always the best judge of such things. "Okay, why don't you come in and sit down?"

I gestured to the couch and took a seat in my favorite chair, wrapping my hands around my crossed knee in what I considered my professional listening posture, which was probably seriously undermined by the owls, but whatever.

"We need to ask you about your relationship with Babs Norton," said Blaszczyk.

"I already told him everything I knew down at the station," I said, gesturing to the younger officer.

Ryan nodded. "You did, but some new information has come to our attention, and we wanted to follow up."

I took a deep breath and did my best impersonation of someone staying calm. "New information, huh? And did that happen to come from someone named Stefan Pierce?"

"We can't comment on that," said Ryan. But the look on his face was comment enough. It was Stefan. I should've known he'd go to the police. He must have driven there straight from Margot's house.

"Never mind." I waved my hand to withdraw the question. "You don't have to tell me. He just accused me of killing Babs in front of sixty or so colleagues at the reception after the funeral."

The two policemen looked at each other. I could tell from the look on their faces that Stefan hadn't mentioned our very public confrontation.

Blaszczyk crossed his arms in front of his barrel chest. "There have been some pretty serious accusations against you, Miss McKenna."

"Look, I don't know what Stefan's beef with me is, but let me set the record straight: The thought that I could have killed Babs Norton is preposterous. I had absolutely nothing against her, and even if I did, I never could have done something like that."

"Be that as it may," Blaszczyk said, "it seems like you might have left out a few details last time."

I furrowed my brow. "Like what?"

"Like the fact that you didn't tell us how you ended up with Ms. Norton's clients in the first place."

"There was nothing to tell. They came to me. End of story."

"Why don't you walk us through everything that happened one more time?" said Ryan.

I recounted the whole story for them once again, making sure I went slow enough to keep all the details straight. I didn't want them to doubt my version of events just because I said "bear claw" when I meant "cream puff." I explained the whole situation with Haley and Christopher and assured the officers there was no contract worth killing over.

"And where were you the night of the murder?" Blaszczyk asked.

"We've already been over this!" I protested.

"Humor us," said Blaszczyk.

"I was at home, watching TV."

"And there's no one who can back up your story?" he asked.

"It's not a story! It's the truth." I told them I'd talked to Brody for about fifteen minutes and gave them the name of the Chinese restaurant I'd ordered takeout from in case they wanted to confirm my order of kung pao chicken. I wished I had a better alibi, but then again, I couldn't believe I even needed one.

Blaszczyk jotted something in his notepad and showed it to Ryan, who glanced at me and nodded. Blaszczyk stood and tucked the notepad into his back pocket. "We'll be in touch."

Just like that? I mean, not that I was complaining, but I did wonder what Blaszczyk's little note to Ryan had said.

"In the meantime," said Ryan, "I suggest you steer clear of Mr. Pierce."

"Oh, believe me, it's my new goal in life." I walked them to the door.

Detective Ryan pulled a business card out of his pocket and scribbled something on the back. "If you think of anything, call me." Blaszczyk shot him a look, and he quickly corrected himself. "Us. Call us. Either one of us. Day or night." Did I dare hope he was on my side?

"And in the meantime, stay out of trouble," said Blaszczyk. His tone was more gruff than concerned. "You don't want us to have to come back here."

After they left, I closed the door behind them and flipped the dead bolt into the locked position. It must have gone pretty well, as evidenced by the absence of handcuffs at the end of the conversation. Then again, all that meant was that they didn't feel like they had enough evidence yet. It didn't mean they wouldn't keep digging.

Thanks a lot, Stefan.

I grabbed my phone and called Brody, and all it took to get him to come over was saying the magic words: "Stefan called the cops." Half an hour later, Brody was in my kitchen, pouring us both a glass of wine.

"Wait, slow down. So Stefan called the cops on you?"

"Apparently. And since this is an active investigation, they have to take it seriously."

"What a jerk. I can't believe he'd do that."

"Really? Because I can. I wouldn't put anything past him after the scene he caused at the reception."

I munched thoughtfully on some Cheetos that I'd put out in a bowl. My refrigerator wasn't really stocked for entertaining, but I was taught to always offer your guests a snack.

"You're right," Brody said. "I guess I thought his little hissy fit would have tided him over for a day or two. Guess he didn't get it out of his system."

I sighed. "I don't know what to do. He seems to be fully committed to ruining my life instead of trying to find out what actually happened to Babs."

"Yeah, I agree. It's like he's waging a one-man anti-Kelsey campaign."

"He's probably having T-shirts made."

Brody's face brightened. "Oooh, I want one."

I opened my mouth wide in mock outrage. "Thanks a lot!"

"Not to wear, just as a collector's item. I'll have one printed that says 'Team McKenna' if it makes you feel any better."

"A little. Can it have baby goats on it?"

"Goats? Why goats?"

"I just think they're cute."

"Oh, I thought it's because they eat everything. Which . . ."

Brody paused to give me that up-and-down look he'd perfected so well, and I threw some Cheetos at him to express my displeasure.

"Okay, forget the goats, you ruiner of dreams. Point is, I've got to do something. First he accused me in front of everybody, and then he got the police involved. I have a feeling he's not going to let this drop."

Brody looked at me warily. "What exactly are you going to do, though? It seems like you'd be better off staying far away from him. Isn't that what the detective said?"

"I know, and I'm going to, but I still want to clear my name. I can't stand thinking that anyone might think I had something to do with Babs' death."

"I know it sucks being accused, but the police will figure it out eventually."

I stood up from the couch and started to pace. "I don't know if I can wait that long. And in the meantime, Stefan could do a lot of damage. I mean, what if a potential client hears about this? It wouldn't matter whether it's true or not. You think they're going to call me? And if those detectives start asking around about me, it's just going to add fuel to the fire."

"You have a point," Brody said. "It's one thing for Stefan to say it, but it's going to look really bad if the police are actually investigating you."

I was silent for a moment as I pondered my future as a person of interest. I didn't want to wait around and hope for the best. That would be seriously bad for business, not to mention my own peace of mind. No, there was only one logical solution. "All right then, so you agree?"

"With what?" Brody asked. "That being a murder suspect is bad for business? I said I did."

"No, that we should investigate!"

"I don't know, Kelsey. You of all people should know that getting involved in a murder investigation is a big decision."

"So is getting married, and people do *that* all the time." I stared at Brody, my mind whirring with the possibilities. "I mean, we do have some experience in this area."

"Don't you think we should leave this to the police to figure out? It's kind of their job and all."

"I'm sure they're on it, but that doesn't mean we can't help them out in the meantime."

"You'd better be careful you don't piss them off. How would you feel if they showed up at one of your weddings and started telling people where to sit?"

"Oh, right, like it's that easy. Have you ever tried doing a seating chart? It's a nightmare."

"So you think a seating chart is a nightmare, but a murder investigation is a piece of cake?"

"I'm not saying that. I'm just saying that we could help speed things along. And now I want cake. Thanks a lot."

I went to the refrigerator and got out the pink box I'd tried to hide from myself on one of the lower shelves. Inside was a beautifully decorated eight-inch cake a bakery had sent over to woo me into throwing some work their way. I'd been planning on saving it for breakfast, but I needed some white chocolate ganache filling to help me think.

I returned with the cake and two forks and set them down on the table. Brody just stared at me.

"What?"

Sighing, he got up and went to the kitchen, returning with two plates and a knife. "Let me show you how adult humans eat."

"What? It's not like I smushed it in your face or something."

Ignoring me, he sliced off two pieces, doled them out onto the plates, and handed me my individual serving complete with a napkin.

"Anyway," I said, sneaking in a bite mid-sentence, "it doesn't have to be a big deal. We'll just speed things along. We'll ask around, see what we can find out, and pass the information on to San Francisco's finest. I'm sure they'd appreciate the help."

Brody shot me a look. "Oh, yeah, cops love volunteer vigilantes."

"You know what I mean. They're all understaffed. Don't you watch the news? Tip lines and all that? We could just help point them in the right direction."

Brody took a bite and chewed thoughtfully. "So you're really doing this?"

I paused and picked at a perfectly executed fondant flower. "I don't think I have a choice."

CHAPTER 9

The next morning, I hopped out of bed and got to the office early. I was eager to get going on my little extracurricular project, but first I had some business to tend to. After telling Laurel about the visit from the police—and reassuring her that I wasn't going to be going to jail anytime soon—I settled in to clear my plate.

Lucas Higgins had left me a message about the wedding at Higgins Estate, so I returned his call and set up a meeting for the next day. With any luck, he'd be able to fill in some of the blanks about what Babs had orchestrated for Haley and Christopher's wedding, since Stefan was refusing to talk.

By midafternoon, my mind was churning and my thoughts kept turning back to Babs. I had so many questions. What had happened to her? Who was responsible? And where was I even going to begin? I had just started making a list when my phone buzzed with a text from Brody:

Are you in the office?

I confirmed that I was.

You with a client?

Negatory. I told him I was just logging some expenses.

Don't go anywhere. I'm dropping off the DVD of the
Bixby wedding and I have a surprise for you.

Half an hour later, I heard a banging noise coming from the front door. I poked my head out of my office in time to see Brody entering with a large, rectangular something that I had yet to identify.

"Brody, what on earth?"

He came into my office and dropped a fresh, new whiteboard onto the floor, then dug into his jacket pocket and pulled out a package of dry-erase markers.

"What is that?" I asked. "Office supplies?"

"What do you give the amateur sleuth who has everything?" he asked.

"I don't know, what?"

He held out his arms in a presentational flourish. "A murder board!"

"Excuse me? It just looks like a whiteboard to me."

"Remember that one night we watched that crime show you like? They put all the suspects up on a murder board. I thought it might help."

"That's actually a really good idea. I think better when I can make lists."

"I know! I'm supersmart. Besides, I know last night it probably seemed like I wasn't totally onboard with this, so I wanted to let you know that I get it."

"Seriously? You don't think I'm nuts?"

"I didn't say that. But I know you won't be able to let this go until it's resolved, and that's one of the things I love about you."

"*Awww,* thanks. You're the best, Brody Marx."

"I know. Now, where can we set it up?"

"Not in here. I don't want anyone thinking we're opening a private eye firm. Oh!" I snapped my fingers. "We can put it down the hall. There's an office down there that's been sitting empty for months. No one ever goes down there."

Part of our office co-op, the room was at the back of the building and rarely stayed rented. It was too small, under-ventilated, and right next to the shared bathroom—which meant every time someone flushed, the office was filled with the racket of pipes clanging in protest.

I poked my head out to see if anyone was around, then gave Brody the all clear.

We carried it past the kitchen, me leading the way and Brody holding up the back end.

"Hey, guys, whatcha doing with that whiteboard?" I was so startled to hear Laurel's voice I nearly dropped the board.

"Nothing!" I don't know why I was acting so suspicious. I hadn't done anything wrong. I mean, wasn't that the point of the whole thing anyway? To prove that I hadn't done anything wrong?

She leaned over to get a better look. "What's wrong with it? Are you throwing it out? I could use one of those in my office."

"No, it's . . . Brody's. He's—" I fumbled for an explanation. I don't know why I felt sheepish, except for the fact that I hadn't told her yet that I was turning my attention to crime-fighting.

"Working on a project," Brody interjected. "I'm just going to—"

"Use the empty office for a few days," I said, pointing down the hall. "Just until—"

"They finish painting in my office," he finished.

"Yeah," I said, staring dumbly at her.

She looked back and forth between us. "Oh, okay. We're out of coffee, so I'm going to run down to the store. Anybody want anything?"

"No!" I said, a little too loudly.

"I'm good," Brody said.

"All right, then, see you in a few." I listened as she walked down the hall, and sagged with relief when I heard the front door close behind her.

"Well, luckily you kept it cool," Brody said. "Why were you acting like we're up to something? All we're doing is transporting oversized office supplies."

"I know," I said. "I'm just nervous. Sorry."

"Sheesh," he responded. "If we're going to prove you're innocent, you're going to have to stop acting so guilty."

We got the whiteboard into the spare office and closed the door behind us. Even though the room was dank, windowless, and probably last painted around the time of the Second World War, it was perfectly suited for our purposes.

"Okay," said Brody, opening up the package of pens. "What color marker should we start with?"

"Green. No, blue. Wait, on TV they always start with the victim. In red."

He took the cap off a marker and scribbled the word "Victim" on the left side of the board. "Babs Norton." Under that, he added for clarity: "Wedding planner."

"You don't have to put that. We know who she is."

Brody's marker froze in midair. "Look, do you want me to help, or not?"

"I do, but—"

"But what?" Brody put his hands on his hips and stared at me.

I bit my lip. "Can I write it?"

"Why? What's wrong with the way I did it?"

"It's not *wrong*." I wrinkled my nose and pointed at the board. "It's just—your handwriting's really messy."

"It is not!" he said, incredulous.

"Here, just give it to me."

He replaced the cap on the marker and threw it at me. "I can't believe you're calling me out for bad penmanship."

"Sorry," I said, "just because it's a murder board doesn't mean it can't look nice."

I rubbed off the words he'd written with the sleeve of my sweater and started again. In my tidiest handwriting, I wrote Babs' name in all caps on the left side of the board. We wrote out bullet points under her name—well, *I* wrote out the bullets while Brody offered a few suggestions and pretended to pout.

"This is great," I said. "Now, suspects."

I uncapped the black marker and drew several columns to the right of Babs' name.

"I suppose we should start with Margot," Brody said.

"Margot Norton," I said, writing her name at the top of the next column. Just to be thorough, I wrote the words "Babs' sister" under Margot's name. "Okay, what've we got?"

Brody crossed his arms in front of his chest. "Well, they're sisters. Sometimes that's all the motive you need."

I thought of all the sisters I'd worked with over the years. He had a point. Under her name I wrote the words "Motive: guilt by siblingry."

"That's not a word," Brody said.

"You're just mad because I won't let you write. Now, if they really did own real estate together, that's a huge motive."

"It depends on how it was set up," Brody said. "If they were tenants in common, it would go to whoever Babs named as her heir, but if they were joint tenants with right of survivorship, then yeah, it would immediately go to Margot."

I looked at him, surprised. "What are you, some sort of real estate lawyer?"

"What?" he said. "I know things."

"I underestimated you, Brody Marx. Continue."

"Now, if they were joint tenants, then it all depends on who her beneficiaries were. Did she have any children?"

I thought for a second. "Not that I know of."

"Then it's possible it would all go to Margot."

Under Margot's name I wrote:

- *Owned real estate together?*
- *Beneficiary of the will?*
- *Possible drinking problem?*

I turned back to Brody. "So how do we find out more about Margot? Do you think they'll make Babs' will public?"

"Not right away. It's not like in those movies where everyone gathers in the library for the reading of the will with lots of old white men in suits."

"Too bad. That would certainly be handy. What about real estate records?"

"They don't read those aloud in the library, either."

"I know, smarty-pants, but couldn't we go down to the court-house and look them up?"

"Probably. Maybe. I don't know. I'm sure you can if you know what to look for."

"Or maybe there's an easier way," I said, mulling over the building where Babs' office was located.

"What's that?"

"Pay a visit to Babs' office building and have a talk with the office manager."

"Are you sure they even owned the building? How do you know she didn't rent that space?"

"Either way, it seems like talking to the office manager would be the easiest way to find out. Besides, who knows what I might learn that isn't in the public record?"

"Okay, fair point," Brody said. "But what are you going to do? Go in and flash your fake police badge or something? The build-ing manager isn't going to tell you anything."

"Not if I come right out and ask." A thought was forming at the back of my mind. "But say I were to casually inquire?"

"How are you going to do that?" Brody furrowed his brows in an expression that could best be described as "dubious."

I crossed my arms and smiled. "Let's just say it might be time for me and Laurel to consider a new office."

"So you're going to pretend you're a potential renter?"

"Why not? And if it doesn't work, we can still try the records office."

"I guess it couldn't hurt." Brody gestured to the board. "Who's next?"

"We have to consider the possibility that it was Stefan." I wrote his name on the board next to Margot's.

Brody mulled my words for a moment. "I wouldn't put it past him, but what's the motive?"

"I don't know," I admitted. "It seems pretty stupid to me because I'm not sure there can be a 'Weddings by Babs' without, you know, *Babs.* Which means he's basically out of a job. It would have had to have been something pretty major."

"Or it was a crime of passion."

"True. She couldn't have been easy to work for." I tapped my chin with the marker while I thought out loud. "They could have gotten into an argument, and she could have threatened to fire him. And we know he has a temper."

"Yeah," Brody said. "There are any number of things that could have set him off."

"Besides," I added, "on crime shows, it's always the husband who did it, and he was like her work husband."

I jotted some points under his name:

- *Access to the victim*
- *Motive: crime of passion*
- *Hot-tempered*

I drew a tidy line between Margot's column and Stefan's column to keep them apart. "Who else?"

"One of her clients?"

I shuddered a little. "I suppose it could happen, but that kind of freaks me out a little bit."

"Sorry, but you of all people know how emotional people can get about their weddings."

Over on the right side of the board, I started a new list to help us brainstorm. Under the heading of "Other Possibilities" I wrote the words "Unhappy clients."

"There's just one problem," I said, staring at the list.

"What's that?"

"I don't know who any of her clients are—or were. And I doubt I could get Stefan to tell me."

"Just tell him you're hoping to sign a few more couples in time for wedding season," Brody said with a smirk.

"Ha. Yeah, I'm sure that would go over well."

"What about Haley and Christopher?" Brody said.

"What? No!" I said. "I didn't mean them!"

"Yeah, but they qualify, don't they?"

"Technically, yeah, but I don't see it. They weren't mad or anything. They were just ready to move on."

"All right," he said. I was glad he was dropping it. It would be hard to plan a wedding for someone who I thought was capable of murder.

We stared at the list, unsure what to do next.

"Sheesh," I said. "It could be anybody. Jealous ex . . ."

"A disgruntled vendor . . . ," Brody said.

"A random intruder . . . ," I added, writing all three possibilities on my list.

"Mafia hit?" Brody said.

I shot Brody a quizzical look. "Why do you think it was the Mafia?"

"I don't! I thought we were brainstorming."

We sat in silence for a moment. I was forgetting something. I stared at the board, trying to capture the thought dodging around the back of my mind. Was there another suspect we should put on the board? Some evidence that we needed to add? "Pictures!"

"Pictures?" Brody asked.

"Yeah, there are always pictures of the suspects on the murder board."

Brody looked puzzled. "Why? We know what everyone looks like."

"C'mon, if something's worth doing, it's worth doing right."

Brody sighed. "Okay, fine, I'll print you up some pictures to put on here."

I jumped up and hugged my friend around the neck. "You're the best, Brody."

He wriggled out of my grasp, laughing. "And you're a control freak."

CHAPTER 10

It seemed like Margot and Stefan were my two best leads if I was going to find out what happened to Babs, but I didn't even know where to start with Stefan; he wasn't going to let me anywhere near him. So the next morning I set to work on my plan to find out more about the sisters' deepest, darkest, most real-estate-oriented secrets.

With housing prices booming in San Francisco, real estate was serious business. And if what Danielle said was true, Margot might well have had a major financial motive to want Babs out of the picture.

Step one? Make sure I wouldn't run into Stefan. I assumed the office he'd shared with Babs was out of commission, but I had no doubt that if I ran into him there he'd accuse me of returning to the scene of the crime.

After picking up a cheap burner phone from Walgreens with sixty prepaid minutes—I'd learned my lesson about caller ID—I had Laurel call him, pretending to be a newly engaged bride who wanted to come into his office for a consultation.

Stefan was accepting new clients, but he told Laurel they'd

have to meet somewhere else, since his office was "being reno-vated." He didn't mention that the renovation involved finger-print dust and crime scene tape.

He suggested they meet at a Starbucks of Laurel's choosing, and Laurel promised to check with her fake fiancé and call back later to set up the consultation.

The coast was clear.

Step two was to make an appointment with Linda, the prop-erty manager whose number I'd gotten off the sign hanging outside of Babs' building. She said I could come by the next morning, which gave me plenty of time before my afternoon ap-pointment at Higgins Estate Winery.

Step three, pick out an outfit that says, *I really am here to rent an office space and not just ply you with questions.* I flipped through the hangers in my closet. Green dress that makes my eyes pop? Gray slacks and heels? What had I worn when I rented my office space? Realizing I was overthinking it, I grabbed a skirt and blouse that would also be appropriate for my meeting with Lucas Higgins and set them out with my favorite pair of heels.

There'd be no sneaking in this time. When I arrived at Babs' building the next morning, I pressed the button next to the front door and waited until I was buzzed in, then strode through the lead-glass doors that still had bright blue painter's tape on them indicating their recent repair.

A moment later, I heard the click of heels on marble and turned to greet the businesslike blonde who was descending the staircase. "You must be Linda."

"And you must be Kelsey," she said, sticking out her hand. "Nice to meet you."

"Likewise," I said as we shook hands.

"You were looking for something under a thousand square feet, right? I have a couple of options I can show you upstairs."

She walked over to an ornate doorway and pressed a button on the wall, sending gears whirring as they lowered the century-old birdcage elevator to meet us.

"Nice," I said, pretending I'd never seen the decorative metal-work. "Is that art nouveau?"

"It is," Linda said. "All original. Isn't it beautiful?"

"It's lovely," I said as she slid the doors open and we climbed on board. "How old is the building?"

"Built in 1909, a couple years after the Great Earthquake. They just don't make them like this anymore."

"Whoever owns it sure must be proud of it. . . ." I let the statement hang in the air for a second to see how she'd respond.

"You're right about that. It's been in the same family for decades." The elevator groaned to a halt, and Linda opened the door once again.

"Oh, yeah?" I exited the elevator and looked around the landing. "Lucky family. I think I read an article about them. Wasn't their name Norton or something?"

"Yes, that's right," she said as I followed her down the hall. There was one question answered. Not that it told me much, but at least I was on the right track.

"Now, this office," she said, taking the keys from her pocket and opening a door, "doesn't face the street, but it gets plenty of natural light."

I nodded thoughtfully, looking around the empty room and pretending I was trying to figure out where my furniture would go. What I was really wondering was how I could get her to divulge more information about the Nortons' real estate holdings.

I walked from the reception area into what would theoretically be my office if any of this were real. Nice, spacious, beautiful wainscoting. Not bad at all. If only I really were office-shopping. "Does it have a bathroom?"

"There's a shared bathroom, down the hall."

I managed to look concerned. "Hmm, that might be a problem."

"These old buildings have their charm, but they don't always have every modern amenity. Most people end up loving it, despite its quirks."

"I don't suppose the owners would consider adding a bathroom into the layout?" I gestured to a small room that was theoretically expendable. "Maybe in here?"

"I don't know. Ms. Norton doesn't usually—" She stopped herself. "Well, I don't really know. Let's just say things are in a little bit of flux around here."

Well, there was one question answered. The building was definitely owned by a Ms. Norton. But which Ms. Norton was she referring to?

"In flux?" I said. "Anything I should be concerned about? I mean, as a potential renter?"

She shook her head. "Oh, no, nothing like that. It's just that there's been a death in the family. It was unexpected."

"Oh, I'm sorry to hear that. But . . . well, I hate to even bring this up, but is there going to be a change in ownership? I only ask that because if I signed a lease and then the building was sold . . ."

"I'm not sure, but I don't think so." She was waffling, but I couldn't blame her.

"Well, I don't know if I'd feel comfortable signing a lease right now if the building is changing hands." I still hadn't figured out a way to come right out and ask who would inherit Babs' portion, but I was definitely making headway.

Linda paused. "I really don't think so, but hold on a second. Let me see if I can get you some answers."

Linda pulled a walkie-talkie from a case clipped to her belt and pressed the button on the side. "This is Linda. Can you meet us down in 4B?"

A staticky voice came over the line. "4B. Copy. Give me just a minute."

My skin prickled with adrenaline, starting at my fingertips and working its way up my arms. Was it my imagination, or did the voice sound familiar? I waved my arms to get Linda's attention. "That's not necessary," I whispered. "Really. I hate to bother anyone."

Linda pressed the button again. "Copy that. Over." She replaced the receiver into her belt clip and smiled warmly. "Oh, it's really no trouble. She's right upstairs."

Who? Who was right upstairs? I couldn't be sure, but it had sounded like Margot's voice on the other end. *Dang it.* I hadn't expected to run into her. What ever happened to just owning a building and letting the building manager do her job?

I starting edging toward the door. The flaw in my plan was now apparent. I'd thought I could sneak in, snoop around, and sneak back out again without anyone being the wiser.

I wanted to make a break for it, but Linda was pointing out the lovely crown molding, and a discussion about crown molding isn't something that can be rushed.

"Hey, about that bathroom," I said. "Can I borrow it?"

"Sure, it's right this way. I'll show you." Darn it! Did I really look like I needed an escort? I was hoping she'd just point the way and I could make a break for it, but she probably wanted to enumerate the many fine properties of the copper plumbing.

She pulled out her key ring once again and unlocked the door, holding it open for me. Not only had I not been able to escape, but this unexpected visit to the little girls' room was actually wasting valuable seconds. I went inside and shut the door, then stood there for the very minimum amount of time I thought it might have taken to use the facilities. Then I ran the water for a few seconds in what I hoped would be a convincing piece of theater in case Linda could hear me from the other side of the door.

I came back out to find Linda waiting—*alone,* thank God.

I checked the time on my phone, then pointed at it in the universal symbol for having somewhere else to be. "I'm sorry, Linda, I hadn't realized how late it had gotten. How about if I call you later? Do you have a card?"

"Sure," she said, looking confused and maybe a little disappointed. It wasn't her fault I wasn't going to take the office, but of course I couldn't tell *her* that. She offered me a card, then pressed the elevator call button, once again sending the gears into a whir.

I tried not to look too nervous as I checked the stairs. The brass dial indicated the elevator's progress, but why did it have to go so slow?

Eight.

Seven.

Six.

I could have run down the stairs in the time it took the elevator to come. *C'mon!*

Five.

Four.

As the wrought-iron elevator compartment descended into

view, I could see a pair of women's shoes, followed by a pair of women's legs, followed by—"Oh, Margot!" Linda said as Margot slid open the antique elevator door. "Good! I'd like to introduce you to—"

"Kelsey?" Margot said, stepping out of the elevator.

Linda looked from Margot to me and back again. "You two know each other?"

"Hi, Margot." I tried desperately to come up with some explanation for my presence that would make sense. "Yes, of course. I hadn't realized . . ."

You know how sometimes someone will start talking and they say so many different things that you can't follow any of it and eventually you give up?

Yeah, that was pretty much my strategy. I started talking—babbling really—about crown molding and renovations and my current lease, and by the time I stopped neither of them could remember what they had meant to ask me.

"So you were hoping to rent office space?" Margot asked, looking unsure. "Here?"

"That's right," I said. "Well, I'm looking at my options anyway."

Margot's eyes narrowed. "Uh-huh. And you were hoping to move into *this* building?"

"Sure! It's a great building."

"Right on the heels of my sister's death?"

"I'll admit the timing is a little . . ." I waved my hand instead of finishing.

Margot stared at me matter-of-factly. "And you're not scared off by her murder?"

Linda looked at Margot and gasped. "I thought we weren't telling anyone about that?"

"Oh, Kelsey knows," Margot said. "In fact, she's the one who found my sister."

"What?" Linda's voice echoed down the hall. "You pretended you'd never set foot in this building before."

"I didn't mean to imply—"

"What are you *really* doing here, Kelsey?" I couldn't read Margot's expression, but I knew it wasn't good. What if she told Stefan? He'd have a field day with this information.

"Look, guys. I'm sorry. This was a bad idea. I didn't mean to be insensitive. I just . . . well, to be honest, I always loved Babs' office. I didn't know what you were planning on doing with it, and I knew it was too soon to ask. I just thought maybe I'd see what else you had."

Linda seemed unmoved by my speech. "Then why were you asking so many questions about who owned the building? Sounds like you already knew."

"Is that true, Kelsey? Because I don't think what we're planning on doing with the building is any of your business."

I took a shot in the dark: "Babs told me she owned this building, so I figured there might be some changes, that's all."

Margot's eyes narrowed. "I think you need to go."

"I'm sorry, I thought that's what she'd said. Does that mean *you're* the owner?"

"Unless you're ready to sign a lease, I'd say that's none of your business. Now I don't know what your game is, but I think it's best if you leave before I call the police."

I wasn't sure exactly what she was going to tell the police: *I'd like to report a rental inquiry?* Nonetheless, I apologized for the intrusion and left.

Had Margot killed her sister over real estate? If so, she knew *exactly* why I was there. And if not, then I probably looked pretty guilty myself—returning to the scene of the crime and all that. Of course, if I'd really had nefarious intentions, would I have made an appointment?

What had made me think I could just waltz in there, ask a few questions, and have someone blab the whole family history to me?

Too many reruns of *CSI,* that's what.

CHAPTER 11

*I*f my encounter with Margot and Linda was any indication, I seriously needed to rethink my approach. I'd verified that the Nortons owned the building, but that was about as far as I'd gotten. I still didn't know how the two women had gotten along, what Margot stood to gain from Babs' death, or even whether electricity was included in the rent.

I still had a couple of hours before it was time to drive up to the wine country for my meeting at Higgins Estate, so I headed back to the office to regroup. I also wanted to spend a few minutes researching the winery. Based on their website, Higgins Estate really seemed to be pushing weddings and events. There were tons of beautifully lit photographs of happy couples toasting in the vineyard and a contact form that promised someone would be in touch within twenty-four hours.

From the "About Us" page, I learned that Lucas was the CEO and business manager, and his brother, Miles, was the winemaker. There were a couple of pictures of Lucas, but Miles seemed to be more of a behind-the-scenes guy. His focus was on

Zinfandels, for which he'd won several awards. Higgins Estate looked like it had changed a lot since I'd been up there last. Formal gardens, a brand-new tasting room—this place was high-end all the way.

By 1:00, I was cruising up Silverado Trail toward St. Helena. It was a beautiful day, with blue skies, fluffy clouds, and the lightest of breezes. In other words, wedding weather.

I pulled through the entrance to Higgins Estate and headed up the hill to the château looming in the distance. Rows of old-growth grapevines lined the road, with scarlet roses in full bloom at the end of each row.

Wineries didn't plant the rosebushes just for looks. They used them as an early warning of plant fungus, which, I'd learned, showed up on the rosebushes earlier than on the vines. Not that I'd ever share that trivia fact with my brides. Most of them don't want to hear the word "fungus" while we're talking about nuptials.

I pulled my car into the parking lot and headed up the sidewalk. The château was even more impressive up close, with its turrets, balconies, and patios with views of the rolling hills. A chalkboard easel pointed me toward the tasting room and invited me to meet inside for a 2:00 tour.

I swung open one of the large wooden doors and found myself in the gift shop, where visitors could load up on coasters, fancy condiments, and epicurean accessories to take home with their cases of Chardonnay and Zinfandel. Smart to filter everyone through here on their way in and on their way out.

A twentysomething woman with long, dark hair and a name-plate reading *Zara* greeted me at the door. "Hi, welcome to Higgins Estate."

"Hi, I have an appointment with Lucas. My name is Kelsey McKenna."

She smiled and picked up the phone. "I'll let him know you're here."

I waited by a rack full of aprons and oven mitts embroidered with a sprig of ripe olives. Come to think of it, I could use an oven mitt. I checked the price tag. Twenty-four bucks? For an oversized mitten with no mate? I didn't even want to know what the matching tea towel cost.

"Kelsey," said a deep voice behind me.

I turned to see Lucas standing there. Although he was dressed much more casually than when we'd met, he still had a refined elegance to him. I wasn't surprised the family had chosen him to be the face of Higgins Estate. He certainly dressed the part.

"Hi, Lucas, good to see you," I said, bumping into a display of wineglasses with a picture of the château etched on to them. The glasses tinkled together merrily, and for a second I thought I was about to buy a matched set of broken drinkware, but they quickly settled back down again.

"Thanks for coming in. I was thinking I could give you a quick tour and then we could sit down and talk, if that's okay with you. Would you like a glass of wine?"

"Oh, no thank you. Maybe later, but I'm afraid business and wine don't mix."

"That's too bad. I think they go together rather well, myself, but then again . . ." He smiled broadly and gestured toward the front door. "Anyway, shall we?"

He led me down the hallway, our steps echoing off the marble tiles. "We have weddings here almost every weekend during the busy season. The courtyard patio holds about eighty, and there are picnic tables under the oaks up there for smaller, more casual gatherings. Now, I checked my calendar and your couple is supposed to be on the Vintners Terrace."

He led the way through a pair of French doors to a large outdoor space that overlooked the vineyards. It was indeed impressive, and I immediately started making a mental checklist of things we would need to furnish it. I walked over to the railing to check out the view, and Lucas pointed to the top of a hill. "Up there is our wine cave that we built last year. Remind me to take you there later. We built a dining room inside it for special events."

"How cool. I definitely want to see that." Wine caves were becoming more and more popular in the wine country. Not the naturally occurring kind with stalactites and tales of hidden treasure, but the newfangled kind that wineries excavate out of the hills to make underground wine cellars that stay cool all year long. Instead of hauling the sixty-gallon barrels of wine off to a commercial cellar, they just store them under the very ground where the grapes had grown—and who doesn't need extra storage space?

But more importantly—okay, well, at least for me—caves make a great setting for small weddings and rehearsal dinners. They're dark and atmospheric and don't require much more than a bunch of candles to create instant drama.

After showing me the rest of the château, Lucas led me to his office, a high-ceilinged room on the second floor with sweeping views of the vineyard. He sat down at his antique banker's desk and motioned for me to take a seat in one of his elegant leather guest chairs that probably cost about two thousand dollars each.

I had a feeling he didn't spend much time at Ikea.

"Thanks for the tour," I said, settling in. "You have a beautiful winery."

"Thanks," said Lucas. "I'm glad to hear you say that. I'm hoping I can convince you to spend more time up here. But first, you had some questions?"

"Well, yes. I'm coordinating a wedding that Babs had planned before . . . well, you know, *before*."

Lucas nodded gravely.

"And I'm afraid I don't have much information on what she'd been planning. Unfortunately, I haven't been able to coordinate with Stefan"—I was super proud of my diplomatic skills on that one, and it wasn't technically a lie—"so I was hoping you might be able to fill in some of the blanks?"

"Hmmm . . . we kind of let Babs do her thing. What do you need to know?"

"Oh, basically, everything." I explained my predicament in more detail, but I didn't get much more than sympathetic nods.

"I'm sorry, I don't know much—but I might be able to help narrow it down for you." He walked over to a credenza in the corner of the room and opened a drawer, then dug through some papers until he produced a printed list. "These are the caterers who are approved to work here," he said, handing the list to me. "It would have been one of them."

"Thank you," I said, scanning the list. "This will definitely help."

"As for the rest, I can't really say. I guess she did so many weddings here, I stopped paying attention after a while." There was a pause. "Speaking of that, how do you feel about taking over some of her workload?"

"I'm definitely open to that," I said.

"If you can hold on one second," Lucas said, picking up his cell phone. "I'm going to try to call my brother Miles real quick. I was hoping he could join us." A few seconds later he shook his head. "I'm getting his voice mail." Another moment passed as he waited for the beep. "Miles, I have Kelsey in my office. Come on up if you can." He clicked off the phone and laid it on his desk. "I apologize. I really wanted him to meet you."

"Tell me more about what you're looking for," I prompted.

"The long and short of it is, we got so used to sending inquiries to Babs, we never really tried to bring in anyone else. So now that she's gone, it's left a pretty big hole in our team. Eventually, we'll probably hire someone to be our on-site planner, but in the meantime, we need to get some new referrals lined up."

I pictured the calendar hanging on the wall of my office. Weddings, weddings, and more weddings. "I'd love to help out, but wedding season is about to hit and we're pretty booked up."

Lucas shook his head. "I get it. The irony is, anyone who's available isn't that good, and anyone who's good isn't available."

I paused. I was dying to know where Stefan fell on that spectrum. "But what about Babs' assistant?"

Lucas sighed. "Who, Stefan? The verdict's still out on that one."

"What do you mean?"

"Honestly? I was surprised to learn at Babs' funeral that they were still working together."

"Really? Why? I mean, don't get me wrong, I was surprised she even hired him in the first place, but that's neither here nor there."

"I don't want to go into too much detail, but he screwed up one of our weddings pretty badly. It caused a lot of problems for us."

"So wasn't he working with Babs on this wedding?"

"No, after that whole debacle, she promised to personally oversee all of our events, so we hadn't seen him around in months. She kind of hinted that he was on his way out, but I guess it never happened."

Wow. Stefan and Babs were on the outs? That was news to me. If she had intended to fire him, that would certainly be motive—and definitely worth adding to the murder board. "So where does that leave you with the weddings she was doing?"

"That's what's ironic. The contracts were with her company, not her specifically, so now he's back up here. Unfortunately, there's not much we can do about it except keep a close watch on him. But I sure don't want to refer more business to him."

I nodded diplomatically, glad he'd already come to that conclusion on his own. "Of course."

"So you can see why I wanted to reach out to you," he said. "I know you probably aren't interested in the on-site position since you have your own business, but I'd love to add you to the list of approved vendors."

I was definitely interested. Not everyone has the budget to fly off to Reykjavík to get married under the aurora borealis or to have an underwater scuba-diving wedding in the Maldives. Adding more wine country weddings to our portfolio would certainly help pay the bills.

Before I could reply, the door to Lucas' office swung open. I twisted around in my chair to see a sunburned man in his forties wearing grungy jeans and a fleece pullover embroidered with the Higgins Estate logo. His hair needed a trim and he was sporting a three-day stubble—a shaggy contrast to the clean-cut Lucas.

"Oh, good. Miles, this is Kelsey. She's a wedding planner. Kelsey, meet my brother Miles."

"Hi," I said. "Nice to meet you."

"Hey," he grunted, plopping down into the seat next to me. Don't ask me how, but I knew there would be no *pleased to make your acquaintance* to follow. I'm kind of psychic that way.

"I've been talking to Kelsey about helping out with our

wedding program," Lucas said, "and I thought you might like to meet her."

Miles looked at me and shrugged as if to say, *She'll do.*

Lucas smiled patiently. "Kelsey comes highly recommended, and I'm trying to charm her into saving our backsides, so maybe you could help me out a little here and talk to her a little about our wines."

"You mean the wines I should be making right now instead of sitting in here in your overpriced office talking about weddings?"

"Now, Miles, play nice."

"I'm sorry," said Miles—not sounding sorry at all—"but you know how I feel about weddings."

"And *you* know how important they are to our business," Lucas said, irritation edging into his voice.

Miles scowled. "I don't know about you, but I'm in the wine-making business. Not the 'be nice to spoiled brats' business."

"Be that as it may, we have a pile of contracts, and unless you want me to put you in charge of hand-holding the brides, we're going to need someone to take over for Babs."

Miles' face turned red at the mention of her name. "If there's one thing this place doesn't need, it's another Babs."

"Kelsey isn't 'another Babs.' Maybe if you stopped being so damned stubborn, we could work out a solution that we'd all be happy with."

This was getting interesting. What did Miles have against Babs Norton? Was it the mere fact that she was a wedding planner and he didn't like our kind in general, or did he specifically have a beef with her?

I turned in my chair to face him. "I take it you're not a fan of weddings?"

Miles' scowl softened into a glower. "I don't even know why we do them. If I had my way, I'd return every one of their deposits and tell them to go find someone else's vineyard to stomp around in."

"Is there anything specific?" I asked. "Maybe it would help if we could implement some guidelines?"

"How about 'no brides, no grooms, and no wedding planners coming in here acting like they own the place'?"

I opened my mouth to speak, then quickly closed it again. If only I had done that in the first place. "I'm sorry. I didn't mean to overstep."

Miles turned in his chair and made eye contact with me for the first time since he'd entered the room. "I guess there's nothing I can do to stop my brother from letting people hold weddings here. So I'll tell you what: you stay out of my way, and I'll stay out of yours."

I blinked a couple of times and nodded. "That seems fair."

And with that he got up and stalked out of the room. I stared after him as he slammed the door with a loud bang.

"I think he liked you," Lucas said, a big grin spreading across his face.

CHAPTER 12

*H*e said *what?*"

I'd returned to the office to fill Laurel in on the day's events, lugging a case of wine that Lucas had sent home with me. It was an obvious bribe, but a good one, and Laurel and I had locked the doors and declared it happy hour.

"Yep, he's a real charmer," I replied, topping off Laurel's glass of Higgins Estate Zinfandel. "But he does make good wine."

"Cheers to that," Laurel said, raising her glass. "Was Lucas at least nice to you?"

"Oh, he was great. Not bad looking, either."

"I can't believe he's still single," Laurel said.

"You looked him up?"

"Of course. The Internet is our friend." Laurel smiled mischievously. "Wanna do a coin toss? Heads, you date him; tails, I date him?"

"No way. Neither one of us gets to date him."

"Oh, come on," she teased. "Why are you so against love?"

"I'm not against love! But believe me, you don't want to go out with anyone who's in the industry."

"They're not in the industry, remember? They're in the wine business."

"Yeah, but close enough. When you break up, it makes things really awkward."

"Who says we're breaking up?" she asked, pretending to be offended on behalf of her imaginary relationship with a man she wasn't actually dating.

"You know what I mean. *If* you broke up." I took a sip of wine while Laurel pretended to pout. "Oh, never mind, I'm sure you'll be very happy together."

"That's more like it," she said, smiling.

"Anyway, he said it was no problem putting us on the approved-vendor list. In fact, he seemed pretty enthusiastic about throwing some more weddings our way."

"That's great!" Laurel studied my face. "Isn't it?"

"Of course," I said halfheartedly.

"Then why does it make you look like you need twenty units of Botox?"

"What do you mean?"

"You were making that scowly face you make when you're concentrating or you're worried."

"Sorry," I said, rubbing the spot right between my eyebrows that always gave me away. "I was just thinking about Stefan."

"What about him?"

"Well, Lucas said that Babs was thinking about firing him."

"No way!"

"I know. If that's true, then . . ."

"Then maybe he's the one who offed her?"

"Listen to you! Get a glass of wine in you and you sound like a street detective."

"Sorry," she said. "I got caught up in the moment."

"But yeah, I hadn't really taken him that seriously as a potential suspect. I mean, sure, he's a jerk, but I always thought he had too much to lose to have killed her."

Laurel took a sip of wine. "But if she was about to fire him—"

"Then he had nothing to lose."

We both sat in silence for a moment as we considered it. Should I go to the police and tell them what I'd learned? Without proof, they'd just think it was mutual finger-pointing. Stefan would probably say that she'd promoted him or something.

"Botox!" Laurel said.

"What? Oh, sorry." I shook my head briskly, trying to relax my forehead. I had to stop doing that.

"Well, anyway," Laurel said, "I promise if you ever try to fire me, I won't kill you."

"Much appreciated."

"But you probably shouldn't fire me, in case I'm lying."

"Fair enough. And now I'm officially scared of you."

"It's always the ones you least suspect." She drained the last bit of wine and set the empty glass on the table in front of her. "Now, let's get out of here and pretend we have a life."

The next morning, I got up early so I could make a dent in my ever-growing to-do list. I started with my neglected e-mails, culling my inbox down to a more manageable number, and noticed with dismay that a prospective client had canceled our initial meeting with no real explanation. Surely it was a coincidence, right? I shook my head. *Stop being silly. Sure, people talk, but people also cancel meetings for no reason. It happens. Now stop being a weirdo and get back to work.*

It was time to roll up my sleeves and start using my skills of deduction to solve the mystery of Haley and Christopher's caterer, since that was one of the bigger vendors. Maybe I'd even call it the Great Caterer Caper. That made it sound a lot more fun.

I settled in on the couch with my laptop and the list of approved caterers Lucas Higgins had provided me. It was a healthy list, about twenty caterers altogether, but it definitely helped narrow it down from "someplace with 'Wine' in the name."

I'd just have to start calling them one by one until I figured out which one Babs had hired for Haley and Christopher. I mentally rehearsed how to explain the situation, then took a deep breath and dialed the first number.

"Hi, this is Kelsey McKenna. I was wondering if you could tell me whether you're catering a wedding at Higgins Estate on the eighteenth?"

"Sorry, we're booked on the eighteenth." The man's voice was brusque, as if he were in the middle of piping filling into an infinite number of miniature cupcakes that had to be at the White House or else the Prime Minister would be left without dessert and all diplomatic relations would be severed.

Maybe I'm exaggerating, but he really did sound busy.

"No, I'm not trying to hire a caterer. I'm trying to find out if you're the caterer for this particular wedding."

"Who is this?" Clearly those cupcakes weren't going to fill themselves.

"My name is Kelsey. I'm the wedding planner."

"And you don't know who their caterer is?"

"It's complicated. See, I took over their wedding and—"

"Our scheduling person isn't here right now. You'll have to call back later."

This wasn't going to be easy. I went down the list one by one, leaving a string of voice-mail messages and confused caterers in my wake. With practice, I got my spiel down to something that invited fewer questions.

"Hi, my name is Kelsey"—I'd stopped offering my last name out of sheer professional pride—"and I've been asked to help with some last-minute wedding arrangements. Can you tell me if you're catering a wedding at Higgins Estate the Saturday after next?"

The woman on the other end of the line paused. "That's, what? The eighteenth?"

"Yes, that's right. At Higgins Estate."

"Ohhh." Her voice had taken on a somber tone. "Was this the wedding for Babs Norton?"

"Yes! I mean, probably. It would be under the name Bennett or possibly Riegert?"

"Bennett. Yep, I remember them."

Jackpot. It had taken almost an hour, but I'd finally nailed down the caterer.

"Where should we send the check?" she asked.

"The what?"

"I assume you're calling to get their money back. We'll cut them a check. Minus the fifty percent nonrefundable deposit of course."

"I think there's been some sort of mistake," I said. "This is for Haley Bennett and Christopher Riegert."

"Right. They canceled the wedding."

"No, no, no. It's not canceled. I was calling to confirm."

"Hold on. Let me check." She set down the phone and returned a moment later. "Yep, it says right here: 'Canceled.'"

"That can't be right. I'm calling to confirm." When in doubt, repeat things, only louder.

"Look, I'm sorry. But Stefan told us we could release the date. So do you want the check or—"

I felt a surge of adrenaline flood my system, and my neck grew disproportionately warm. "Stefan called you? When?"

"Last week. I don't know, Wednesday."

Wednesday. He must have called right after he found out they were working with us. Man, I knew he was petty, but I never thought he would do something so vindictive.

I took a deep breath. I had to fix this. "No, I don't want a check. I want a caterer. The wedding is one hundred percent happening, so just un-cancel it."

Awkward pause. "I'm not sure if I can. I think we've already rebooked it."

I silently counted to five before responding. "Look, they're counting on you. You had a contract, and I expect you to honor it."

"Hang on." I could hear her clicking away at the computer keyboard. "Yeah, I'm sorry. I wish I could help you out, but that date is fully booked. We don't have the staff."

I was so shocked I hardly knew what to say. There wasn't going to be any winning this one. I'd have to find a new caterer. However, there was one thing I could do. After all, negotiating is part of my job. "Okay, you said you rebooked it, right?"

"That's right."

"So it's not causing you to miss out on another opportunity. Plus it's still far enough out that you haven't bought the food yet, which means you're not out any expenses. So since I have to go find a new caterer, I'd sure appreciate it if you could cut us a break on the deposit."

I held my breath awaiting her response. If I could at least get some of their money back, it would be a big help.

A pause. "What were you thinking?"

"Full refund, minus any actual expenses? They're a really sweet couple, and I'd hate to see them suffer from this . . . miscommunication."

"I do feel bad for them." More typing on the keyboard—possibly a stalling tactic, but I'd give her that. "Okay, I'll tell you what, I can refund ninety percent since we were able to re-book it."

"I'll take it. Thank you so much."

"Oh—except . . . I'm looking at the order now. Technically, the contract was with Weddings by Babs, and since the deposit came through them, I can only refund it to them. I know it's kind of a pain, but I'm sure you guys can work it out."

I didn't share her optimism, but she was already doing me a huge favor by offering a refund. I'd just have to make it work. It wasn't going to be easy, but I was sure I'd be able to get the check back from Stefan. I didn't care if he was mad at me; the money wasn't his to keep and I wasn't going to take no for an answer.

I gritted my teeth. "I'm sure we can. Thank you so much for being flexible."

"My pleasure."

I hung up the phone and stared at the table in shock. No caterer. *Are you kidding me? No freakin' caterer?* What was I going to do? Call in a taco truck? Send word to all the guests that it was now a potluck? Drive through In-N-Out Burger on the way there and order Double-Doubles and onion rings for all?

Part of my job is to freak out so my clients don't have to. And today I was really earning my paycheck.

CHAPTER 13

*T*here's no wedding-planner oath, but if there were, it would definitely include the idea that you shouldn't sabotage a wedding, anyone's wedding, for any reason.

I still couldn't believe Stefan had done this to us, and it made me wonder what else he was capable of. If he could destroy someone's wedding out of spite, was it that much of a stretch to think he might have killed Babs?

Whether he liked it or not, we needed to talk. Although I knew the odds of him answering were slim, I picked up the phone and dialed his number. No big surprise: it went to voice mail. Listening to his outgoing message, I tried to remain calm, and I steadied myself so I wouldn't unleash on him.

"Hi, Stefan, this is Kelsey. Will you give me a call, please?" Oh, who was I kidding? There was no way he was going to call me back out of common courtesy. "I know you're mad, but we need to talk. I'm looking at a pile of canceled contracts here, and you know as well as I do that that's a major ethical violation, and probably illegal, too. I don't want to have to get lawyers involved, but if you don't fix this immediately, I'm not going to have any choice. Now call me back."

I rubbed my forehead, trying to figure out what to do next. My wedding worksheet—the one that should be filled out with the names of all the vendors we were using—stared back at me blankly. If I could make a dent in it, I'd feel a lot better.

Haley had said the florist was located in St. Helena. That would be easy enough to find. A quick search showed that there were only three on the main street through town. I called Brides in Bloom, thinking they'd be the most likely candidate.

"Oh, you mean the canceled wedding?" said the voice on the other end of the line. "What about it?"

Aaarrgh!

I didn't want to drag the florist into our drama, so in my calmest, most patient voice I explained that the wedding was back on again. They were happy to reinstate the order, and with a little finagling I even managed to have them throw in free delivery.

Next up, the cake. Easy enough. Babs had worked almost exclusively with Renee at The Sweet Spot, ever since they'd been featured on that Food Network show about wedding cakes.

With trepidation, I dialed their number. Sure enough, Renee told me that Babs had hired them to do the cake, but that Stefan had canceled it last week. How many contracts was I going to have to uncancel? If he was trying to make my job as difficult as possible, he'd succeeded.

I begged Renee to help us out, but she wasn't as easy to win back as Brides in Bloom. "I'm sorry, Kelsey, I can't do it."

I wasn't above wheedling. "Why not? The wedding hasn't been canceled, which means we *have* to have a cake!"

"Look, canceled, not canceled, whatever. Weddings by Babs

has thrown a lot of business our way, and I can't afford to get involved in this feud between you and Stefan."

"We're fine," I lied. "Just a misunderstanding."

"I heard about Babs' funeral. It sounds like a lot more than just a misunderstanding."

"Okay, fine, yes, there's been some tension, but right now I need a wedding cake and I am begging you."

"He said you stole his clients."

"That's so not true! They came to me first."

"It doesn't matter. I can't afford to get in the middle of it."

"Are you sure I can't change your mind?"

"I'm sorry, Kelsey. You're going to have to find someone else."

My shoulders sagged in defeat. "Can you at least share with me what they ordered so we don't have to start from scratch?"

She laughed. "What?" I said defensively.

"Sorry, you said 'from scratch.' I thought you were trying to use baking humor to win me over."

"Believe me, this is no joke."

"Okay, look, I'll e-mail you their order, okay? Just don't mention it to anyone."

At this point, I'd take whatever I could get. "Okay, thanks, Renee."

I hung up and headed for the kitchen, where I dug through the trash to find the empty box from the cake Brody and I had demolished. Yep, everyone thinks being a destination wedding planner is nothing but international flights and cocktail receptions, but if only they could see me elbow-deep in my garbage can.

"You want business, you've got it," I mumbled under my breath as I retrieved the pink packaging. Normally, I'd take the bride and groom for a tasting, but I made the executive decision not to worry them with it. I'd been impressed by my own informal tasting, and with the help of Renee's instructions Haley and Christopher would probably never know the difference.

Twenty minutes later, I'd secured a cake for the wedding, along with one happy cake shop that was willing to do whatever it took to please their newest client.

I still had no idea where to even start with the rest of the vendors. Photographer? Linens and silverware? Music? I didn't know who Babs' go-to people were, and it would take a miracle to figure it out.

For the twentieth time, I checked my voice mail. Nothing. Who was I kidding? Stefan had to know that I'd discovered the cancellations by now, and there was no way he was going to answer the phone, much less call me back.

It was time for Plan B.

I punched in Laurel's number.

"Hello?"

"Hey, it's me. I need you to do something for me."

Ten minutes and one fake accent later, we had an appointment with Stefan. Or perhaps I should say, Stefan had an appointment with Kate, the make-believe bride Laurel had pretended to be last time she'd called him, and her fiancé, Will. They'd made plans to meet a couple days later at a coffee shop downtown, which was a short walk from Kate's made-up job as a financial planner.

We were in.

In the meantime, I needed to talk to Haley and Christopher, so I called an emergency family meeting. The couple arrived at my office a few hours later with an extra person in tow. "Hi, Kelsey.

I thought I'd bring my dad, since he's helping pay for all this. This is my dad, Stanley Bennett."

"Nice to meet you." I could see a resemblance between Haley and her father, especially in their intense green eyes with extra-long lashes. He must have come straight from work, because he was wearing a crisp button-down shirt with a suit and tie.

Haley had told me he worked in software, so I'd pictured him wearing a T-shirt and hoodie and perhaps carrying a light saber he'd built himself. Turned out he was more of a salesman. She'd mentioned something about "software in the cloud" or "software as a solution," and I nodded along, pretending I knew anything more than "software is what makes my computer turn on."

"Thanks for helping out," he said. "I guess you know we had some troubles with the last wedding planner, but Haley said you've really got our back." I must have looked startled when he alluded to Babs, because he quickly backtracked. "I'm sorry. Was she a friend of yours?"

I pressed my lips together and nodded. "I knew her, but we weren't close."

"Sorry, I suppose that was insensitive."

"It's okay," I said.

"I only met her the one time, but she seemed like a nice enough person. There were just some . . . budgetary issues."

"I heard."

"I should have been more involved, I guess. But we've been pretty busy launching our new analytics platform. I'm sure you've heard about it."

"Oh, sure," I said. "Those analytics platforms are . . ." I gave a vague wave in lieu of finishing my thought, which I'd known was going nowhere as soon as I'd started it.

"It's pretty cool, actually. You can embed your dashboard across any cloud service to get a consistent view—"

"Dad," Haley interrupted, raising her eyebrows in my still-smiling-and-nodding direction.

"Right." He brushed his slacks. "Anyway. That's why I wanted to tag along today."

"I'm glad you did. Some things have come up, so it's good you're here." He wasn't going to be happy when he heard what Stefan had done, but if he wanted to be more involved he could start by dealing with that whole mess.

"Why don't we go to the conference room?" I gestured for the three of them to follow me down the hall, and I could hear Haley and Mr. Bennett mumbling to each other as we walked. From what I could pick up, "secure data exploration was tougher than people thought," but it was also "something that could probably wait until after this meeting, Dad, don't you think?"

"So," I said to Haley and Christopher once we'd all gotten settled in. "Since we last met, I've been trying to piece together the plans for your wedding."

Haley held up a spiral-bound blank book with glittery stars on the cover. "I brought my notes like you told me to."

"That's great," I said. Maybe there would be something in there I could work with. The photographer, rentals, musicians—there were still a lot of holes that needed to be filled in. "But first—"

"And I remembered the name of the caterer," Christopher said. Haley smiled proudly and took Christopher's hand.

"Yeah, about that," I said. "Before we get started, I need to fill you in on what I've found out the last couple of days. There've been a couple of hiccups."

Haley and Christopher exchanged nervous glances while

Mr. Bennett leaned forward in his chair. "Hiccups. What kind of hiccups?"

I took a deep breath. "There seems to be a problem with a few of your contracts."

"But Babs told us that negotiating contracts was something we wouldn't have to worry about," Christopher said.

"It's not the contracts themselves that are the problem. It's the fact that Stefan seems to have canceled several of them."

"He *what*?" Mr. Bennett's face flushed with anger.

"What do you mean?" Haley asked. "Which ones?"

"Well, the florist and the cake, both of which I was able to salvage. But there's definitely a problem with the caterer. They've rebooked and they're no longer available that day."

Haley's eyes grew big. "No caterer? But what about the shrimp kebabs?"

"I don't know. Believe me, I'm going to try to get to the bottom of this, but we might have to get creative."

"What about the money?" Mr. Bennett said, his voice taut with tension.

"You'll have to look at your contract. I did manage to talk the caterer into refunding most of your money, but unfortunately it'll go back into Babs' account, so that will take some figuring out."

Mr. Bennett gripped the armrest of his chair. "That son of a bitch."

"I assume you'll be able to get it back eventually—I mean, there's no way he can keep it, legally—but that's something you'll have to work out with him." I could only imagine how that conversation was going to go.

"I'm not going to let that bastard get away with this," Mr. Bennett said.

"Now, Daddy, it's okay." Haley put her hand reassuringly on her father's arm.

"No, it's not okay," he said, jumping up from his chair. "First that Babs woman and now *this*?"

I froze, not sure what to say. He had every right to be angry at Stefan, but what had he meant by, *First that Babs woman?* I was a little stunned by the sudden outburst, and it made me wonder if there was more to it than an overextended budget.

"Now, Daddy," Haley said. "I'm sure Kelsey will be able to work all this out, but in the meantime—"

"In the meantime, nothing," he shouted as he headed toward the door. "He picked the wrong man to mess with! We'll sue him for everything he's worth. By the time this is through, we'll *own* Weddings by Babs." And with that, he stormed out of the office, slamming the door behind him.

CHAPTER 14

*A*fter Mr. Bennett's unexpected departure, Haley apologized profusely for her father's behavior and I insisted everything was fine and that it was totally not a big deal for the father of the bride to threaten to run someone out of business.

Of course, I couldn't help but wonder if he deserved a spot on the murder board, but there would be time for that later. Right now we had a wedding to figure out, so Haley, Christopher, and I worked out a plan that involved a little bit of teamwork and a whole lot of improvisation, and they left with a to-do list that would take some of the pressure off of mine.

The main priority was resolving the caterer dilemma once and for all, so after they left I settled in with the list of caterers Lucas had given me and started calling. I found three candidates who were willing to work with us on short notice, probably because they wanted to hold on to their "approved vendor" status at Higgins. My top choice was a restaurant called Cask and Vine, and I was so relieved I practically booked them over the phone, but in the interest of due diligence I made dinner reservations and then called Brody. "Whatcha doing tomorrow? I have to go check out a restaurant."

"*Have* to? Jeez, I'm sorry. You have it rough."

"Tell me about it. Anyway, come with me and we'll eat ourselves silly. You in?"

"I can't," said Brody. "I have to drive up to Sonoma tomorrow."

"You're in luck! The restaurant's in Napa."

"I don't know if I'll be done in time. I'm doing a favor for a friend."

"Ah, come on! Who is this so-called friend and what's so important that it's infringing on our dinner plans?"

"Guy named Jake. He wants me to shoot some pictures of his winery that he can use on his website."

"Jake, schmake. He can't be all that good a friend. I've never even heard of him."

"You have too. I mentioned him the other day and I also tried to set you up with him last year."

"You did? What did I say?"

"I believe you said, 'Jake, schmake'—which . . . just because it rhymes doesn't make it mean anything."

"What do you mean?"

"You can't just go adding the *schm* sound to someone's name when you want them to go away."

"Sure you can!"

"Schmelsey McSchmenna."

"Hmm. You're right. I'm not crazy about it when you put it that way."

"Anyway," Brody said, "I guess if you wanted to tag along, we could go to dinner afterward. It'd be fun. I could use the company, and you'd get to spend time with your favorite person."

"Who, Jake Schmake?"

"That's not his name, and you know perfectly well that I'm talking about me."

"You're not trying to set me up, are you?" I hated setups, mostly because every bride I ever worked with has tried to set me up with someone in their wedding party because they think everyone should find a love as deep and profound as their own.

"Nope, I gave up on that a long time ago."

"Hey! What are you saying, I'm a lost cause?"

"C'mon, stop being argumentative. It's a nice drive and we can go to that cute bakery you like that has those fancy macaroons."

"Okay, fine, but I get to pick the music."

Brody had been right about one thing: it was a beautiful drive, especially once we got off the interstate and were cruising down a two-lane road lined with fields of vines on either side. We rode with the windows down, and I held my arm out, riding a wave of fresh air and inviting the warm breeze to circulate freely through the car. It felt good to get out of the office, even if it wasn't as far away as I would have liked.

While we drove, I caught Brody up on everything that I'd learned in the last couple of days, starting with my awkward meeting at Higgins Estate.

"So this Miles guy," he said. "Did you add him to the murder board?"

"I sure did. I mean, he's not a hard-core suspect, but he is a person of interest, what with him hating weddings and all."

"I'm sure he doesn't hate weddings; he just doesn't want them at his winery."

I shook my head. "Nope, he hates weddings. And kittens and puppies and love itself."

"Wow. Lock him up and throw away the key."

"Right? He's pretty nasty."

"And you're going to be working with him. Yay for you. Were they at least able to fill in some blanks with Haley and Christopher's wedding?"

"Well, that's the second part of my story." I proceeded to tell him about Stefan's efforts to sabotage the wedding.

"Unbelievable. Do you think you'll be able to get everything done?"

"I don't have a choice. I'm just going to have to let go of perfection."

"Says the girl who won't let me write on her whiteboard."

"I know, I know. I may have to lower my standards a little bit. Oh, and I may need your help if I can't find a photographer."

"Hey! What the—?"

"No! That's not what I mean! Those two thoughts were unrelated."

Even though he was watching the road, he still managed to scowl at me.

"I'm sorry, Brody. You know I love you best. So is there any chance you can help me out if I find myself without a photographer?"

"Well, as much as your offer sounds super tempting and not at all rooted in desperation, I can't do it."

"Why not?"

"The same reason no one else can! I'm booked. You may not realize it, but I'm kind of a big deal."

"I know you are." I said, smiling at him fondly. "You remind me all the time."

"That's more like it."

"Anyway, what are you booked with?" I knew I didn't have much of a shot at him being available, but a girl can dream. "If it's just engagement portraits or something, you can move it."

"Oh, like you'd take it so well if I tried to move an appointment with one of your clients."

I shrugged. "I'm just saying."

"Well, it's a wedding, for your information, and I'm pretty sure it's too late for me to request they reschedule."

Hmph. I wasn't surprised, really, but I wasn't ready to accept defeat. "What time is the wedding?"

"I think it's at two."

"Okay, so Haley and Christopher's wedding isn't until seven. You can still make it."

"I don't know. I'd have to haul you-know-what to get up there in time. Not to mention the fact that doing two weddings back-to-back would kill me."

"C'mon, Brody, don't make me cheat on you with another photographer! What if I like them better and they become my new BFF?"

Brody laughed. "Oh, right, as if you're going to be able to find anyone you like as much me with such short notice."

"You never know. I'm very resourceful."

"I'll take my chances."

"Just think about it." I hoped I wouldn't need him, but why have best friends if you can't beg and plead until they do your bidding?

A few minutes later Brody turned off the main road onto a narrow drive lined with eucalyptus trees. "What is this place? There's not even a sign."

"I know. Jake's just getting started. He took over a couple of fields of vines, and this year is his first release as Prentice Vineyard. He doesn't even have a tasting room yet, so he's got a lot of work to do."

"What are you taking pictures of?"

"Some shots for the website. Maybe a brochure."

"Is he paying you in wine? Because if so, then I'm in."

"You're in, regardless, because we're here." Brody pulled up in front of a wooden farmhouse with a wraparound porch and shuttered windows situated under a canopy of sprawling live oaks. In every direction were rolling hills covered in grapevines. "Wow. This is beautiful."

Brody gestured toward the house. "That's going to be the tasting room. He's almost done with the renovations. Speak of the devil . . ." He gestured toward the old house, where a tall guy with an enormous smile waved to us from the porch.

"*That's* Jake Schmake?" I asked. He was tan and muscular—not *too* tan or *too* muscular, mind you, just enough to look like he spent a lot of time outdoors—and he had light-brown hair that was perfectly tousled in a way that looked like it required zero effort. "Why didn't you tell me?"

"Tell you what?" Brody looked puzzled.

"That he looks like that," I whispered.

Brody scrunched up his nose and looked at his friend, who was dressed in paint-spattered jeans and a T-shirt and who was striding down the walk to greet us. "That he looks like what?"

"Like my future boyfriend."

Brody got out of the car and greeted Jake, then gestured toward me while I stood stood gawking. "This is my friend Kelsey McKenna. She's just along for the ride."

"I'm his assistant for the day," I said, giving Jake a quick wave and trying not to blush. "Nice to meet you."

Jake's blue eyes crinkled playfully as he smiled. "Watch out. I might put you to work."

Surprising myself, I did *not* blurt out anything idiotic about being his love slave but instead smiled back and—mercifully—managed to keep my mouth shut.

"The light's great right now," said Brody, holding his camera up and pointing out toward the rolling hills covered in grapevines that were, in fact, positively glowing in the late afternoon light. "So I was thinking I'd get some outdoor shots first. Do you want to give Kelsey a tour?"

"That would be great," I said, ignoring the obvious follow-up comment that Jake had beautiful eyes.

"You sure you can live without her?" Jake asked.

"Ah, she's not really very helpful," Brody said with a wink.

I smiled and gave Brody a sweet smile that I hoped he understood meant, "Thank you and I'm going to punch you later."

While Brody wandered off to capture his magical vineyard lighting, Jake showed me around the grounds, starting with the house. "Be careful not to touch the walls. They're still wet."

"This is so charming," I said, looking around the room that had probably been a parlor.

Jake grinned handsomely. "Wait until you see it when it's not covered in drop cloths. I'm going to build a counter out of reclaimed wood across this wall." He pointed out several of the room's best features while I secretly checked out some of his. After we finished exploring the house, he led me out into the backyard. The screen door swung shut behind us with a satisfying *bang,* sending a flock of chickens scurrying for the rosebushes.

"We're going to put in a bocce ball court back here," he said, pointing, "and over here will be a patio."

"I love bocce ball!" I said, wondering if that was the one that worked like shuffleboard or the one with the mallets and the little metal dealies. No, that was croquet. It must be the former.

I shielded my eyes from the sun as I mentally filled in a sprawling flagstone patio, then went ahead and strung it with theoretical party lights while I was at it.

"Down there is the old barn," he said. "I haven't decided what to do with it yet."

"Besides store your cows?" I asked.

He laughed. *Thank God he laughed.* Agrarian humor isn't for everyone.

"No cows," he said. "But we do have a small herd of goats that we use to keep the weeds in check, and if you're lucky maybe they'll put in an appearance later."

"Baby goats?" I asked, my eyes widening.

"A couple."

"Now I'm officially excited. I've never met a real baby goat before. Do they have pajamas?"

Jake laughed. "I don't think goats wear pajamas."

"They do on YouTube," I said, vowing to send him some links when I got home.

We walked down a path to the big, rustic barn shaded by humongous live oak trees. Painted a deep red with white trim, it had broad double doors, a tall, rounded roof, and the kind of weatherworn patina that comes only with age.

Jake slid one of the doors open and sunlight flooded the inside, revealing an extra-large space with high ceilings and open rafters made of thick wooden beams.

"Wow," I said. "This is amazing. Are you going to use it as an event space?"

"Maybe. I haven't even had time to think about that. What do you think?"

"I think this would make an incredible place to throw a wedding is what I think." I immediately started decorating the place in my mind. "You could probably fit over a hundred guests in here. I'd put a stage down at that end and string lots of lights from the ceiling."

"Huh," Jake said, running his fingers through his hair. "I've never thought of this for weddings. Don't brides want something a little more . . . sophisticated?"

"No way! Rustic is *in*. Besides, have you ever tried giving a hotel ballroom ambience? Trust me, brides would flip out for this space."

His eyes met mine. "Oh, that's right! Brody mentioned you're a wedding planner, so I guess you would know what brides want." Jake looked around the room, as if seeing it for the first time, then shook his head. "Maybe someday. I wouldn't even know where to start."

"Pictures!" I blurted.

"What?"

"Start with pictures. Put them on your website—you're building a website, right?"

Jake nodded.

"So make a section called 'Weddings,' put up some pictures and the dimensions, maybe make up a few rules to make it look like you've been doing this for a while, and *voila*! Wedding venue."

"You make it sound so easy!"

"It is pretty easy, honestly. I'd be happy to make a list of everything you need."

Jake looked surprised. "You would?"

"Sure! I've rented enough venues that I can tell you exactly what information wedding planners would be looking for."

"Wow, that would be great. I mean, if it's not too much trouble."

"Easy-peasy. Brody could take some shots while he's here." An idea tickled at the back of my brain. "Oooh! You know what we need?"

"Floors?" he said, kicking at the loose, brownish-gray dirt.

"Nah, you can rent those. We need pictures of it all set up for a wedding so potential clients can visualize it better."

"Okay, that makes sense, but where do I get a wedding on short notice?"

I glanced over at Jake—which I'd been trying not to do because every time I did I found it hard to look away. "We stage one."

"We do?"

"Sure! It's easy. I can help you figure out the details. Mostly decor, like flowers and lights, but that stuff's easy. Maybe we even borrow a Styrofoam dummy cake." Without having an actual bride and groom stressing about every detail, I could plan this in my sleep. All I'd have to do was make a few calls, and then it would just be a matter of setting everything up. Besides, it would be a nice diversion from everything else going on in my life.

"So who will attend this fake wedding? You want to be my date?" He smiled playfully, and my heart did a flip.

"No guests necessary," I regretted to inform him. "It just has to look like everyone will be arriving at any moment. Not that I wouldn't love attending a fake wedding with you."

He paused and looked around the room again. "If you're serious, I think this is a fantastic idea. I don't know what it would cost, but I'd be happy to pay you for your time."

"Honestly, it won't take that long. Besides, it'll be fun. You can just trade me some wine or something."

"Or something," he said. He smiled and held my gaze for a moment until I blushed and looked away.

CHAPTER 15

I can't believe you've been keeping Jake a secret from me!" I told Brody as soon as we pulled out of the driveway of Prentice.

"What are you talking about? I've been trying to set you two up for ages."

"I guess I'm going to have to start listening to you."

Brody glanced over at me and smiled. "I *am* pretty wise."

"What did you say?" I asked, pulling my phone from my purse. "I wasn't listening."

"Just that you can thank me by paying for dinner."

"Fair enough."

On our way to Cask and Vine, I made a list of staging ideas for our photo shoot. I'd need flowers. Place settings. And lights, lots of lights. It would be fun planning a wedding without having to get everything approved by the bride and groom. Not to mention having an excuse to go back and see Jake again.

The restaurant was packed, but luckily, I'd made a reservation. The hostess assured us our table would be ready soon, and

I took a seat on the patio near the outdoor fire pit while I waited for Brody to go wash up.

The couple next to me were enjoying a before-dinner beverage and what looked like bacon-wrapped figs. My stomach growled appreciatively. I was in the middle of weighing how rude it would be to ask how the figs tasted in the hopes they'd offer me one when Brody came trotting back to the table, a gleam in his eye. "You'll never guess who I was just talking to."

"Who?"

"Guess," he said, sliding into his chair.

"C'mon, Brody, just tell me." We knew hundreds of people in common, and the odds of me figuring out who he'd bumped into were slim.

"Oh, okay, spoilsport. Corey. He's one of the bartenders."

The name didn't ring a bell, but Brody clearly thought I'd be excited about the news. "Does this end with one of those cocktail thingies? Because suddenly I'm interested."

"Oh, you're definitely going to be interested in hearing this."

I motioned for him to continue. "All right, go."

"Corey is a friend of mine who I know from around the neighborhood. And you'll never guess who he used to date."

"Who?"

"You'll like this: Stefan."

"Nuh-uh!" I sat up, my focus fully on Brody. "Stefan Pierce?"

"Yep. There's no accounting for taste. Anyway, you want to meet him?"

"Disgruntled ex, ready to blab? Heck, yeah!" I hadn't known exactly how to proceed with my suspicions about Stefan. After all, I had to be careful around our mutual colleagues. But who knew what sort of intel the ex-boyfriend could provide.

"I told him we'd stop by after dinner," Brody said.

I eyed the bacon-wrapped figs longingly. "Good idea. I hate being nosy on an empty stomach."

Soon enough the hostess called our name. She led us through the dining room to a table near a large stone fireplace. *Nice place.* Upscale, but not stuffy, with exposed brick walls, soaring ceilings, and a warm glow given off by candles at every table.

Not only did Brody and I get our own plate of bacon-wrapped figs, we also sampled so many starters that we didn't have room for entrees. I sighed contentedly as I leaned back onto the banquette. Yep, they would definitely do.

After I paid—and no, Brody didn't even reach—we headed for the bar.

"Kelsey, this is Corey," Brody said. "Corey, this is Kelsey."

The bartender stopped moving long enough to shake my hand. "Nice to meet you."

"Same here," I said as I pulled up a chair. "Brody tells me we have a friend in common."

"You mean Stefan?" He rolled his eyes. "Or Lord Voldemort, as my friends now call him."

"Nice. We call him the Ankle Biter."

Corey laughed an easygoing laugh. "That works, too."

Brody's phone rang and he checked the display. "It's Jake. If you don't mind, I'll step outside and take this and you two can chat amongst yourselves."

"Jake?" Maybe Brody would get some scoop. "You should definitely take it. And tell him yes."

"To what?"

"To whatever he asks." I sat down at the bar and turned my attention back to Corey. "So, you and Stefan. I take it things didn't end well?"

"You could say that. You could also say that he is an evil jerk who made my life hell."

That sounded about right. "Why? What did he do?"

"How much time do you have?"

"That bad, huh?"

"He not only dumped me over text message, but he got me kicked out of my rent-controlled apartment. What did he do to win *you* over?" While he talked, he continued to buzz around the bar area, pouring, shaking, stirring, and garnishing an endless string of cocktails.

"Well, he accused me of stealing his clients a couple of times now."

"Yikes. So you're a wedding planner, too?"

"Yep. Our paths don't cross that often, though, since I'm a destination wedding planner."

He paused and stared at me for a second. "I think he might have mentioned you before. He had wanted to get into destination weddings himself."

Great. That's all I needed: Stefan vying for my job.

"Anyway," Corey said. "So he thought you were stealing clients?"

"Yeah, and he's also trying to sabotage one of the weddings because the couple I'm working with had fired him and Babs."

Corey looked up from the bottle of wine he was uncorking. "Oh my God, are you serious?"

"Yep. Oh, and speaking of Babs, he accused me of murdering her at the funeral."

"He did *not*!" Corey grabbed a glass and poured the wine, then replaced the bottle on the bar behind him.

"Oh, he did. The police showed up at my house and everything."

He shook his head in disbelief. "Can I get you a drink? On the house?"

I was enjoying our bonding session, and besides, Brody was driving. "Sure, why not?"

"You like gin?" he asked, pointing to the backlit bottles on the shelf behind him. "I'm working on a new recipe."

I nodded enthusiastically and Corey started grabbing ingredients. "I can't believe he accused you of killing Babs. That's extreme, even for him. The police didn't believe him, did they?"

"I don't know. They didn't arrest me, so there's that. But in the meantime, people are starting to talk."

"That really sucks. I'm sorry. I wonder if he just needed to blame someone because he was upset? I know I sound pretty bitter toward him, but he really isn't all bad. If he was, I wouldn't have stayed with him as long as I did."

I managed a weak smile. "I'll have to take your word for it."

"I know, I'm probably not very convincing." Corey finished my concoction and set it on the bar in front of me. "Taste that."

I took a sip. Sweet, but not too sweet. Hints of elderflower. Something citrusy that I couldn't identify. "Mmmm. Perfect. Thank you."

Corey nodded as I took another sip. I stirred my drink and thought about what Corey had said. Maybe Stefan was acting out of grief. But it sure seemed like there was more to it than that. "The thing is," I said at last, "it's occurred to me that maybe he's pointing the finger at me to deflect attention away from himself."

Corey scrunched his face into a quizzical expression. "You mean, you think he might have had something to do with it?"

"I don't know. It's crossed my mind."

"Wow, I don't know." Corey picked up a tray of freshly washed glasses and began polishing them. "Just because he's a jerk doesn't mean he's a murderer."

"Yeah, I know what you mean. I just wish we knew what happened. Not just because of Stefan, but because it was Babs. I really want them to find out who did this."

"Do they have any other leads?"

"You mean besides me?" I shrugged. "I don't know. Someone told me Babs' sister might have had something to do with it."

"Who, Margot?"

"Oh, you know her?"

"Yeah, we used to have dinner with them sometimes."

"So what do you think? Any chance there's anything to that?"

Corey leaned against the bar and folded his arms in front of his chest, still for the first time since I'd sat down. "It's hard to imagine. They weren't best friends or anything, but she seemed like a pretty okay person."

"You never know what people are capable of when there's money involved."

Corey tilted his head to one side. "How do you mean?"

"Well, it's just that there's a motive, you know? All that real estate?"

"Real estate?"

"Yeah, you know, the buildings they'd inherited from their parents?"

"Oh, yeah." He shook his head. "No. Those are long gone."

Now it was my turn to be confused. "I thought they still owned them."

"Oh, well, Margot does, but Babs sold her share years ago."

"So she doesn't own anything with Margot?"

"Nah, Margot bought her out. Babs wanted to focus on wedding planning, so she took a payout and reinvested it in her business. Seems to have paid off, too."

I thought about Babs' Mercedes and the extravagant clothes she always wore. I'd assumed she'd figured out the secret to a wildly lucrative career in wedding planning, but it sounded like it was more the good luck of being born to parents with a knack for snatching up real estate.

I knew I was grasping at straws, but I wasn't ready to cross one of my prime suspects off the list. "But surely Babs still had some assets. And since she didn't have any children, wouldn't it all go to Margot?"

Corey shook his head. "Babs was doing okay, but Margot has cash to burn. That house she lives in? Totally paid for. Plus, she still owns several office buildings that bring in tons of cash every month, including the one where their office was. I'm telling you, she had nothing to gain from Babs' death."

Well, there went that theory. Without a motive, I had nothing. "So I wonder who gets the business now?"

Corey froze for a second. "Oh, wow."

"What?"

"Well, I don't know what ever came of it, but I know Stefan had been trying to talk Babs into making him a partner."

That was news to me—although I wasn't surprised Stefan had tried to grab a share of the business. "So, did she?"

"Not that I know of. She said she wasn't ready to take on a partner. Stefan complained about it a lot. Sometimes to her face, but usually just to me. He said that if anything ever happened to Babs, he wouldn't be able to afford to keep the business open."

"It doesn't exactly sound like he won the lottery in this deal."

"I just thought of something, though. Babs told Stefan that if anything ever happened to her, he'd be taken care of."

I set down my drink. "She said that?"

"Yeah. At first, he thought she was just blowing smoke, but a couple of weeks later, she told him she'd had her lawyer set up a life insurance policy—and I'm talking one with a sizable payout—in case she died. Apparently, CEOs do it all the time."

"Sizable? How sizable are we talking?"

He blew out a breath as he realized the full impact of his words. "Motive sized."

Wow. An insurance policy? I'd thought that if Stefan had killed Babs, it was probably in the heat of the moment. But if what Lucas had told me was true—that Babs was considering firing Stefan—then that gave Stefan a pretty big incentive to take control of the situation before she had a chance to cancel the policy.

"So I realize that a bitter ex might not be the best person to ask—"

He looked surprised. "Bitter?"

"Sorry, poor choice of words."

"No, that's fair. I'm probably kind of bitter."

"Anyway, we've established that Stefan has a temper, but . . ."

"But do I think he's actually capable of hurting someone?"

"Well, yeah."

He ran one hand over his chin, then made a noncommittal movement with his head, neither yes nor no. "I wouldn't necessarily have thought so before." He folded a towel he'd been wiping the bar with. "But between you, Margot, and Stefan? My money would be on Stefan."

CHAPTER 16

*T*urns out, bartenders make great confidential informants. Not only had Corey convinced me that it was time to cross Margot off the murder board, he'd also given me plenty of material to add under Stefan's name. Well, only one thing, really, but it was an all-caps, double-underline piece of intel.

Babs had wanted to make sure that Stefan would be taken care of, and how had he shown his thanks? By making sure Babs was taken care of—permanently.

My list of things I wanted to talk to Stefan about was growing by the minute: *I need Haley and Christopher's catering deposit back.* Also, *please kindly cease and desist with the wedding sabotage.* And oh, yeah, by the way, *Did you kill your boss?*

Luckily, today was the day the fictional Kate and Will were supposed to have their consultation with Stefan. And with any luck, I'd be able to get some answers.

Wedding planners always show up early, so Laurel and I got to the coffee shop half an hour ahead of time.

Laurel tucked her long blond hair up under a hat and donned a pair of oversized sunglasses, then took an outside table so she could act as my lookout and text me when Stefan arrived. Inside, I found a corner table that was out of view of the counter. *Perfect.*

I settled in with my newspaper and a caramel latte. When Laurel gave the heads-up, I'd hide behind the newspaper until Stefan walked in. Then, when the moment was right, in I'd swoop. *Why, Stefan, what a coincidence,* I would say as I pulled up a chair. Who knew if he'd actually talk to me, but I was hoping the imminent arrival of Kate and Will—bless their make-believe hearts—would keep him from bolting.

I took another drag off my coffee and noticed my hands were shaking a little. I wasn't sure if I was nervous about our little sting operation or just hopped up on caffeine. *I'm really going to have to switch to decaf.* I took a few deep breaths, glad I had extra time to calm my nerves.

By the time 4:00 arrived, I was ready. I was surprised Stefan hadn't gotten there early. You never want the client to beat you there. Babs would have had a fit.

Having already caught up on all the front-page news, I flipped through the entertainment section and skimmed a profile on a Cuban funk band for lack of anything else to do. *Huh.* Still no sign of Stefan.

At 4:05, I texted Laurel.

Nothing?

My phone buzzed immediately.

Not yet

I wrote back:

Have Kate text him

I'd already read the entire paper, so I chose the sports section to hide behind for the rest of my wait, figuring he'd never suspect to find me reading about a blocked punt return that apparently was really fascinating to people who care about such things.

I checked the time. Ten after four. I was getting antsy and my coffee was cold. I drank it anyway. *Great.* Now it was empty and I had to pee. How did policemen do it? Well, I kind of suspected how policemen did it, but policewomen must be at a severe disadvantage when it comes to stakeouts.

I sat for another twenty minutes, jiggling my leg and checking the time. Laurel and I texted back and forth a few more times. She'd gotten no response texting from the burner phone, and when she tried calling him it went straight to voice mail.

We'd been made.

I tossed my cup in the recycling bin, then wondered if it was meant to go in the compost bin, then decided not to worry about it as I tossed my newspaper in after it. After a much-needed bathroom break, I met Laurel outside.

"He must have recognized you," I said, eyeing her hat.

"No way. I was watching for him. I would have seen him coming way before he saw me."

"Maybe he knew from the beginning and was just toying with us." I was disappointed that I wouldn't even get the chance to *try* to talk to Stefan, but I guess I wasn't as clever as I'd thought.

Our sting was a bust.

We went back to the office and pretended to work, but I was

distracted. I couldn't believe Stefan had stood us up. I knew I should leave the whole deposit business up to Haley's dad, let them sue him and get the money back themselves.

But there was more to it than that.

If Stefan really *had* had anything to do with Babs' death, then we had much more important things to discuss. Like the fact that he'd accused me of murdering Babs right in the middle of the memorial service. Was he just acting out in a grief-stricken rage, or had he been trying to cover up his own involvement? Either way, it was *not okay.* If the cops had a murder board of their own, I was probably on it. And I wasn't willing to sit around and wait for them to clear my name. After all, brides are notoriously skittish about signing on with wedding planners who were also murder suspects.

It's not like I'd expected him to confess, but who knew what else I could learn if I could actually get him to talk to me? Now I might not ever get the chance.

There was only one solution that I could think of.

"You up for an adventure?" I asked Brody when he answered his cell.

"Like a fun adventure, or just something where I come along because you don't want to go alone?"

"Um . . . it'll be fun." My voice wasn't even slightly convincing. Who was I kidding?

"Nope, you're not fooling me. You want a favor, and favors are never fun. They're just favors. Besides, I'm busy."

"Busy doing what? You don't sound busy."

"I'm painting." Brody had been updating his home office with a chocolate-brown accent wall, but I was sure he'd finished days ago.

"You're still painting? I thought you'd be done by now."

"Yeah, someone keeps interrupting me, remember?"

"I need you to help me hunt down Stefan. I thought we'd try his house in Bernal Heights."

"I don't think that's a very good idea."

"C'mon, please? I have to talk to him, and he won't return my calls."

"Yeah, because he doesn't want to talk to you. And going to his apartment isn't going to change that fact."

He had a point, but I wasn't ready to give up without a fight. "I have to at least try."

"You know this is going to go poorly," Brody said.

"I know."

"And you're probably going to end up regretting it."

"I do."

"Isn't there anything I can do to change your mind?" he asked.

"You could invent a time machine so I could go back in time and mind my own business. Instead of going to the Wine Country Wedding Faire to help you out, I could stay home and go to Pilates. Then I never would have met Haley and Christopher, and I'd have a stronger core."

"That's a much better idea. I'll get right on it."

"Okay, but just in case you don't succeed, let's go talk to Stefan. If you do succeed, then whatever happens won't matter once we go back in time."

"I'm really sorry, Kelsey, I have to finish painting, then I have an appointment at four, and then I have to work on the time machine. Busy, busy, busy!"

"Oh, okay, fine. I'll get Laurel to go with me."

"Call me later and tell me how it went?"

"Nope, if you're so danged curious, you shoulda come with me." I hung up the phone and thought for a second. If there was any chance Stefan was responsible for Babs' death, there was no way I was going to go talk to him alone. No wonder cops always have partners.

"Laurel?"

She ran into my office, a little too quickly. I guess she was as bad at pretending to work as I was.

"This is probably a little beyond the call of duty, but—"

"I'll do it!"

"You don't even know what it is."

"Does it involve investigating Stefan?"

"Well, as a matter of fact—"

"I knew it!" she said. "I'm in."

"I thought you wanted to be a wedding planner, but now I'm thinking you'd rather be a private eye."

"Nah, I'm just mad he didn't show up to our stakeout."

Half an hour later, we pulled up to Stefan's house in Bernal Heights. The boxy, modern structure sat above a garage with a steep flight of stairs leading up to Stefan's front door, so it wasn't until we'd reached the top that we saw a vase full of white lilies sitting on his porch—a classic bereavement bouquet.

"Doesn't look like he's home," Laurel said, pointing at the arrangement.

I knocked anyway and we waited. Nothing. I peeked through his bay window, but there was no sign of activity inside.

Laurel studied the flowers. "These don't look very fresh. Either the florist did a pretty lousy job or they've been sitting here awhile."

I knocked again, but still no answer. Looking through Stefan's mail slot, I saw what appeared to be several days' worth of mail littering the parquet flooring.

"He's not here," I said, a knot forming in the pit of my stomach.

Laurel stood on her tiptoes to peer through a window. "He must be out of town."

I thought about everything that had happened the last few days. Maybe I wasn't the only one who'd started to think Stefan had something to do with Babs' death. Maybe people had started to talk. "Or maybe he *skipped* town."

Forget the fact that I wouldn't be able to get Haley and Christopher's deposits back. This was serious. Had anyone heard from Stefan in the last couple of days, or had he ghosted? I pulled my phone out of my pocket and called Lucas Higgins.

He answered quickly and sounded rushed: "Hey, Kelsey, what's up?"

"Hi, Lucas. Hey, have you seen Stefan? I need to talk to him."

"You and me both. We're having sort of a situation here."

"That doesn't sound good."

"It's not. In fact. . . " There was a pause as he covered the phone and said something to someone in the background, but then he was back. "What are you doing right now?"

"Right now, you mean, like *right* now?" I looked at Stefan's front door, not wanting to admit we'd been stalking him. "Just some . . . paperwork. Why?"

"Stefan is supposed to be at the winery for an engagement party tonight, but I don't think he's going to show. He's already two hours late, and no one can get hold of him."

"That's awful!" I looked over at Laurel and mouthed the words, *"Oh my God,"* pointing at the phone, then emphatically pointing at the door, hoping she would piece together what we were saying, but she just stared at me with a quizzical expression, as if she didn't speak mime.

"I know. They're beside themselves. I can't believe he screwed us over again."

I gritted my teeth in frustration. It hadn't been my imagination. Stefan was gone.

"Anyway," Lucas continued, "any chance you could help me out? It's only about twenty people. The dad is one of our biggest clients. He owns a couple of restaurants, and they buy wine by the truckload."

I thought about it for a second. I had no idea what I was getting myself into, but I was sure I could wing it. "What time do you need me there?"

"What time can you be here?"

I checked my watch. "Two hours, give or take? It depends on traffic."

"You're a lifesaver."

CHAPTER 17

*E*ven after dropping Laurel back at the office and running home for a costume change, I'd made it out of the city in record time. The late afternoon sun slanted through the oak trees, making long shadows that stretched across the two-lane highway. I rolled down my car window to feel the warm breeze on my face and soaked in the views of tidy rows of grapevines lining the hills. Nice and orderly, like I hoped tonight would be.

Oh, who was I kidding? If I'd planned the evening's festivities, I'd have been sure it would go off without a hitch. Heck, if I even knew what the plan was meant to be, I'd feel a whole lot better, but I had to admit: I had no idea what I was walking into.

I punched the code Lucas had given me into the keypad at the front entrance and waited while the grand wrought-iron gates swung slowly open. Then I wound my way up the hill and parked my car, taking one last deep breath before I transitioned into work mode.

It was go time.

Zara was on the back patio, setting up for the wine-tasting

portion of the evening. There were twenty places set, each with six stemmed glasses lined up in front of it so that the buttery Chardonnays wouldn't have to intermingle with the spicy Zins as guests worked their way through the wine menu.

"Zara, hi. I'm Kelsey. Lucas sent me?"

Relief flooded the girl's face. "Oh, thank God. I was supposed to get off at five when the tasting room closed, but Lucas roped me into staying. You're a wedding planner?"

"Yep."

She blew her black bangs out of her eyes as she polished one of the glasses with her apron. "Thank God. Brides make me nervous."

"Not to worry. I can handle them."

"Perfect. They're doing a tasting on the patio first; then dinner is up in the wine cave." She pointed toward the door that led into the tasting room. "The floral arrangements are all over there, and the rental place dropped off the linens and dishware earlier. Hector will be here in a minute to take you up to the wine cave, and I can send up a few guys to help set up. But if you can make some executive decisions about where everything should go, that would be a big help. Normally, this would have all been done hours ago, but, well, you know."

"No problem," I said. "I know my way around a place setting."

She waved me into the kitchen, where she opened a drawer and pulled out a notepad and pen. After scribbling something on the top sheet of paper, she tore it off and handed it to me. "Here's the door code to the wine cave. When the green light blinks, it means you're in; then you can prop the doors open after that."

"Got it." I grabbed some hydrangeas and headed toward my car, but my trajectory was interrupted by a well-dressed couple strolling up the stairs, her in high heels and him in a jacket.

Guests were already arriving? Maybe I could invite them to roam the gardens while they waited. I set the flowers aside and put on my game face.

"Hi," said the pretty brunette, beating me to the punch as I turned to greet her. "I'm Monica, and this is Gordon."

"Welcome to Higgins Estate," I said, sounding all official as if I'd worked there for years. "Are you here for the Maxwell party?"

"We *are* the Maxwell party," the man said, looking confusedly at me.

"I'm Monica," the woman repeated, as if I hadn't heard her the first time. I'd heard her, but Lucas hadn't told me the couple's first names, just their last, and I didn't want to tell her what happens when you assume.

"Of course! The bride and groom. We've been expecting you. I'm Kelsey, and I'll be filling in for Stefan tonight. I'm so sorry for the confusion today." Not that I had anything to apologize for, but I didn't think saying, *I'm sorry Stefan is a jerkface,* would strike quite the right tone.

She crinkled her eyebrows in confusion. "Are you his assistant?" Deep breath. Count to ten.

"No, but I am a wedding planner myself, and Lucas told me how important it is that everything go smoothly for you tonight, so don't you worry about a thing. All you have to do is relax and have a good time." *While I pretend I know what's going on and what Stefan had planned.*

"All right," Monica said, still looking unsure.

I put on my best smile. "Now let's get you set up on the patio with a glass of champagne."

Gordon put his arm around his fiancée and gave her a squeeze. "See, sweetie? I told you everything would be okay."

She actually seemed to relax a little. *Whew.* Everyone knows if the bride's not relaxed, then *nobody's* relaxed.

I led them up to the patio, where I left them in Zara's capable hands. In the meantime, Hector had shown up and was carrying floral arrangements off to the official Higgins Estate SUV, which would be shuttling guests up and down the hill later in the evening.

After introducing myself, I rescued my abandoned hydrangeas and headed to the parking lot, a bee following me the whole way. As Hector and I were loading the SUV, a white truck with the words "A Moveable Feast" painted on the side pulled into the spot next to us.

The driver—a dark-haired man with a goatee, a white jacket, and a tattoo of a whisk on his forearm—rolled down his window as I approached.

"You must be the caterer. I'm Kelsey. I'm the . . . wedding planner."

"You sure about that?" he said, smiling broadly.

"Oh, yeah, sorry. I'm definitely *a* wedding planner; I just wasn't supposed to be *this* wedding planner."

He shrugged. "All right. Where do you want me to set up?"

"Just up the road. You want to follow us?"

"Will do."

Hector and I took the SUV, winding our way up a narrow road with the catering van close behind. The sun was about to dip behind the mountain, and the sky was a brilliant blue punctuated with pink streaks. I hoped Monica and Gordon were enjoying the sunset. As it turned out, they'd made the right choice in showing up early.

Hector pulled up near the arched door of the wine cave, and the catering van rolled to a stop behind us. I jumped down from the SUV and checked my watch. We didn't have long to get everything ready.

Next to the door, there was a pile of dish crates marked "A-1 Party Rentals." I hoped they'd left me everything I needed, because there wouldn't be time for them to come back out if anything was missing. On the bright side—or maybe the not-so-bright side—the cave would be lit by nothing but candles and a chandelier, and dim lighting can cover a multitude of woes.

"Would you mind helping us move some things into the cave?" I asked Whisk Guy. "Zara's sending up reinforcements, but we don't have a ton of time."

"Sure, point the way," he said, shutting the door to his van.

"Thanks. I owe you one. What was your name again?"

"Pete."

"Okay, Pete, give me one second to get these crates open so I can take a quick inventory."

Grabbing my flashlight so I could see what I had to work with, I opened the first box and found a pile of plates separated by little squares of cardboard. *Whew.* Plates are important.

I opened the second box and shined the light inside. More plates. Subsequent boxes unearthed silverware, tablecloths, and water glasses. Where were the wineglasses? I'd have to send Hector down to make sure we had enough.

"Hey, Kelsey?" Hector asked.

"Yeah," I said, distracted as I counted out how many wineglasses we were going to need.

"I can't open the door."

"Hold on," I said, trying to do the math in my head as I multiplied the number of guests we were expecting by the number of glasses per guests. I didn't even know what they were serving.

Champagne and wine? Just wine? Maybe Zara already had them ready to go down at the château.

"Okay, sorry. Let me try." I took the slip of paper over and punched in the numbers Zara had written down for me. The light on the keypad flickered green. "There you go," I said as I turned the doorknob and pushed.

Nothing.

I tried again, pushing as hard as I could, and still the door didn't budge. *Dang it!* Was it so much to ask that this evening go smoothly?

"I don't think it's the lock," I said. "The door seems to be stuck."

"Here, let me try," said Pete. He threw his weight against the door, and after a couple of tries he was able to crack it open. "Something seems to be blocking it."

I couldn't see inside the cave, but the smell of oak and wine came wafting out, stronger than I remembered it. It was starting to get dark and the cave was nothing but a black hole, so I clicked my flashlight on again and shined it through the crack in the door. The light reflected back to me, and it took a moment for me to realize it was coming from a dark puddle on the floor.

"Is that . . . ?" Hector asked.

"It looks like blood," Pete said.

My heart thudded in my chest. *Blood?* No. This could not be happening.

Leaning in closer, I was hit with the strong smell of Cabernet Sauvignon. The dark puddle stretched as far as my flashlight beam could see. "No, there's too much for it to be blood. I'm sure it's . . ." I shimmied my arm into the cave and held my breath while I touched my finger to the liquid. I laughed. "It's just wine."

As relieved as I was that it wasn't blood, I still had a major problem on my hands. How was I going to clean this mess up before the guests arrived? "Um, I don't suppose anyone thought to bring a mop?"

"I think there's a wet vac down at the château," said Hector. "Want me to go get it?"

I never thought I'd be so happy to hear the words "wet vac." "Great. Help me get this door open first, okay?"

The three of us lined up again, putting our shoulders against the door.

"Okay, on three," Hector said. "One, two, *three*." We pushed hard and the door opened.

A huge puddle filled the entryway, along with splintered pieces of Hungarian oak. I didn't even have time to wonder how it had happened. All I knew was that a barrel held three hundred bottles' worth of wine, which meant there was literally thousands of dollars' worth of breakage on the floor of the cave.

"Wow, talk about the angel's share," Pete said.

"What?"

"You know, when wine evaporates, they call it the angel's share?"

"Oh, yeah. Lucky angels."

"*Drunk* angels," he added. "They don't usually get this much at once."

"True. And they really can't hold their liquor." I tucked the flashlight under one arm and took off my shoes, glad I was wearing a dress, so I wouldn't have to roll up my pant legs. This was going to make a *mess*.

Trying not to slosh, I took a step into the room. I moved the beam from side to side, surveying the mess. I'd never get it cleaned up in time. Maybe there was another entrance we could bring them through.

Someone mumbled something I didn't hear over my left shoulder.

"I'm sorry?"

"I didn't say anything," Pete said from over my right shoulder.

I spun around and shined the flashlight on him and he shrugged.

"Sorry," I said. "I thought you—never mind. Okay, you grab that, and—"

"Wait!" Pete said, holding a finger in the air. "Shhhh."

I froze in place. Was someone else in the cave with us? Pete pointed behind me and I turned and peered into the darkness, using my flashlight beam to sweep back and forth. Nothing.

"Wait. What was that?" Hector said.

"Where?" I asked.

"To your right."

I slowly arced the beam back to the right and saw a large section of barrel and something white. Something lifeless. Something with fingers.

I jumped back and grabbed Pete's arm, a full-body shudder running down my spine. "It's a dead body!"

"What the—?" Hector said as we leaned in to have a look. Sure enough, there was a human hand reaching out from behind one of the barrels

Male, from the looks of it. Could it be? No. Surely not.

My heart pounded as I crept forward. I had to find out who the arm belonged to. Just as I got close enough to see behind the barrel, the fingers twitched.

I let out a yelp and jumped backwards, dropping the flashlight in the process. It landed with a splash and bounced out of reach. I scampered over to fish it out of the puddle, but before I could get to it, the batteries shorted out and we were engulfed in darkness.

"Guys?" I whispered.

"Yeah?" Pete answered back.

"Cover your ears, because I think I'm going to scream."

CHAPTER 18

I blinked in the darkness, trying to steady my breathing. I stared toward where I'd seen the fingers move, but without the flashlight I couldn't see a thing. "Hello?" I called out. "Can you hear me?"

My heartbeat thudded in my ears, drowning out the silence.

"Hang on," said Hector. "Let me find the light switch." He fumbled his way across the debris, and a few seconds later the cave was flooded with light. Quickly but carefully I scrambled across the broken fragments of barrel to find out who was connected to the hand.

Stefan. His skin was pale, but he was breathing. "Call 911!" I yelled, sending Pete fumbling for his cell phone.

"There's no reception in here," Hector said. "You'll have to go outside."

Pete hurried toward the door, and I leaned over and gave Stefan a little nudge. "Stefan, can you hear me?" His eyelids fluttered briefly, but he didn't respond. "Stefan!" No wonder he hadn't shown up for any of his appointments today. He hadn't skipped town; he'd been otherwise occupied on the floor of the wine cave.

Hector hurried over to join me. "Is he still alive?"

"Yeah, but he's unconscious."

"Should we try to move him outside?"

My head was swimming. "We'd better not. We don't know what his injuries are."

Hector leaned down for a closer look. "What about CPR?"

"He seems to be breathing okay."

"Maybe if you slapped him? That's what they always do on TV."

I paused. *Tempting, but no.* "We'd better not do anything until the ambulance gets here."

"All right." Hector pushed a splintered piece of oak aside with his foot. "At least let me clean some of this up before we set up for the party."

The engagement party! In all the excitement, I'd forgotten about the guests waiting down at the villa. "There isn't time. We're going to have to figure out a Plan B, and *fast.*"

Pete stepped back inside the door to the cave. "The ambulance is on its way. They should be here soon."

I let out the breath I'd been holding. "Thank God. There's no telling how long he's been in here."

"So what should we do in the meantime?" Pete said.

"We can't leave him alone. But I should probably get down to the château before they start sending people up here. Do you mind staying with him?"

"Of course not. I'll wait outside so the ambulance knows where to go."

Minutes later, Hector and I were hurtling down the hill in the waning light. As soon as we hit the parking lot, I jumped out and ran inside, nearly colliding with Zara as I rounded the corner. "We need you to stall!" I told her.

She motioned with her head to follow her into the kitchen, and she closed the door behind us. "What happened?" she whispered frantically.

I lowered my voice so the waitstaff wouldn't hear me. "It's Stefan. We found him unconscious in the wine cave. I think some barrels might have fallen on him."

Her eyes widened in shock. "That's horrible! Is he okay?"

"I don't know. We've called an ambulance, but we're going to need everyone to stay down here."

She looked anxiously toward the guests, who were happily chatting and sipping their wine. "Okay, ummm . . ." She paused for a second, considering her options. "No one's on the Vintners Terrace tonight. We can put them out there."

"Perfect. I'll have Hector help me bring the place settings back down."

"Do you mind letting them know?" She pointed toward the courtyard, where the sommelier was instructing the wedding party on the proper way to taste wine. "Like I said, brides make me nervous."

"Fair enough." I steeled myself for a moment before approaching the bride and groom. Monica and Gordon would be disappointed, but it's not like we had any choice in the matter. What was I going to say? *Come on in, folks. Don't mind the mess—or the unconscious wedding planner lying on the floor. Just climb on over here and enjoy your dinner!*

I paused for a moment as the sommelier showed them how to stick their nose into their glasses and inhale deeply to experience the wine through their sense of smell. He swirled the wine in his glass as he spoke. "See if you can detect the grapefruit and the subtle notes of sweet Thai basil."

While everyone stuck their nose in their glasses and inhaled on command, I crept up next to the bride and leaned in close.

"Monica? Can I talk to you for a second?" I kept my voice low and discreet.

"Yes?" She took a sip of the wine and aerated it against her palate, like she'd been taught.

"I'm sorry for the last-minute notice, but we're going to need to move you to the Vintners Terrace for dinner."

She swallowed her wine and set her glass down abruptly. "But we were promised the wine cave!"

One of the other girls laughed with an unsympathetic snort—probably Monica's sister if I knew my bridal parties. "Oh, no. She's been going on about that damned wine cave all week."

"What's the problem?" asked Gordon, the groom-to-be. "I confirmed yesterday."

"Yes, well . . ." I had half the table's attention, and they were all staring at me expectantly. What was I going to say? Cave-wide electrical outage? Excessive limestone deposits? A colony of rabid bats?

"There was an earthquake," I said, trying my best to sound like I wasn't making it up on the spot.

"I thought I felt something!" said an older woman I'd pegged as Monica's grandmother. Her gray hair was cropped short, and she wore a loud purple dress that made her stand out from the rest of the family.

"Huh," said Gordon, looking skeptical. "I didn't feel anything."

"This building's pretty solid," I said, "but believe me, you could really feel it in the cave. It was pretty scary."

Grandma's face lit up. "Didn't I tell you all I'd felt something? No one ever listens to me!"

"Anyway, I'm afraid there was some damage in the cave, and it's not safe to go in there." As if on cue, the sound of an ambulance siren wailed in the distance, causing our guests to look at one another in alarm.

"Don't worry." I said, waving a hand nonchalantly. "One of the staff got bumped in the head by some falling debris, so we called an ambulance to come make sure he doesn't have a concussion." That was putting it mildly. "But it's a beautiful evening to be out on the terrace, and we'll get you all set up. In the meantime, enjoy your wine, and let Zara know if you need anything at all."

Monica looked disappointed, but she nodded her consent as she downed the rest of the wine. The sommelier immediately topped her off, giving her a slightly more generous pour than usual, then started opening the next bottle. *Good man.*

I could have used a glass myself, but there was work to be done. We'd have to load everything up and bring it back down, then set up the terrace and make it look twice as good to make up for the fact that it wasn't underground. I had already sent Hector up with the winery's SUV, so I hopped into my car and made my way back up the hill, hoping I didn't take a wrong turn on one of the many narrow dirt roads leading through the vineyard. A few minutes later, I pulled up in front of the wine cave, where the lights from the ambulance bathed the hillside in a pulsating red light.

Pete and Hector stood near the door of the cave, smoking and talking in hushed voices, and I hurried over to join them. "How is he?"

"I don't know," Hector replied. "They asked us to wait out here."

I peeked through the door to the cave. One paramedic worked on Stefan, while the other seemed to be clearing a path for the stretcher. "They look like they've got everything under control. So in the meantime, we're moving this party down the hill. Can you guys help me get everything loaded up?"

"Sure thing," said Pete. He took a drag off his cigarette, then dropped it to the ground, smashing it out with the toe of his rubber-soled chef clog.

"Are we going to the terrace?" Hector asked.

I nodded. We all swung into action, the men lifting the heavy dish crates and me stuffing my car full of floral arrangements. While I was trying to coax an extra-tall cymbidium orchid into my back seat, the paramedics came rushing out of the cave pushing Stefan on a stretcher. *Rushing.* That meant he was still alive. I breathed a sigh of relief, then jogged over to them as they loaded him into the back of the ambulance. Stefan's eyes were closed, an oxygen mask over his face.

"Is he going to be okay?" I asked.

"We're doing everything we can for him," said the female paramedic, stoic and noncommittal. "You can follow us to the hospital if you want."

"Oh! No, that's okay. I'm sure he's in good hands."

"Suit yourself," she said, striding toward the driver's seat and not giving me a second thought.

The next few hours were a blur. The first order of business? Resetting the party on the Vintners Terrace in record time. Zara sent the waitstaff up to the cave to help us move everything back down, and they set up while I made executive decisions about where the flowers, candles, and place settings should go. I hoped Monica would approve.

Despite the mad scramble, we were able to pull it off, and before long I was able to say the words that every girl longs to hear: "Dinner is served."

The guests murmured appreciatively as they gathered on the terrace, and even the bride-and-groom-to-be looked pleased with the results. Once everyone was seated, I retreated back into the château and locked myself in a bathroom, ready to collapse into a heap in the corner.

I felt like a frazzled mess, and the mirror helped confirm that I looked like one, too. I wasn't sure if the guests had noticed the splotches of red wine on the hem of my tangerine-colored dress, but if they had, they hadn't said anything.

Next time someone told me they were envious of my job, I'd have to be sure to mention tonight.

I splashed some cold water on my face and thought about Stefan. No matter what I was feeling, he'd had a much worse night than I had. I just hoped we'd found him in time.

I shuddered. First Babs, and now this? What was going on here?

A knock at the door made me jump.

"Kelsey, you in there?" It was Zara.

"Be right out!" I dried my hands on an extra-luxurious paper towel and tossed it in the trash can.

"Sorry, just wanted to make sure you're okay," Zara said. "Pete made us a snack. You hungry?"

"Starving." I hadn't eaten since breakfast and was running on fumes.

"Follow me." We went into the kitchen and Pete motioned to some seats at the end of a large, stainless steel worktable. The cold, hard stools weren't exactly comfortable, but it felt good to finally sit down.

"You want wine?" Zara asked.

My mind quickly flashed to the mess on the floor of the wine cave, and I flinched a little bit. I shook my head, banishing the vision from my mind. "That would be great, thanks."

Zara ducked into a storeroom and returned a minute later, an open bottle dangling from one hand and two empty glasses in the other. "I don't know about you, but after everything that's happened tonight, I could use a drink."

I held the glass aloft for a moment before taking a sip. "Yeah, it's been quite an evening."

Pete swooped in long enough to set two plates in front of us. "Fennel-crusted ahi tuna over couscous. Enjoy."

"Thank you," I said, eyeing the dish while my stomach rumbled. "This looks delicious."

We invited Pete to join us, but he wanted to start cleaning, so he left us to chat amongst ourselves while we gratefully polished off his meal.

"I'm glad Miles wasn't here tonight." Zara swept her long, dark hair over to one side, still somehow managing to look elegant even at the end of a long day.

"Tell me about it." I hadn't even really had time to process everything, but based on Miles' grumpiness toward all things wedding related, I knew he wouldn't be happy.

"I don't want to be anywhere near him when he finds out about the damage in the cave," Zara continued.

"How do you think he'll react?"

"He's going to go ballistic. And the fact that it was Stefan . . ."

"Well, it's not like he did it on purpose." I couldn't believe I was defending Stefan, but I was pretty sure he hadn't pulled the wine barrels over onto himself just to mess with Miles.

"It doesn't matter. Miles has been against the wine dinners from the beginning. Said he doesn't want anyone going into those caves unless they have a forklift or a degree in viticulture. Lucas overruled him, of course, but it's been a point of contention between them for a long time."

"I don't get it. Why is he so against weddings? I mean, sure, I'm biased, but even if he doesn't like them, it's an easy way for the winery to pull in money."

Zara cocked her head to one side. "Lucas didn't tell you?"

I shook my head.

"A few years ago, there was a wedding party who bought out the whole place for the night. Couple of tech millionaires from Silicon Valley. You know, young and kind of entitled. Anyway, some of the guys got drunk and decided it would be super hilarious to play hide-and-seek in the vineyard. Didn't ask or anything, of course. Suddenly they were just gone."

Uh-oh. Rogue wedding parties. I'd seen my share of those.

"They were running all over the hills, laughing and shooting off fireworks."

"Fireworks?! Are you kidding me?" During the dry season, that could take out the entire county.

"We kept begging them to come back in, but it was like herding cats. Then the best man decided it would be a really great idea to get in his SUV and drive up to the top of the hill, but he was drunk and ended up plowing right into the vineyard."

"No!"

"Yep. He destroyed about ten vines that were over a hundred

years old. He kept saying, 'Don't worry, bro, I'll pay for them,' but you can't really replace something like that."

"Wow, I bet Miles was mad."

"You can't even imagine. If Miles had to choose between people and grapes, he'd choose the grapes every time. Those vines are like his children."

I cringed. "Who was in charge?"

"It was supposed to be Babs, but she was double-booked so she sent Stefan instead. Miles was ready to pull the plug on weddings after that, but Lucas said they needed the business, and he's the money guy. So they compromised: They'd still have weddings, but no more Stefan."

I nodded. "Except that when Babs died . . . ?"

"They didn't have a choice but to let him come back."

No wonder Miles had such a chip on his shoulder. I'd have to be sure to tell Haley and Christopher no fireworks. Probably no birdseed or bubbles, either. I hoped Miles would be okay with some flower arrangements, as long as I promised none of them were invasive species.

I shook my head. "I'm doing a wedding up here on the eighteenth. Any advice on how to stay on Miles' good side?"

Zara shook her head. "I'm not sure he has a good side. But the more you can stay out of his hair, the better."

CHAPTER 19

After a day that had been approximately forty-three hours long—or at least felt like it—the last of the guests finally got in their cars and wound their way down the hill.

Was Stefan going to be okay? I hoped so, despite everything he'd put me through. I mean, sure, we weren't best friends, but seeing him lying there on the floor of the cave had really rattled me, even if I didn't fully care to admit it. I knew I wouldn't be able to rest until I found out what had happened to him, so when I got to the bottom of the hill I turned my car toward the hospital instead of home.

Twenty minutes later, I pulled into a spot near the emergency room. The temperature must have dropped twenty degrees since sunset, and I pulled my sweater tight around me as I entered through the brightly lit automatic doors. The waiting room was crowded with people in various states of emergency, and I half-expected to see Stefan sitting in a chair holding an ice pack to his head. *Wishful thinking.*

At the front desk, a harried, heavyset woman was checking

in a young man with a high blood alcohol content and a large piece of glass sticking out of his arm. Or at least she was trying to. He was babbling incoherently and was having trouble remembering exactly where he lived. I waited patiently as she gave him the third, fourth, and fifth degree.

"Sir, I need you to help me out here so I can get you checked in."

"Fremont," he slurred.

"Is that the street, or the town?"

"Freeeeeemonnnt!" He must have thought exaggerated enunciation would clear things right up.

I waited while she dragged information out of him one bit at a time. Finally, she spun her chair around and retrieved some documents off the printer, handed them to the man, and pointed him to a chair. "Have a seat right over there."

Then she turned her attention to me. "Can I help you?"

I slid my phone into the side pocket of my bag and gave her what I hoped would come across as a winning smile. "Hi, yes. I wanted to check on someone who was brought in earlier. Stefan Pierce?"

She didn't respond but typed something into her computer. She stared at the screen, then back up at me. "Are you family?"

"No, I'm, uh . . ."

"Then have a seat over there and someone will be with you in a couple of minutes." *A couple of minutes.* I'd been in emergency rooms before, and "a couple of minutes" usually translated into at least an hour, if you were lucky—and since I had all my vital organs intact and nothing protruding from them, I doubted I would be.

I smiled my best smile, hoisted my bag up on my shoulder, and tried to look as friendly, undemanding, and not-drunk as possible. "I don't really need to talk to anyone. I just wanted a quick update."

She leveled a stare at me. "Well, I can't give you one. HIPAA rules. Have a seat."

"Okay, look, I could tell you I'm his wife or something, but you and I both know I'd be lying. And if he made a list of visitors, let's just say I'm one of the last people who'd be on it. But I'm the one who found him earlier, so I feel kind of responsible for him. I just want to make sure he made it."

There was a long pause while she stared at me, trying to decide whether she was going to help me out or not. She turned and typed something on the computer, then turned back to me. "I'm sorry, ma'am, visitors are restricted to family only."

"Family only?"

She nodded while maintaining eye contact, then raised her eyebrows at me pointedly to make sure I got it.

"Ohhhh, family only. So I can't visit him?"

"You got it."

"But I could maybe try tomorrow?"

"You can try, but I'd call first. The main desk."

I blew out a sigh of relief. *He was still alive.* "Thank you so much. You don't know how happy I am to hear that."

The desk attendant nodded efficiently and turned her attention back to her computer screen.

When I got home, I sent Laurel an e-mail summarizing the night's events and told her not to expect me before noon. Good thing I'd turned off my ringer before I went to sleep, because when I finally did wake up I could tell my phone had had a busy morning without me.

There were two messages from Lucas, the first asking me to call him when I had a chance and the second one insisting that he *really* needed to talk to me. He probably wanted to hear my version of what had happened at the winery, but I wasn't quite ready to talk to him yet. Not until I'd at least gotten properly caffeinated.

There was also a message from Brody, asking me how the dinner had gone. Based on the number of text messages I'd gotten that morning, he was the only one who *didn't* know how my evening had gone.

There was also a message from Danielle Turpin, wondering if I'd heard the news yet. I hadn't talked to the gossipy wedding planner since the reception at Margot's house, and I had no doubt she was fishing for information. Heck, she'd probably already confirmed with her sources that I was the one who found Stefan.

Up until that moment, I hadn't really thought about how this was going to look to other people—especially after my very public altercation with Stefan. As much as I didn't want to have to talk to her, I'd have to call her back to make sure the rumor mill was at least running on accurate information.

When I got into the office, I dropped my things and went to find Laurel. She wasn't at her desk, so I went to the kitchen in search of coffee.

The fancy coffee machine was all fired up and ready to go. Jabbing at the buttons, I coaxed out a tiny quantity of liquid that must have been an espresso. That wasn't going to do. Where was my trusty old Mr. Coffee when I needed him?

I poked my head out into the hallway. "Laurel?" No answer. I pulled out my phone and dialed her cell, ignoring all the new text alerts that had popped up since the last time I'd checked.

"Hey, Kelsey," she said as she picked up. "Are you in the office?"

"Yeah. Where are you?"

"Down the hall. Looking at your murder board."

"My what now?" I hadn't realized she even knew about it, but I guess Brody and I hadn't been as discreet as we thought.

"You know, the big dry-erase board you and Brody set up in the spare conference room?"

"How did you know it was a murder board?" Considering how eager she'd been to play Nancy Drew with me, I wasn't sure why I'd felt the need to keep it a secret, but I had.

"Because it says real big up at the top: 'Murder Board.' Nice handwriting, by the way."

"Thanks," I said. "I'm in the kitchen, trying to make coffee, but I seem to be failing."

"Blue button."

"Got it. See you in a second." I clicked off the phone, brewed a grown-up-size cup of coffee, and headed down the hall. Laurel was staring at the board deep in thought, tapping the side of her face with a dry-erase marker, which thankfully still had its cap on.

"Oh, hey." She jumped up to hug me, then pulled back to look at my face, her eyes filled with concern. "Did you get *any* sleep?"

"Some, but I'm still exhausted. Thus my inability to work basic office machinery," I said, holding my coffee mug in the air, then taking a drink. "I kept replaying the whole scene in my head all night."

"I'll bet. It must have been awful."

I filled her in on everything that had happened, including my late-night visit to the emergency room to make sure Stefan was okay.

"Wow, he's lucky you found him in time," she said. "You probably even saved his life."

I smiled and took a sip of my coffee. "Ironic, isn't it?"

"Don't expect a thank-you card," Laurel said, laughing.

"So, what do you think?" I asked, jerking my chin toward the murder board.

Laurel sighed. "I don't even know where to start."

"Welcome to my world." I studied the names Brody and I had written on the board. "Yesterday I was sure Stefan had killed Babs and skipped town, but now I don't know what to think."

"It doesn't mean he didn't do it. I mean, whatever happened to him could have been an accident."

"I guess it's possible. But as much as I'd like to think he was in the wrong place at the wrong time or that it was the universe's way of telling him he's a jerk, I can't help but think someone did this on purpose."

Laurel's eyebrows furrowed with concern. "Yeah? How come?"

"First Babs, and then Stefan? It just seems like too much of a coincidence."

"So you think, what? That someone's picking off wedding planners?"

Yikes. I'd never thought of wedding planning as a profession that's fraught with peril, but that *was* one obvious thing that Babs and Stefan had in common. "I don't know what to think. But sooner or later the cops are going to want to talk to me, and I'm going to need to give them something more than just my assurances that I didn't do it."

"Surely they're not going to think *you* did anything. You're the one who found him!"

"I know, but I wouldn't be the first person to return to the scene of the crime."

"Kelsey! Don't even joke about that!"

"I'm not kidding. At the funeral, Stefan accused me of murdering Babs, and now he's in the hospital. You can see how that looks bad. I'm just saying, don't be surprised if they show up here wanting to know what happened."

Laurel shook her head with conviction. "It won't come to that. I'm sure they'll talk to Stefan and he'll tell them you weren't there."

"Great plan—if he even remembers what happened. And if he doesn't still hate me. And if he's had a personality transplant."

Laurel's face brightened. "Maybe we could go talk to him!"

"Who, Stefan? Have you *met* Stefan?"

"I know you guys have had your differences—"

"That's putting it mildly."

"—but he has to know you're the one who saved his life, and maybe he can tell us what happened."

"Laurel, we don't even know if he's *conscious,* or if they'll even let us visit him, for that matter."

"We at least have to try."

It seemed ironic to ask for Stefan's help in clearing my name, especially since he was the one who'd pointed the finger in the first place. But maybe if he did remember what happened, he'd let me try to help. For his sake and for Babs.

"Okay, but we shouldn't get our hopes up. In the meantime, we need to figure out how last night fits into all of this. I have a feeling that if we can figure out what happened to Stefan, it will lead us to Babs' killer."

"You mean lead the *police* to Babs' killer."

"Of course. I'm not going to go chasing down bad guys myself." Especially since the bad guys seemed to have a penchant for wedding planners.

Laurel chewed her lip for a moment. "Okay, then let's make a list. Who might have wanted to kill Stefan?"

I blew out a long breath as I mentally scrolled through a long roster of people he had wronged. "Jeez, try *everyone*?"

"Kelsey!" Laurel made a scoldy face and tsked in my general direction.

"What? It's true!" I started ticking off possible suspects on my fingers to prove my point. "His ex-boyfriend, Haley's dad, *me* . . ."

"Okay, okay. I retract my question. Who actually rates a spot on your suspect board?"

"Murder board," I corrected.

"Sorry, murder board."

"I can think of one person." I uncapped a black dry-erase marker and approached the board.

"Who's that?"

"Someone who's cranky, temperamental, and had a big fat grudge against Stefan." I wrote the answer out in all caps. "Miles Higgins."

CHAPTER 20

Laurel's eyebrows shot up. "Miles Higgins? Because it happened in his wine cave?"

"Well, yeah, for starters, but there's more to it than that." I filled Laurel in on everything Zara had told me the night before: the out-of-control wedding party, the demolished vines, Miles' lack of a good side. "And the time I met him, he didn't seem very fond of Babs, either."

"That's perfect! I mean, that's horrible, but he makes a way better suspect than you."

"I'd like to think so."

"So?" Laurel made an impatient gesture in my general direction.

"So what?" I replaced the cap on the marker and folded my arms in front of me. "It's not like I can go arrest him."

"No, but you have to tell the police!"

"I know. I will. I just feel like they're going to want more to go on than that."

"What do you mean?"

"They're not going to arrest him based on gossip, speculation, and general bad manners." I thought for a minute. "Maybe we could find out more. Like actual evidence or proof so they'll take us seriously. After all, with Haley and Christopher's wedding coming up, we do still have business there. And if I had to guess, Lucas is going to need our help more than ever."

"I don't know, Kelsey, doesn't that seem kind of dangerous?"

She had a point. I wasn't on Miles' bad side yet, and I wanted to try to avoid it if at all possible. Still, I didn't really have an option. Stefan had accused me of murdering Babs in front of everybody, and now he was in the hospital. People were surely going to talk. And it was probably just a matter of time before the police started asking around. Being questioned about Babs was one thing, but it was going to be a lot harder to convince the police that I wouldn't have hurt Stefan, given our history.

No, if I wanted to clear my name, I was going to have to find out what happened—the sooner, the better. "It'll be fine."

Laurel chewed her lip. "How do you know?"

"I don't. I'm just trying to make you feel better."

"That doesn't make me feel better at all. Can you at least make something up?"

"Because . . ." I thought about it for a second. "Okay, how about this? If Miles had anything to do with any of this, it would be way too risky for him to turn around and hurt us, too. I mean, don't you think he'd need to lay kind of low after last night?"

"Hey, that's not bad!"

"Yeah, for something I made up just now."

"Okay, fine, but I'm coming with you."

"I don't know, Laurel. I don't want to put you in danger—"

"You just said it wouldn't be dangerous! Besides, like you always say, there's safety in numbers."

Having Laurel there *would* make me feel a little better. Not that she would be all that effective a bodyguard, but killing two wedding planners takes a lot more time and planning than only killing one.

"Okay, fine. Lucas has been trying to call me this morning. Let's find out what he knows and then make ourselves indispensable to him in his time of need."

Lucas picked up on the third ring. "Lucas Higgins."

"Hi, Lucas, it's Kelsey McKenna."

"Kelsey! Thanks for calling me back. Hold on. Let me shut the door." There was silence for a moment and then he was back. "Zara told me everything that happened with Stefan last night. Are you okay?"

"I'm fine. I'm just glad we found him in time." I paused. "Any idea what happened to him?"

There was an audible sigh on the other end of the line. "That's the million-dollar question. From the looks of it, he got himself locked in and tried to escape."

"What? I mean, how? He knew the code. Doesn't it work the same way going out as it does going in?"

"Good question. Miles is looking into it. Anyway, we're devastated by what happened. Thank God we have insurance."

Did Lucas know more than he was letting on? If his brother had been responsible, I had no doubt Lucas would help protect him. After all, a homicidal winemaker isn't usually considered an asset in the winery business.

"Anyway, thank you again for helping us out in a pinch. You're a lifesaver. Both literally and figuratively."

"Thanks. I was happy to help, despite everything." I had to force a smile so that I sounded like I meant it. If I was going to learn more about Miles or find out what happened in the wine cave, I couldn't let on that his brother seriously creeped me out with his creepy creepface. No, it was time to secure our all-access pass to the winery. "So, what are you going to do now that Stefan's out of commission?"

"I wanted to talk to you about that. We're going to need someone to keep things afloat and I was hoping I could talk you into helping us out some more—if we haven't already traumatized you."

Bingo. "I'm sure we can work out something. How about if I come up and meet with you and we can talk about what needs to be done?" Laurel waved her arms to get my attention and pointed dramatically at herself. "And I'd like to bring Laurel along, if it's okay with you. I won't be able to do this without her." Laurel nodded encouragingly.

"That sounds fine," Lucas said, and I gave my assistant a thumbs-up. We made plans to meet the next day, and I hung up the phone.

"We're in."

I spent the rest of the afternoon working on Haley and Christopher's wedding. After confirming with Cask and Vine that they were available on the eighteenth, I got the contract all filled out and sent, relieved that Laurel and I weren't going to have to whip up dinner for the guests. Now that I had the major vendors in place, the rest would be easy.

While I reviewed the seating chart Haley had provided me, I found myself distracted. I couldn't stop thinking about Stefan. Was he okay? Was he even conscious? And would he possibly, maybe, potentially be willing to talk to me?

After work, I faced a tough choice: go home and stew about it or drive up to the hospital to see if I could get some answers.

As much as I missed hanging out on my couch, I knew I'd sleep better if I could at least get some word on Stefan's condition. Besides, if I could get him to talk, maybe I could get to the bottom of all this. Surely he'd be willing, right? Having a close call like that gives you lots of time to think about things, and there was a really good chance that he'd be less antagonistic. Plus, he was probably drugged, which would also be a major point in my favor.

If he knew who had locked him in the cave, then he knew it wasn't me, which would mean the majority of his rage would now be focused on someone else. Even if he didn't know who did it, he must know that I was the one who had found him and called the ambulance. Would his attacker have done that? No way.

But more importantly, we had something pretty major in common: we both wanted to catch Babs' killer.

After completing my must-dos for the day, I scooted out a little early and drove to the hospital. Okay, so maybe I should have called first like the ER lady had suggested, but I didn't want anyone to dampen my resolve. I figured he'd been transferred from the ER into the hospital—after all, they weren't going to just put a Band-Aid on him and send him home—so I marched up to the front desk and confidently announced, "I'm here to see Stefan Pierce."

With a few strokes on the keyboard and barely a glance in my direction, the front desk attendant directed me to the fourth floor.

This was good. He was here, and he wasn't in the ICU.

On the way to the elevator, I passed the hospital gift shop, with its window display featuring frilly ladies' pajamas, stuffed bears, and whimsical coffee mugs. *Flowers couldn't hurt.* I hurried inside and searched the refrigerated floral display in the back for something suitable. Roses? Too romantic. Carnations? Too cheap. I was about to grab a handsome display featuring birds-of-paradise, those prickly tropical flowers that look like they could poke an eye out, when I saw the perfect choice: a peace plant. What better way to make a peace offering than that?

Right as I was reaching toward the potted plant with the broad dark-green leaves, a voice behind me said, "Kelsey?"

I turned and recognized Corey, the bartender who used to date Stefan, holding a toothbrush and an unopened bottle of Diet Coke. Giving him a quick hug, I said, "Corey! What a surprise!"

"Sorry, I probably look awful." He ran his fingers through his hair, self-consciously trying to untangle the mess on top of his head. "I've been here all day."

"Oh! Who are you—I mean, what are you—?"

"Doing here? You're not going to believe this, but . . ." He smiled sheepishly. "I'm here with Stefan."

"But I thought—"

"I know, I know. He still had me programmed into his phone as his emergency contact, and, well, he doesn't have anyone else."

"How is he?" I asked, ignoring the part of me that wanted to say, *Are you kidding me?!?*

"He was injured pretty badly," Corey said. "And they've got him pretty heavily sedated."

"Oh, no!" I said. "I knew it was bad, but . . ."

"On the plus side, it cuts down on the awkward ex-boyfriend conversations about who did what to whom."

I retrieved the peace plant from the shelf and held it up for approval. "I was just going to take this up to him. Are you heading back up?"

Corey nodded. "Sure. I'll take you to him."

We paid for our purchases and walked toward the elevator.

"I know this probably seems super dysfunctional, me being here after everything I told you," Corey said while we waited. "And just for the record, this does *not* mean we're back together. I'm only here as a friend."

"I'm not here to judge," I said. "To be honest, I'm glad you're here. I wasn't sure if my visit would be welcome or not, so it's nice to see a friendly face."

Corey punched the Up button a couple more times to hurry things along. "I heard you were the one who found him?"

"It's true." I smiled. "I don't suppose he knows that, does he?"

Corey laughed. "I don't know. He's been out of it the whole time. He woke up for a bit, but he just kept mumbling 'Higgins.' That's the name of the winery where he was, right?"

"That's right. They asked me to come up for an event when he didn't show up, but it turns out he'd been there the entire time."

"Well, I'm just glad you guys got to him in time. If you hadn't . . ." A loud *ding* interrupted us and the elevator doors slid open. As we rode up in silence, I thought how glad I was to have a friendly escort to take me to Stefan. It made it a lot easier—as did the knowledge that Stefan would be asleep. But when I walked into the room, a weird surge of emotion tugged at me. "He looks so peaceful when . . ." I paused as I considered my word choice.

"When he's not yelling at you?"

I smiled and nodded. "That's the basic gist." I set the plant on the bedside table. The room was dark and quiet, except for the occasional blip of the heart rate monitor. Corey sat on the edge of the empty second bed and motioned toward the taupe guest chair.

"Have the doctors been able to tell you anything?" I asked.

Corey shook his head. "Not much, since I'm not next of kin. But I called his sister and she's flying up tonight. I'm hoping she can find out more."

"That's good. I don't suppose you've talked to the police, have you? I'd really like to know what happened to him."

"You and me both. One of the nurses told me the police had been here, but she didn't tell me much more than that. You think they're investigating?"

I shuddered. "I don't know. It looked like an accident, but after what happened to Babs . . ."

"I know," said Corey. "I thought the same thing."

I looked over at Stefan, frail and motionless. "Can you think of anyone who might have wanted to hurt him?"

Corey shook his head. "I don't know. He could be a handful, and it's impossible to say who he might have pushed too far."

We both sat in silence for a moment, listening to the heart rate monitor and Stefan's shallow breathing. They always say people can hear you even when they're unconscious, and I wondered if Stefan could hear us talking. If so, he was probably having a fit. Not because of the subject matter, but because I was hanging out in his hospital room and he was helpless to do anything about it.

How had we gotten off on the wrong foot, anyway? It wasn't like we were bitter rivals or anything. I barely knew the guy. I shook my head. It didn't have to be that way.

I stood and gestured for Corey to follow me out into the hall-way. Once we were outside, I closed the door behind us. "So, do you remember that night at your restaurant when we talked?"

He nodded. "Yeah?"

"It sounded like you'd heard Stefan mention me before. I was just curious. Did he ever say anything about why he has it out for me?" Corey seemed taken aback by my question, so I quickly added, "Don't worry. I know he hates me. I just want to know why."

He paused while he considered his answer. "Well, 'hate' is a strong word, but he was certainly jealous of you."

"Jealous?" I asked. "Of me? Why?"

Corey looked around as if to make sure Stefan hadn't snuck up behind him. "You really don't know?"

I shook my head. "I barely know him."

"Well, I told you he wanted to be a destination wedding planner."

"You mentioned that, but it's not like I'm stopping him."

"He said when he applied for a job as your assistant, you blew him off."

"What?!" This was news to me. "I don't even remember seeing his résumé!"

"There's no reason you would have recognized his name at the time. Apparently, he met you at a party once and he thought you'd remember him. Besides, you did send him a polite form letter, but he said you'd snubbed him."

My eyes widened in surprise. "I didn't mean to. I got literally hundreds of applications. There's no way I could have personally responded to every one of them." I didn't feel bad that I didn't hire him, because I'd clearly dodged a bullet, but I did feel a little bad that he'd felt slighted.

"I know; that's what I told him," Corey said, his tone reassuring. He paused. "But it was more than just that."

I took a deep breath. "Okay, what else?"

Corey shrugged. "Oh, it was lots of little things. Someone brought him pictures from a wedding you'd done and asked if he could do something like that. He saw that feature *Bride's Life Magazine* did on you. And then there was Babs. . . ."

"Babs? What did she have to do with it?"

He shook his head and laughed. "I suppose she thought it would motivate him, but she used you as an example on more than one occasion. In fact, one time he got mad and said if you were so great, maybe she should go hire you instead."

"Yikes," I said, feeling both flattered and embarrassed by the praise. "What did Babs say to that?"

"She said she would if she thought you'd accept."

Ouch. It didn't totally make up for the way Stefan had treated me, but it certainly helped explain it. Maybe once he regained consciousness, we could put this all behind us. "Thanks for telling me," I said. "I had no idea."

A voice over the intercom let us know that visiting hours were almost over, so we went back into the room and I gathered my things. Corey promised to call me when Stefan was awake and able to talk, and also to let him know that I'd been to visit.

"Let me know if you need anything," I said, giving him a hug. "And try to get some rest, okay?"

"Will do."

I crept up beside Stefan and leaned down toward his ear. "Stefan, I don't know if you can hear me, but this is Kelsey. I want you to get better so we can find out who did this to you. Meanwhile, Corey is here with you, and when you wake up I want you to be really nice to him, because he's a great guy, okay?"

Stefan's lip twitched a little, but his eyes remained closed.

I smiled over at Corey and gave him a wink. "I'll take that as a yes."

CHAPTER 21

The next morning, Laurel and I had an appointment with Lucas Higgins to talk about how we could help with their upcoming weddings—or at least, that was the official plan. Off the record? We were there to snoop.

When I got to the turnoff to the parking lot, I slowed down until the car rolled to a stop, influenced by a strong pull toward the top of the hill.

"What are you doing?" Laurel asked.

"I think we should go up to the wine cave."

Laurel bit her lip. "I don't know, Kelsey. It's one thing to be in the château, since we're meeting with Lucas, but we have no excuse to be up there."

"Come on. I never even got a chance to look around that night, everything happened so fast."

"What if we get caught?"

"We'll just say I was showing you the view. Haven't you always been curious about the view from up there?"

Laurel looked unconvinced, but she didn't jump out of the car in protest or anything, so I kept driving.

As we pulled up to the entrance, I breathed a sigh of relief. No cars, no police officers, no sign of what had taken place inside except for the pile of shattered wood stacked outside the door, waiting to be hauled off.

"Let's just see if they changed the door code," I said.

"Kelsey! What if it's a crime scene?"

"There'd be yellow tape up. I just want to peek."

Laurel crossed her arms in front of her chest. "I want no part of this. I'm staying here."

"I thought you were Laurel Quinn, Private Eye."

"You need a lookout, don't you? That seems like a highly valuable role in this operation."

"Okay, fine. I'll only be a minute."

I dug into the side pocket of my purse, where I still had the key code scribbled on a piece of paper, then climbed out of the car and approached the entrance. I punched in the number, and the light on the keypad flashed green. I was in.

As I swung open the door, I was struck by the dueling odors of wine, bleach, and Mop & Glo. The concrete floors gleamed beneath my feet as if to say, *What mess?* Someone had certainly been on top of things. I stepped inside and turned on the lights. It was as quiet as—well, as quiet as a cave. No metaphor needed.

Along the walls were racks full of wine barrels stacked on their sides, reaching almost to the ceiling. The only thing that seemed out of place was the rack nearest the front door. It was broken at the top and appeared to be two barrels short of a full load. Just out of reach, there was a vent to the outside that a reasonable-sized person might be able to wiggle their way through, provided they could kick it out of its casing.

Maybe Lucas was right. Maybe Stefan had climbed up, tried

to dislodge the vent, and fallen, breaking the rack and taking a couple of wine barrels with him.

That still didn't explain how he'd gotten locked in in the first place.

The main hall of the cave stretched far back under the ground, with additional passageways branching off from it. I peeked down one of the hallways and saw that it was lined with dozens of barrels, stretching back into the darkness.

Off to the right of the hall was an actual door that was partially open, so I poked my head in to see what was inside. Although it was dark, I found a dimmer switch right inside and slid it upward, revealing the event room. I gasped—but in a good way. The switch had illuminated thousands of twinkle lights woven through a canopy of grapevines. Too bad I hadn't been able to have the dinner in here; I would have loved to have seen it fully decked out. If Zara was right and Miles got his way, this room would never see another wine dinner again. Too bad.

I walked around the room, soaking it all in, and as I rounded the table my foot hit something and sent it skittering across the floor. I knelt down to see what it was. A set of keys. Whoever had cleaned up must have missed them since all the action had happened in the main room. Were they Stefan's? I scooped them up and dropped them into my purse. Maybe they'd come in handy, but at the very least I could take them to the lost and found.

Suddenly, I heard a sound from the front door. Actually, I realized, the sound *was* the front door. Laurel?

"Who's in here?" a masculine voice bellowed from the front of the cave.

Definitely not Laurel.

I looked around frantically, trying to decide between fight, flight, or the seldom-mentioned third option: diving under the table and hoping whoever it was would give up and go away. It would never work. Whoever it was already knew I was here. Hiding would just make me look suspicious.

"Hello?" I called. I exited the room, prepared to explain that I was taking measurements for some wedding-related something or other, which, by the way, is totally a thing that wedding planners do all the time in the real world. Too bad I didn't have a tape measure on me to back up my story.

"What the hell are you doing here?" *Miles.* My heart sank. I had hoped it would be, well, pretty much anyone else in the world, but there he was, the decidedly less friendly of the Higgins brothers.

"I was just making sure there were enough chairs for the Maxwell wedding!" I said brightly, relying heavily on the assumption that Miles wouldn't be up to date on the wedding happenings since he didn't want anything to do with them.

"I told Lucas, no more dinners. Not in my cave!" Miles' face turned red as he reached past me to close the door to the dining room. His gruff voice boomed off the cave walls, creating an intimidating echo.

"My mistake. I should have checked with Lucas first. I'll go get this straightened out right now." I racewalked for the door, not daring to look back to see Miles' response.

"You're not allowed in my cave," Miles bellowed after me. "You hear me?"

"Got it!" I called over my shoulder.

"I'm changing the code," he yelled.

"That would probably be for the best," I replied, trying to

keep my voice light as I scooted out the door, almost knocking Laurel over on my way out. She was crouched down, cell phone in hand, finger poised over the 9 button.

We dashed to the car, and I didn't even bother putting my seat belt on before practically peeling out. I sped down the hill, slowing down only when we hit the parking lot. I wish I could say my heart did the same, but it was still thumping wildly in my chest. "Why didn't you honk or something?"

"I didn't want him to see me!" Laurel's voice sounded contrite.

"Making you officially the worst lookout ever."

"I'm so sorry, Kelsey! I panicked. I didn't want it to look like I was warning you."

"Which is exactly what you were supposed to be doing!"

"Well, sure, but then he'd know that you were snooping instead of taking measurements."

I took a deep breath and blew it out, counting to ten. "I guess you're right."

"You did great," she said. "And for what it's worth, I had your back. I was listening through the door and ready to call 911 if he made a move."

"That's great, except for one thing."

"What's that?"

"If he'd made a move, 911 wouldn't have gotten here in time."

As tempting as it was to abandon our plan, we still had work to do. Surely we'd be safe down in the château. Almost definitely. Or at least probably.

I pulled into a spot and we went inside and found Lucas in

the tasting room. Even though I was still shaking, I tried not to let my nerves show as I greeted him.

"Thanks for coming up," he said.

"Happy to help out. You remember my assistant Laurel?"

"Hi, good to see you again." He smiled broadly and held out his hand, and I swear Laurel blushed a little as she took it.

"Good to see *you*." She bobbed her head and dipped at the knees a little, and I made a mental note to tease her later for what had almost become a curtsy.

"Let's meet down here," he said, leading the way down the hall. "We've got an office that Babs uses to meet with couples when she's here." He paused for a second, then corrected himself: "*Used*. Sorry, I hope that isn't weird for you."

No weirder than anything else that's happened the last couple of weeks.

He opened the door to reveal a room that was the perfect blend of form and function. Decorated in French-provincial-meets-wine-country chic, it was anchored at one end with a large mahogany desk and at the other with a cozy seating area.

"Wow, nice setup."

"Thanks. You're free to use it whenever you're up here. We set it aside specifically for wedding consultations." Lucas gestured for us to take a seat and slid a slim black spiral-bound book across the desk. "Here's the calendar we use for events. I thought we could start by seeing which dates you're free."

Flipping the book open, I scanned through the upcoming events. "It's hard to say until I know what we're dealing with. How many people, that sort of thing."

"Well, you're in luck," Lucas said, rolling his chair over to an office credenza. "Stefan's been working out of here the last few weeks while his office is out of commission, so this time I have all the information you need." He opened up a drawer and started thumbing through it. "I can't tell how he's arranged everything, though. It's certainly not alphabetical."

"Don't tell Kelsey that," Laurel said. "She'll end up reorganizing the whole thing."

He pulled out a large stack of folders and set them on the desk between us. "Be my guest."

I quickly glanced through a couple of folders, including one that contained Haley and Christopher's information. "This should come in handy," I said, sliding it across the table to Laurel. While I looked through the rest, I kept an eye out for any tidbits of information that might be of use. Lots of vendor agreements and proposals, but nothing that was evidence of anything other than Babs' exquisite taste and penchant for weddings with large budgets.

Maybe I could use the files as an excuse to poke around a little more. "I'll tell you what," I said to Lucas, "why don't Laurel and I spend some time looking through all of this? We'll check our calendars and figure out which ones we can take on, and then we can reconvene in a bit."

Lucas paused while he considered it. "Sure. I've got some calls I need to make anyway." He stood to go. "I think you'll find everything you need there, but if you have any questions, I'm right down the hall."

Laurel and I made eye contact, but neither of us spoke until he'd left the room.

"Keep an eye out while I check the desk," I whispered after a minute had passed.

She tiptoed to the door and poked her head out. "All clear." she reported back, then closed the door behind her.

I yanked open the middle drawer and rummaged around in

it. Just your basic office supplies: some highlighters—good to know in case I had a color-coding emergency—some sturdy black-and-silver binder clips, and an assortment of used pens.

The top side drawer held fresh notepads and a stack of glossy brochures from different catering companies, and in the third drawer I found a large binder labeled "Higgins Estate Wedding Program: Rules and Protocols." I pulled the chunky tome from the drawer, surprised it was more than a few pages long. How many rules and protocols did they really need? That had to have been Miles' doing.

"Here's a little light reading for you," I said, handing it to Laurel. "Flip through it and see if there's anything interesting."

"There's a note inside," Laurel said. " 'Babs—Perhaps you need to refresh your memory on our policies. Miles Higgins.' Yikes. I wonder what that's about?"

"Keep reading. Maybe he underlined helpful passages."

While Laurel perused Miles' manifesto, I turned my attention to the credenza. I opened the drawer Lucas had taken the folders from and searched through the remaining files one by one. Nothing major. Pulling all the hanging files forward to check the back of the drawer, I spotted a book that appeared to be a leather-bound desk agenda. A prickly heat crawled up my neck as I pulled it from the drawer, and the name embossed on the cover took my breath away.

Babs Norton.

CHAPTER 22

I silently held up the datebook and showed Laurel.

"What? Are you kidding me?" She abandoned the rule book and came around to my side of the desk to get a closer look. There was a ton of information inside, from vendor lists to planning notes. Stuff that most of us kept on our laptops or tablets these days, but Babs had been an old-fashioned gal.

"There's no telling what we might find in here," I whispered.

"What should we do with it?" Laurel asked. "Photocopy it?"

"That'll take too long. Let's just take it."

"Take it? We can't do that!"

"Why not? No one knew it was there, or they would've already given it to the police."

Laurel crossed her arms in front of her chest. "Which is exactly what we should do."

"And we will," I promised. "Just as soon as we have a look at it."

Laurel looked dubious, but she didn't stop me from hiding the book deep in the bottom of my tote.

Spurred on by our discovery, we searched the rest of the

office, but there were no more major discoveries. That was okay with me. I was already so on edge I felt like I'd had three grande mocha frappuccinos and a fistful of Pixy Stix, and we still needed to scour through the upcoming Higgins events like we'd promised. We finally settled down with our calendars and found some holes we could fill if we divided up the work.

"All right," I said, satisfied that we'd come up with a solid plan. "Let's talk to Lucas, and then we can go." We bundled up our things, took one last look around, and headed down the hall. Halfway there, Laurel stopped. "Do you hear that?"

From the direction of Lucas' office came the sound of muffled voices. None of it was intelligible, but the angry tone came through loud and clear. Laurel and I crept closer a few steps at a time.

We stood outside his door for a moment, me with my hand up in the universal sign for "I was about to knock." I leaned in closer. I wasn't sure, but I thought I heard someone say, "That woman." Which woman? There were so many women to choose from. I sure hoped I wasn't the woman in question.

I made eye contact with Laurel, holding my finger to my lips. Just as I was about to cup my hand against the door to get a better listen, it flew open, knocking me backwards into the wall.

"Hey!" Laurel cried indignantly, rushing to my side.

A red-faced Miles spun around, took one look at me, and spat, "You! What do *you* want?"

It all happened so fast, it took me a second to process the fact that I was flat on my tush in the richly carpeted hallway, the contents of my bag scattered across the floor. A corner of Babs' agenda peeked out of the bag and I quickly shoved it back in. "Well, an apology would be nice, as long as you're offering."

Miles glowered at me in what could only be construed as a

no. He leaned in, saying just loud enough for me and Laurel to hear, "That's what happens to wedding planners who don't watch their step."

As he stalked off down the hall, Laurel and I stared after him in disbelief. Having heard the commotion, Lucas rushed out and helped me to my feet, apologizing profusely for his brother's behavior. "With everything that's been going on, he's just really on edge. I hope you understand that it's nothing personal."

Nothing personal. I'd hate to see what would have happened if it *was* personal.

He explained that Miles had been furious about what had happened with Stefan in the wine cave and had demanded that the wedding program be shut down immediately. Lucas had managed to placate him the best he could, but running into me in the wine cave had set Miles off all over again.

It wasn't exactly the smoking gun that I'd been hoping to find—or the smoldering wine barrel—but I was getting some pretty solid evidence that Miles had a temper, and it was a bad one.

"What were you doing in the wine cave, anyway?" Lucas said, furrowing his brow in our general direction.

I was tempted to say, *Looking for evidence that your brother was trying to kill Stefan—nothing personal,* but luckily Laurel cut in before I had a chance. "She was giving me a tour. Gorgeous view from up there."

I nodded. "I hope we'll still get to do some events up there. Speaking of, we're ready to look at these." I waved the client folders in the air with an excited expression on my face, managing to distract him enough that he dropped the cave.

Snapping into wedding-planning mode, I went through the stack with Lucas, making some vague promises about getting him proposals for the weddings we could do and recommendations for the ones we couldn't. But the whole time, my mind was on other things. I couldn't wait to get home and sort through Babs' agenda and see if I could learn anything that would be of use.

After promising to follow up soon, Laurel and I said goodbye and headed to the car and I tossed Laurel my keys. "You're driving."

"Me? Why?" Laurel looked nervous at her newfound responsibility.

"Because I want to look through *this*," I said, pulling Babs' datebook from my bag.

Once we were safely on the road I cracked open the agenda and started flipping through the pages.

The first thing I noticed? Two different types of handwriting. Babs' elegant cursive, written in blue ink, and what I assumed was Stefan's nearly illegible scrawl in black. He must have taken over the book after her death to keep the wheels turning.

Turning to the calendar section, I looked at the days leading up to Babs' death. She'd had several appointments at Higgins, but as far as I could tell, there was no mention of Miles specifically. And of course there was the Wine Country Wedding Faire that Sunday.

On Monday she'd taken a bride for a makeup consult with someone who wasn't Thierry—the nerve—and had an early evening menu tasting with the Carvers, whoever they were. Had she made it to that last appointment?

I flipped through the weeks prior to her death, searching for anything that stood out about the winery or Miles. There were lots of calendar entries, but most of them seemed pretty innocuous. In fact, I probably would have skipped right over a dinner appointment at the Willows, except that it had been circled twice and annotated in black ink.

"Look at this, Laurel."

"What is this, some sort of test? I can't look; I'm driving."

"Sorry. It's just—at seven o'clock on the Thursday before Babs died, it says 'The Willows' and the initials 'SB.' Then Stefan circled it and wrote Stanley Bennett's name off to the side with two question marks."

"The Thursday before she died? That was right before the wedding fair. That must have been when he met with Babs to talk about the budget."

"Yeah, the night he fired her." I stared out the window, deep in thought. "But why do you think Stefan circled it and wrote out Mr. Bennett's name with question marks? That makes it seem like he didn't know they were meeting."

"True, but it's not like you tell me about every meeting you go to."

"I don't know. Maybe it's nothing." I kept flipping through the calendar, looking for other entries Stefan might have flagged. "It's weird. That's the only one where Babs used initials. She usually wrote out the names of people she was meeting with. Stefan must have thought something was up."

A sudden idea occurred to me. Maybe I could go ask him myself. I fished my phone out of my bag and texted Corey.

How's Stefan? Any change?

Corey didn't answer right away, but a few minutes later his response popped up on my screen.

Can't talk right now, I'll text you later

Shoot. I could really use Stefan's help.

I stared out the window at the rolling hills along the highway leading back into the city. The Willows. Why did that sound familiar?

My cell phone rang and I checked the display. "It's Brody," I told Laurel as I clicked to answer. "Hey, there! Laurel and I are about to go through the tunnel, so if we drop I'll call you back when we're going over the bridge."

There was a pause on the other end. "You forgot, didn't you?"

I searched my memory banks for any sign of what he might be talking about. "No way! Are you kidding me?" The tunnel was still another mile away. Dang it, this was no time for crystal-clear cell reception. I muted the phone. "Laurel, what did I forget? Brody thinks I forgot and I don't want him to know that he's right!"

"I don't know!"

"Kelsey?" I heard Brody's voice coming through the speakers, but he was still on mute. "Are you still there?" Jabbing at the screen, I disconnected the call.

"What'd you do that for?" Laurel asked.

"I don't know. I panicked."

I wracked my brain trying to remember what it was I'd forgotten. Did I owe him a callback? Was I supposed to give him a ride somewhere? It wasn't his birthday, was it? No, that was still another month away.

I thought back to the last time we talked. I'd told him about finding Stefan in the wine cave. He'd told me about some engagement portraits he'd shot. Then we'd talked about Prentice. *Prentice!* We'd made a date with Jake Schmake to plan our staged wedding for the photo shoot.

After we got through the tunnel, I called Brody back. "Sorry 'bout that! You know how bad the reception can be in Marin County. Anyway—"

"Anyway, you forgot."

"I totally did not forget that we were supposed to go up to Jake's this afternoon."

"Great, so are you coming to pick me up?"

"About that . . ."

I filled him in on all the recent developments at Higgins and told him my sleuthing schedule wasn't going to allow for any extra-credit projects, at least not today. After I apologized profusely, he promised to call Jake and see if we could reschedule.

"Okay, thanks," I said. "And, hey, do you know what the Willows is?"

"It's a restaurant over on Geary. Why do you ask?"

"Just following up a lead. That's where Haley's dad met with Babs the night he gave her the boot, and apparently Stefan thought it was suspicious."

"It does seem like an odd choice," Brody said. "Not exactly where you'd expect a business meeting to take place."

"Maybe Mr. Bennett picked it," I said. "Anyway, I'll keep looking through the book and see if there's anything that's actually helpful."

We got off the phone so I could concentrate on Laurel's driving. Traffic was starting to pick up, and it was bringing out my worst backseat-driving tendencies. "Watch out," I said, pointing up ahead. "That light up there has a camera and they take a picture of your license plate if you run it."

"I'm not going to run it."

"I'm just saying, watch out."

"Do you want to drive?"

"No, you're fine. But you might want to slow down a little."
Okay, so I was maybe having some control issues.

"Seriously, I will pull over right here and we can switch."

I waved my hand to dismiss her concern. "No, don't be silly.
I won't say another word."

I waited at least a full thirty seconds before I spoke again.
"Speaking of driving . . ."

"That's it. I'm pulling over."

"No! I was just going to say, as long as we're out, why don't
we go by the Willows?"

Laurel crinkled her nose. "What for?"

"I don't know. Just a hunch. Stefan thought it was suspicious,
and now I can't stop thinking about it."

A quick search showed it wasn't far out of our way, and Laurel
agreed that it was worth a shot. I navigated while she drove, and I
even managed to keep my opinions about her blinker usage to
a minimum. When we arrived, she dropped me off at the front
door so she wouldn't have to find a parking place, or possibly
because she didn't want to parallel park with me watching.

As soon as I walked in the front door of the Willows, I got
what Brody was saying about it being a strange meeting place for
a wedding planner and a client. I guess technically it was a restaurant, but with large-screen TVs on every wall and over thirty
beers on tap, it seemed more like a sports bar—definitely not
Babs' style.

I approached the hostess, who was wiping down the plastic
menu sleeves in advance of that evening's dinner service so that
the ketchup stains wouldn't obscure the various selections of bur-
gers and nachos.

"Hi," I began. "I have kind of a weird question. How far back
do you keep records of your reservations?"

"We don't take reservations. First come, first served."

"Oh, well . . ." I pulled up a picture of Babs on my phone. "Have you ever seen this woman in here?"

The hostess took a look and shook her head. "Not that I remember. But she doesn't look much like our usual crowd."

I asked a few more questions but didn't learn anything that would be of use, except for maybe the fact that they had two-dollar oysters on Wednesday nights.

"That was a bust," I said as I slid into the driver's seat, which Laurel had abandoned. I turned off the hazards and pulled away from the curb, finding it oddly comforting to be behind the wheel again.

I had no idea why Babs and Mr. Bennett had chosen this as a meeting place, and I still didn't know why Stefan had found it significant.

All I knew was I hoped Stefan woke up soon, because we had a lot to talk about.

CHAPTER 23

S o," I asked the pile of papers spread out before me. "Where should I start?" I finally had all the information on Haley and Christopher's wedding, and was eager to finalize their plans. But I also was looking forward to going through Babs' desk agenda line by line to see what else I could uncover.

Before I could make a firm decision one way or the other, my phone rang. It was Corey, and from the sound of it, things had taken a turn. There'd been an emergency surgery. Something about internal injuries. The details were scant, but the outcome was clear. Stefan was in the ICU, and Corey was beside himself.

Poor Corey. Despite their breakup, he obviously still had feelings for his ex, and I found myself promising to help out however I could. I didn't know if Stefan would approve, but it was the one thing I could do.

"Thanks, Kelsey, I appreciate the offer," Corey said, blowing his nose on the other end of the line. "I'll let you know if I think of anything. There's something else I wanted to ask you, though.

I couldn't talk earlier because the police were here asking questions."

My heart sped up a little. "Like what?"

"Like if Stefan had said anything about what happened in the wine cave."

"That's something we'd all like to know. It's not that easy to topple a rack of wine barrels."

"Yeah, and they're also trying to figure out how the glass got there."

"Glass? What glass?"

Corey paused. "Have I not talked to you since then? I'm sorry. Everything's been such a blur. I thought I told you. They found another injury. A head wound. At first, they assumed all his injuries were from the wine barrels, but they found some shards of green glass in the wound."

"Green glass?" My mind was reeling. "Like from a wine bottle?"

"That's the theory. They didn't even notice it at first, with all his other injuries, but now they think he might have been hit on the head before everything else happened."

I thought back to the night in the wine cave. I hadn't seen any broken glass, but there was so much mess I wasn't sure I would have noticed.

"That's not all," Corey said.

"Uh-oh. What else?"

"They were asking me questions about you. Whether I knew you, things like that."

"About me?" I squeaked. "What did you tell them?"

"I told them I'd met you, and that you'd been up to the hospital to visit. I hope that's okay."

"Of course! It's not like I have anything to hide." At least, not in *my* mind. I hoped the cops would agree.

"That's what I figured," he said. "But I thought you should know."

We talked a few more minutes, and he promised to keep me posted.

I hoped Stefan would wake up soon—for everyone's sake. I'd just assumed that when he regained consciousness, he'd be able to tell everyone what happened. I'd even deluded myself into thinking we'd be able to make amends, or at least be solid frenemies. I'd even dared to hope that we'd use our newfound chumminess to figure out what had happened to Babs.

It had been a good plan, but right now I was on my own. And if things took a turn for the worse—no, I wasn't even going to think about that.

What was the proper protocol for being a police suspect, anyway? Did I go into the police station, or did I wait for them to contact me? The former might make me look guilty, while the latter seemed like I had something to hide. *You're being silly,* I told myself.

My dilemma didn't last long, because no sooner had I delved into Haley and Christopher's file than someone began pounding on my door in a way that sounded very unlike the knock of a civilian. Two thoughts popped into my head simultaneously: *Try not to piss them off,* and *I wish I'd ordered dinner.*

"Just a minute," I called as I grabbed Babs' datebook and stashed it under some blankets in my storage ottoman.

After taking a deep breath, I swung open the door to find the two detectives I'd met before, Blaszczyk (the cranky one) and Ryan (the cute one). Neither of them seemed to be packing pizza, but I let them in anyway and even offered them a beverage. Luckily they declined, because I wasn't sure I had anything to serve them besides tap water and a bottle of pricy champagne that I'd been given as a thank-you gift—and that seemed like a gesture that could be misconstrued on many levels.

"I guess you know why we're here," Blaszczyk said, his tone gruff.

I nodded grimly. "You're here about Stefan."

"Very astute," said Blaszczyk. "And now we need to ask you a few questions."

"Of course." There was something that was bugging me about their visit, and it wasn't just the fact that they didn't seem to be hungry even though it was dinnertime. "Wait a minute, though; you're SFPD. The whole thing with Stefan—that was up in Napa."

"Right," Ryan said. "We're working with the Napa police."

I sucked in a breath. "I'm guessing it's not just because they didn't feel like making the drive."

"I'm sorry?"

"I'm just saying, you were investigating Babs' death and now you're looking into what happened to Stefan even though it didn't happen here. You must think they're related."

"What do *you* think?"

"I'd be lying if I said I thought it was a coincidence."

"Last time we were here, I remember telling you to stay away from Stefan." Blaszczyk looked over at his partner. "Do you remember that, Sam?"

Detective Ryan nodded. "We were sitting right here on this very couch."

"So imagine our surprise when we heard you were the one who found the body."

Were they trying to rattle me, or were they just being imprecise with their words?

"I didn't find the body! I found *Stefan,* and he was perfectly fine." The image of Stefan's crumpled body on the floor of the wine cave flashed through my mind. "Okay, well, not perfectly fine, but he was definitely alive."

"Regardless, you were there at the scene of the crime after we specifically told you to stay away from him."

"It's not like I sought him out. Lucas Higgins called me when Stefan didn't show up and he asked me to come help with an event. Then I found Stefan in the cave, and I called an ambulance." I made an exasperated noise, then immediately regretted it. "I was trying to help him."

Blaszczyk grunted. "You want some kind of award? How do we know you weren't the one who put him there in the first place?"

Ryan shot his partner a look, then turned his focus back to me with a diplomatic smile. "Why don't you take us through what happened when you found Mr. Pierce in the cave?"

"Of course," I said, relieved to change the subject. I wanted to help, but Blaszczyk's attitude toward me wasn't making it easy. I took the detective through the events step by step, starting with Lucas' phone call and ending with the ambulance taking Stefan away.

"You have to admit, it's an awful lot to swallow," Blaszczyk said. "Stefan Pierce accuses you of killing Babs Norton, and he ends up in the hospital just a few weeks later."

"Except that he was totally wrong about me and Babs."

"Was he?" Blaszczyk said, leaning forward with a fresh intensity. "It's already been established that you were jealous of Babs because she was more successful than you. Then you had to go steal two of her clients. What's wrong? The wedding business not quite working out for you?"

"I didn't steal Babs' clients! *They* came to *me*."

"You must have loved that, didn't you? Then you went to her office to gloat, and you got into an argument."

"No, it wasn't like that. I just went there to pick up the files. I even brought scones!"

"What happened? Did you snap? You couldn't take it any longer?"

"What? No! I found Babs on the floor of her office."

"Just like you found Stefan on the floor of the wine cave? That must be your—what do you call it, Sam?"

"Modus operandi?"

"Yeah, your MO." His voice had gotten louder to the point where he was practically yelling. "First you killed Babs, then you pretended to find the body, then Stefan was on to you, so you found a way to shut him up."

"I told you, I wasn't even supposed to be there. They called me because he didn't show."

"And when was the last time you'd seen him before that?"

"I hadn't seen him since the funeral. I swear!"

Blaszczyk flung a disgusted expression my way. "Never mind. We'll get the evidence we need. Just don't leave town."

"I'm a destination wedding planner! My whole job is to leave town!"

"I'll be in the car," he said, right before storming out the door and leaving me gasping for air.

"Sorry about that," Ryan said, giving me an embarrassed look. "He can be kind of a—"

"Jerk?" I had "bully" and "jackass" all lined up in case he needed alternative suggestions for finishing his sentence.

"He's passionate about his job, that's all."

I looked up and Ryan's eyes met mine. "He can't really make me stay, can he? I mean, if you're going to charge me, that's different, but I thought that whole 'just don't leave town' bit—I mean, I heard that's not a real thing."

He smiled and shook his head. "No, we can't make you stay. But you should keep in mind how it could look if someone thought you were trying to flee. It would look bad."

"I get it, but I have a wedding in Catalina coming up, and a site visit in Maui. How am I supposed to do my job?"

Ryan relaxed into the sofa. "It would help if you let us know when you're going to be out of town and where you're going. Flight information would be a nice show of faith so we know when you're coming back."

"Sure," I said, relieved at how much more reasonable Sergeant Ryan was being. It was too bad we hadn't met under different circumstances.

"I'm sure we'll get this all cleared up," Ryan said kindly as he pulled a notepad from his pocket. "Now, I just have a couple more questions about the day you found Mr. Pierce in the wine cave. Did you have any other appointments that day?"

"Let's see. That morning, I was in the office with Laurel. Then we—"

I stopped short. *Will and Kate.* Should I tell him that I'd set up a meeting with Stefan, but he didn't show? That was bound to look bad, but it would be even worse if I didn't tell him and he found out.

He cleared his throat after I'd hesitated a moment longer than one normally would when given the chance to provide their alibi, and my mind raced through the pros and cons of telling him.

"It's okay," he said. "If there's something you want to tell me, it's better to go ahead and say it. You don't want things coming out later."

He was right. In fact, I had a feeling he already knew. He was just giving me a chance to tell the truth. "There is something you should probably know," I began.

Wait a minute. There was no way he could possibly have known that Stefan's fake appointment with Will and Kate was with me and Laurel. We'd used a burner phone. Stefan hadn't shown. There was nothing to tell. Even if they suspected, there's no way they could prove it. If I told them, it was just going to give them the so-called evidence they needed.

But then again, Sergeant Ryan was trying to help me. *Look at those big brown eyes.* It was Blaszczyk I had to look out for; Ryan just wanted to learn the truth and—*oh my God, he was good-copping me!*

"You were saying?" Ryan asked, smiling patiently. I couldn't believe I'd almost fallen for the oldest trick in the book. Blaszczyk had been a bully, then Ryan had swooped in, all nicety-nice-nice. He was trying to get me talking, hoping he could lull me into a false sense of security and totally get me to incriminate myself.

I pressed my lips together for a moment, then crossed my arms in front of my chest. "You should know that I visited Stefan in the hospital yesterday." *There, there's your confession, Good Cop.*

Ryan looked slightly peeved, but he corrected his expression back into friendly mode. "Ah, yes, we were aware of that already." He waited for a moment to see what I'd say next. *Let him wait.* "Is there more to the story than that?"

"Nope. Just wanted to be up front with you, since you told me to stay away from him and all. Now, I assumed that was more of a suggestion than a warning—for my own good of course—so I figured it would be okay."

Ryan peered at me. "Anything else I should know?"

"Oh, yes!" I snapped my fingers as if I'd just remembered a crucial detail. Ryan leaned forward, pen poised over his notepad. "I took him a peace plant," I said. "Okay, whew! I'm glad I got that off my chest."

The questions didn't end there, but my naive assumption that Detective Ryan was on my side did. I modified my original plan of blurting out anything that popped into my head and instead politely told him everything I knew that would be of help—the key words being "that would be of help."

I didn't tell him anything that would incriminate myself and send them off on a wild-goose chase; that would be a waste of their time, and I really didn't want to squander taxpayers' money. Okay, I suppose selfishly I didn't want to be arrested, either, so there was that.

After Ryan left, I collapsed onto the couch. *They actually think I might have had something to with this.* I shouldn't have been surprised. I knew they'd want to talk to me after I'd found Stefan in the wine cave. But it was more serious than that.

I'd just been interrogated.

CHAPTER 24

*D*on't leave town." That's what Blaszczyk had said.
But since Ryan had taken a softer position when he
was playing good cop, I'd decided to take my chances. Still,
when I went downstairs to meet Brody the next morning for our
drive up to Prentice, I checked the street for unmarked vehicles—
which wasn't much help since they were all unmarked, so then I
did an extra sweep to look for particularly nondescript sedans.
I hoped the police wouldn't be monitoring my comings and
goings, but a girl can never be too sure.

Brody looked at me in surprise as I climbed in and scrunched
down in the seat. "What are you doing?"

"Making sure we're not being followed."

"And why do you look like you're going on a date?"

"What do you mean?"

"The makeup? That shirt. And are those new shoes?"

"Nothing wrong with a girl looking nice," I said.

"I've been trying to tell you that for years," he said with a
smirk.

I stuck my tongue out at him as he put the car in gear and pulled onto the street.

"I'm just teasing you. I'm glad you like Jake."

"Who said I like Jake?"

"You did, when you agreed to help him stage a fake wedding at his winery out of the goodness of your heart."

"What do you mean? I'm nice!"

"I know you're nice, but you're also busy. Too busy to be taking on an extra-credit project—which makes me think it's more about his devilishly handsome smile than it is your innate altruism."

I smiled sheepishly. "Am I really that transparent?"

"I don't know if I'd call you transparent. 'Obvious' might be the better word."

While we drove, I filled him in on everything that had happened since we'd last talked. He'd only gotten the headlines along the way, but it had been a couple of days since I'd been able to fully catch him up. I started with the visit from the two detectives the night before and then skipped around from the wine cave to Babs' calendar to my run-in with Miles.

"You need to be careful, Kelsey. Miles could be dangerous."

"I know. At least now I do." I hadn't really thought of Miles as a serious threat at first, but I certainly intended to limit our future visits to public spaces in broad daylight. "But I still have to figure out what happened."

"Why can't you leave that to the police?" It was a logical question—or at least it would be under most circumstances. But these were not most circumstances.

"Because they think I'm a suspect!"

"You don't know that for sure."

"They good-cop-bad-copped me!"

"That doesn't mean they seriously think you did it. Sometimes they have to rattle some trees to see what falls out."

I laughed. "So in this metaphor, I'm what? A coconut or something?"

"Something like that. Anyway, the cops want to find out what happened as much as you do. And talking to you—that's just them doing their job. If they didn't talk to you, you'd be complaining they didn't take it seriously enough."

"Maybe you're right. It's not like I think they're putting together an arrest warrant or anything, but they're not the only ones I'm worried about." I thought back to Danielle's voice mail. "People are starting to talk, and I can't just sit back and cross my fingers that the police clear my name."

"Okay, but please, just promise me you'll be careful."

"I promise."

"And if you snoop, be sure to bring backup."

"Already on it. Laurel made me promise that one yesterday." I felt bad for worrying him—not to mention roping him into my drama. "Anyway, that's enough about me. What's going on with you?"

"I've taken up taxidermy since last we spoke." Apparently, Brody didn't like my not-so-subtle attempts to change the subject.

"C'mon, I'm serious!"

"Me too! I built a workshop and everything."

I crossed my arms. "Okay, fine. Don't tell me."

"What? Don't tell me you didn't know that that was my dream all along."

"Sorry, I guess I'm a bad friend."

Brody grinned playfully. "I know, sheesh. You never listen."

DYING ON THE VINE

All right, if that's the way he wanted to play it . . . "I'm sorry,"
I said. "What have you stuffed so far?"

"I found a dead raccoon last night and it's sitting on my
mantle."

"How'd it turn out?"

"Pretty good, considering."

"Considering what?"

"That it's a dead raccoon. Duh."

And so it went until we got to Prentice.

After I checked myself in the mirror one last time, we got
out of the car and walked up the stairs to the front porch.
Brody knocked on the door to the tasting room, but then a loud
whistle came from the vicinity of the barn. "I'm down here!"
Jake called.

He greeted us at the bottom of the path and motioned
toward the side of the barn. "You guys hungry? I made us some
lunch."

As Jake led us to a sunny spot beside a stream, I gave Brody
an excited thumbs-up behind Jake's back.

"I figured it was the least I could do," Jake said. "I'm going to
owe you both big-time, so this is just my first installment."

He gestured to the blankets he'd spread on the ground, where
he'd laid out what might have quite possibly been the perfect picnic spread. There was a colorful fruit salad that was mostly ber-
ries and thoughtfully devoid of filler melons; roasted figs with
goat cheese and a splash of balsamic vinegar; and an assortment
of sandwiches served on crusty baguettes.

After we got settled, he poured us each a glass of sparkling
wine.

Jake raised his glass in a toast. "Here's to the start of something new."

"Cheers," Brody and I said in unison as we clinked glasses. *Something new.* I assumed Jake meant our little project, but it gave me a funny feeling in my stomach nonetheless.

I tucked into my ham and Brie sandwich with slices of green apple that gave it a little crunch, and sighed with happiness. After everything I'd been through the last couple of days, it felt good to relax a bit. I didn't even mind the bumblebees frolicking in my fruit cup.

After we finished eating, Jake pushed his plate aside and wiped the crumbs off his jeans. "So, you wanna talk weddings?"

"That's what we're here for," I said. Well, that and the company, but I wasn't going to tell *him* that.

I pulled my notebook from my bag and flipped it open to share a couple of sketches I'd made the night before. "I was thinking we'd highlight two locations. That great big oak tree over there would make a great setting for an outdoor ceremony. All you'd need is to rent some chairs and get some flowers, maybe an archway or—oooh! We could even drape the tree with flower garlands."

Brody nodded in agreement. "That would make a gorgeous shot."

"Before we get too carried away, though, we should probably talk about your budget." I hated to be a party pooper, but I didn't want to go overboard.

"I've never thrown a wedding before," Jake said, "so I don't know how much they cost, but how bad can it be?"

"You'd be surprised," Brody said. "People can go nuts. But that's what makes this such a good investment."

"And staging a wedding won't cost as much as an actual wedding, since we don't have to worry about food or music or any of that stuff," I said. "I'll write up an estimate for you before we get started so you know what you're getting yourself into, but a couple of rental fees and this thing will pay for itself."

Jake smiled. "I trust you. Let's talk about what we want to do first, and we'll talk about what's actually possible later."

"Perfect," I said, flipping to the next page in my notebook. "Then let's talk about location number two."

"The barn?" Jake asked.

"Exactly," I answered. "We can set it up for a reception. No food, of course, just tables, linens, place settings, and of course lots and lots of flowers."

"Chicks dig flowers," Jake said with a grin.

I smiled back. "I should say that's sexist or something, but it's not untrue."

"Mind if we go have a look?" Brody asked.

"Let's go," Jake said as he stood and offered me his hand, pulling me to a standing position.

"You know what might be cool?" Brody asked as we approached the front entrance. "A wine barrel on each side of the door with a great big bouquet of flowers on top of each."

The mention of wine barrels made me flinch for a second, but it was a great idea even if it did set off a mild case of PTSD. "I like it. Very wine country."

Jake laughed. "I've definitely got a couple of those lying around."

Jake rolled open the big doors that were made to accommodate extra-large farm equipment.

"Now let's talk about what goes up there," I said, pointing to the open beams and high ceiling. "The key is to create drama. We could do chandeliers, or string it with a gazillion café lights. We could even do paper lanterns if you want to go more colorful, or hang some more flower garlands—although the lights are something that would become a permanent fixture."

"Agreed, the lights seem like a good investment."

"Plus," said Brody, holding his hands up to frame the scene, "they'll look great on film."

We talked a while longer, brainstorming ways to show off the venue, and I jotted notes and offered my best guesses on how much the different components would cost.

"And you can help me get everything we need?" Jake said. "I wouldn't know where to start."

"Of course. I'll be here to set it all up and Brody will shoot it."

"Man, this is going to be great. I don't know how to thank you."

"Are you kidding me? This is what I love to do. And it's not often I get to just have fun without having to take two families' worth of opinions into account." It was also a welcome change of pace from all the worrying I'd been doing.

"Excuse me for a minute, guys," Brody said. "I'm going to grab my camera and take a couple of reference shots." I turned my head in time to see Brody bounding up the path toward the house.

"So," I said, feeling nervous about the sudden departure of our chaperone, "I think this'll be great."

"Me too," said Jake. "Hey, while I've got you alone . . . I was wondering if I could bribe you with dinner sometime?"

"You don't have to bribe me. I told you I'm happy to do it."

"Okay, maybe 'bribe' isn't the right word. Tempt?"

Oh, I was tempted all right. "You mean like . . . ?" I wanted to make sure I knew what I was potentially agreeing to before I embarrassed myself.

"Yes, like a date."

I worked hard to play it cool, but my heart was doing jumping jacks and possibly a samba dance inside my chest. "Sure, that'd be great. We can go over the estimate and—"

"Nope," Jake said.

"Nope? Nope what?"

"I told you, it's a date. We can talk about our wedding some other time."

"Our wedding? Oh, our *wedding*. This wedding." I laughed nervously. "I thought you meant—but you just meant this. Okay, good."

Yep, way to play it cool.

Jake seemed nonplussed by my tongue-tied response, but he just smiled. "Good then. Now that we've got that established, I'll call you, okay?"

I nodded but didn't vocalize my consent, for fear of blurting out something equally awkward.

Just then Brody reappeared, and while he snapped a few pictures I watched quietly, still riding high on a wave of giddiness. I was dying to tell Brody about the date, but I patiently waited until we'd said our goodbyes and were pulling out of the driveway.

"I'm not surprised," he said.

"Really? Why not?"

"Because I have an uncanny ability to read people," he said. "And besides, he told me he was going to."

"He did? When?"

"Earlier today, when I called him. Why do you think I made myself scarce back there?"

"But wait, what if I'd said no?"

"Mmm-hmm. Like *that* was going to happen."

"What do you mean?" I crossed my arms in front of my chest in mock indignation. "Are you saying I'm easy?"

"Well, sure. But you already admitted you like him. Besides, I know you well enough to read the subconscious signals."

"Meaning what exactly?"

"Well, correct me if I'm wrong, but I think in the course of one afternoon, the two of you just shared a romantic picnic and then planned your dream wedding."

CHAPTER 25

*A*s Brody and I headed back toward the city, the late afternoon sun bathed the vineyards in a golden glow. Neither of us was in a particular hurry to get home, so I talked Brody into meandering our way along the back roads instead of heading right back to the highway.

"Oh!" I said. "Maybe we'll stop at that place we went to that one time."

Brody flashed me a quizzical look. "Could you be a little more specific?"

"That old general store they fixed up where they sell fancy-pants sandwiches and cool housewares and stuff."

"Oh, yeah. What was it called?"

"I don't remember. The Fancy-Pants Sandwich and Tchotchke Emporium?"

"Pretty sure that's not it, but I bet you can look it up. Maybe we'll grab something to take home for dinner."

"Or an overpriced pair of waffle tongs."

"Waffle tongs? Is that a thing?"

"They're all the rage in Europe," I said as I opened up my Internet app. "And with moms of toddlers."

I held the phone up to the front windshield but couldn't get a signal. "Shoot, I can't connect to the Internet out here. Oh, well, maybe we'll run across it—if we haven't already passed it."

I kept an eye out while we drove. Winery. Winery. Winery. The Willows. *Wait, the Willows?* I spun around to check out the large wooden sign with gold-leaf letters: The Willows. A Bed and Breakfast Inn.

That was weird. "Brody, slow down!"

"What? Why?"

"The Willows. Babs Norton and Haley's dad. It's not a restaurant!"

"Complete thoughts, please."

"Sorry! I saw a sign back there for a bed-and-breakfast called the Willows. Maybe that's the Willows the Babs was referring to in her datebook."

"That makes more sense. That other place is a dump."

I looked back over my shoulder again, trying to see what the place looked like. "Should we go check it out?"

"Why?" Brody asked. "They were probably just scouting a venue, maybe for the rehearsal dinner or something."

"But they'd already booked the rehearsal dinner."

Brody shrugged. "I don't know. Maybe they were looking for someplace for his elderly aunt to stay."

"That seems like it would have been below Babs' pay grade, but I guess it's possible." I tried to let it go, but something was still bothering me. "Can we go back? It'll only take a minute. I want to check it out."

"All right." He didn't sound very enthusiastic, but he did turn around in the parking lot of the next winery and he barely scowled at all. A few minutes later we were winding our way up the long drive.

The main house was small but stately, with manicured rose-bushes along the porch and large white columns framing the door. Behind the main house, several cottages were tucked away behind hedges.

"Nice," Brody said as we got out of the car.

"A little too nice, if you ask me."

Brody quirked an eyebrow at me as I turned to march up to the front door. Locked. I pulled a brochure from the wooden display holder mounted on the wall and read it out loud. " 'The Willows. A romantic retreat in the heart of the wine country.' "

"Hmmm," Brody said. "That doesn't mean anything."

" 'Since 1982,' " I added.

"That *really* doesn't mean anything."

A sign near the door read "Please ring the buzzer if the front door is locked," so I pressed the white button, then peeked through the windows into the front parlor.

"One minute!" came a cheery voice over the intercom. "I'll be right down!"

I looked at Brody and shrugged. A minute later, a woman wearing a floral apron over her khaki pants and T-shirt flung the door open, a huge smile lighting up her face. "Welcome! Are you the Donovan party?"

"No, sorry, we don't have reservations."

"Oh," she said, nodding politely and still smiling—though she seemed confused as to why we were standing on her porch if that was the case. "I'm sorry, we're all full for the night."

"Right. We're not looking for a room. I'm Kelsey." I retrieved a business card from my purse and held it out to her. "I'm a wed-ding planner, and this is my friend Brody."

She smiled and took my hand. "Nice to meet you, Kelsey the wedding planner and her friend Brody. I'm Sandra."

"I'm sorry to stop by without an appointment, but we were up this way, and, well, you came highly recommended by another wedding planner, so I just wanted to stop by and check the place out."

"Oh, fantastic!" She beamed and waved us in. "Come have a glass of sherry and I'll show you around." She led us into the plush front room with its elegant dark-wood wainscoting and overstuffed furniture. "Who did you say told you about us?"

I looked sideways at Brody for a split second and cleared my throat. "Um, Babs Norton."

"Ohhhhhh . . . ," Sandy said, her smile turning from cheery to pitying all in one move. "I heard about what happened. It's just a tragedy."

"Yes, it was," I said.

"You said she recommended us?"

"That's right," I said, hoping it wasn't completely obvious that I was lying. "Apparently she booked parties here sometimes?"

"Well . . ." Sandy smoothed her apron, apparently at a loss for words. "We're not really set up for parties here. Why don't you tell me what size group you have and I'll see if I can make some recommendations?"

"Oh, I don't have anything in particular in mind. Just always on the lookout for new venues," I said, smiling brightly.

"Well, let me give you a brochure. We have a bridal suite that's pretty popular with honeymooners."

I took the brochure and nodded admiringly as I flipped through the pages. Between the Jacuzzi tubs, the beds sprinkled with rose petals, and the much-heralded private cottages, the Willows looked like it was running for Love Nest of the Year.

"I'm sorry," I said. "I guess I misunderstood. So Babs wasn't planning an event here?"

"No, nothing like that," Sandra said. "She just—you know." In lieu of finishing her sentence, she smiled and nodded for a little longer than one might normally under the circumstances.

I peered at Sandra, waiting for her to finish. Which she didn't. "Are you trying to say she was a guest?"

"I'm not really at liberty to say." Sandra looked nervous. "You know how it is."

I knew exactly how it was. Babs had been spending her downtime at a romantic retreat in the heart of the wine country. With Haley's dad.

As much as I admired Sandra's discretion, I wasn't ready to let her off the hook. If I was right about Babs and Stanley, this was big news. "Oh, my mistake! She must have come here with her boyfriend. Stanley Bennett?" I looked at Brody as if to say, *Was that his name?* but Brody looked at me as if to say, *Leave me out of this.*

"I have so many guests, I can't remember all of their names," she said diplomatically.

"Tall guy, brown hair? About yea-high?" I held my hand up to approximate Mr. Bennett's height.

Sandra gave an awkward half shrug. "I can't really divulge . . ."

"Of course not. Sorry." As far as I was concerned, she didn't have to divulge a thing, because her shifty-eyed denial said it all. Not that Sandra was shifty—although you never know; sometimes the cheerful ones are the most dangerous of all—but my questions had clearly struck a nerve. Her sudden need to protect Babs' privacy told me everything I needed to know.

Namely, that there was privacy to protect.

I bit my tongue all the way back to the car, but as soon as we'd closed the car doors behind us, I let it out. "Babs and Mr. Bennett! Brody, can you believe that?"

Brody seemed nonplussed as he started the car and made his way back toward the main road. "C'mon, Kelsey, they're two consenting adults."

"Yeah, but he's a *married* consenting adult."

Brody's eyebrows shot up in surprise. "Whoa, he's married? I thought you said Haley's parents were divorced?"

"I did. They are. But Haley has a stepmom, Yvonne."

Brody let out a low whistle. "That's crazy. No wonder you were all hopped up back there."

"Was it that obvious?"

"No, it's because I know you. She probably just thought you needed to use the restroom."

"Anyway," I continued, ignoring him, "Haley told me her dad had fired Babs over money issues, but maybe there was more to it than that."

"Like maybe his wife found out, or one of them broke it off."

"Exactly. Man, I would never have an affair with one of my clients. That's a total wedding-planner faux pas." I shook my head thinking about Babs and Haley's dad, but trying not to think about it too hard because that was not an image I wanted in my head.

"Definitely not what you would expect from the Queen of Wine Country Weddings, that's for sure."

My mind was racing. "Brody, do you know what this means?"

"That Sandra needs to work on her poker face?"

"Haley's dad lied! He acted like he hardly knew Babs."

"Yeah, well, it sounds like he knew her pretty well."

"Seriously. Like *biblically* well. Don't you think that's pretty suspicious?"

"Definitely." Brody thought for a second. "But he might have just been trying to cover up his affair. . . ."

"Or he might have been trying to cover up a murder." Suddenly the car was feeling kind of stuffy, and I rolled down the window to get some air. "I really, really don't want it to be true. I mean, I don't know them that well, but my clients are always just . . . my clients. And I'm so used to overlooking weird family dynamics that I guess I've been in denial."

"Well, it sounds like it's time to consider the possibility."

I considered it for a moment—and I didn't at all like where it led me. "It's even worse than you realize."

Brody gave me a sidelong glance. "How so?"

"When I told Mr. Bennett about Stefan canceling the contracts, he pretty much flipped out."

"Flipped out how?"

"Somewhere between road rage and a Real Housewives reunion."

"Maybe like Bruce Banner right when he turns into the Incredible Hulk?"

"Yeah, like that. He didn't turn green, but he did threaten to destroy Stefan."

"Yikes. So we know he has anger issues. He was having an affair with Babs—"

"And now she's dead."

"And he was furious with Stefan—"

"Who was locked in a wine cave and left for dead."

My phone began to ring the special ringtone that I assigned to clients, and the name "Stanley Bennett" flashed up on display. A shiver ran down my spine as I held it up for Brody to see.

"And now he's calling me."

CHAPTER 26

There's good news and bad news," I said as I hung up the phone from my brief call with Mr. Bennett.

"What's the good news?" Brody asked.

"He realizes that this job has gone way past a simple day-of-wedding coordination job, and he wants us to send him an invoice so he can pay us for all the extra work."

"That's great," Brody said. "Right?"

I nodded halfheartedly.

"So what's the bad news?"

"Until we figure out what's going on here, I don't know if I want him anywhere near me."

When we got back into the city, Brody dropped me off at my apartment and made me promise to call him if I went anywhere, especially if it involved an investigative mission. My plans were to curl up on the couch with a good book—one with Babs Norton's name on the cover.

After changing into a comfy pair of yoga pants and making myself a soothing cup of French roast, I spent the evening poring over Babs' datebook, going back through months and months of appointments.

In addition to several meetings with Haley and Christopher, there were several more with just "SB"—further proof that the two had been having an affair. And I wasn't the only one who seemed to be on to them: in the back of the book, I found a list in what I assumed was Stefan's handwriting, detailing the dates and locations of each rendezvous. Stefan was obviously on to their secret meetings and possibly even suspected Mr. Bennett of more than just breaking his marriage vows.

That may have been what got him in trouble, I thought with a shudder.

Thumbing through the book, I found hundreds more pieces of information, but nothing else that really stood out. It wasn't like on TV where they can ignore a houseful of clutter and zoom in on the one clothing fiber that shouldn't be there. I had no idea what was significant and what wasn't. Was it the "Publicity shoot at Higgins" on the twenty-second? The notes from the "Dream Wedding Planning Meeting" written out in Babs' tidy hand? Or the list of florists in Sonoma County that was discreetly tucked into the back flap? Heck, for all I knew the phone number she'd jotted down of a handyman named George could turn out to be the key to the whole thing.

I closed the book and set it on the coffee table, trying to decide what my next steps should be. As far as I was concerned, Haley's dad and Lucas' brother both had motives worth looking into. I didn't know what more I could do on the Miles front, but there was someone I could talk to about Mr. Bennett. I picked up my phone.

"Hello, Haley?"

Our quick call confirmed that yes, she was available to meet the next day.

Officially on the agenda? Going through the folder I'd found at Higgins and finalizing her wedding arrangements. My secret agenda? Learning more about Mr. Bennett and gauging his propensity for revenge.

The next day, Haley showed up at my office at 10:00 A.M. for our working session with a handsome golden retriever by her side. "I hope you don't mind," she said. "I had to take him to the vet this morning and didn't have time to drop him off back at our house."

"No, I love meeting people's pooches. He's beautiful!" I leaned over and gave the dog's head a vigorous two-handed rub. "What's his name?"

"This is Farley," she said. "He's our baby."

"Well, hello, Farley." Smiling up at me, the dog wagged his tail with a gentle *thump-thump-thump* against my leg. "Is it just the two of us?"

"Three of us," she said, pointing at Farley, smiling. "He's one of the family."

"Of course. Sorry, Farley." I ruffled his head one more time to make sure there were no hard feelings.

"But yeah, just the three of us. Christopher had to work today."

"And your dad?" I kept my tone nonchalant as I led them into my office.

"Oh! I didn't even think to ask. You probably need a check from him, huh?"

"No, no, this is fine. We'll get a lot more done this way."

Farley had wandered off to smell my trashcan, and Haley patted her leg to get his attention. "Farley, come here, sweetie."

Farley trotted back to Mom, his tags jingling. While she scratched his ear, his hind leg started scratching at the air reflexively.

"Hey!" Haley sat up with a jolt of inspiration. "Do you think we could have Farley be in the wedding?"

"Oh, that would be fun." I hated to squash her enthusiasm, but I was guessing pets were forbidden under Miles' dauntingly thorough rules and protocols manual. "I'll see what I can do, but their rules are pretty strict."

Haley deflated in her seat. "Yeah, I know, them and their rules."

I idly wondered how Brody's time machine was coming along. If he ever got it running, I'd go back and find Haley before she ever hired Babs. I'd keep Haley a million miles away from Higgins, and I'd keep her dad a million miles away from Babs.

I shook my head to get the thought out of my mind before I mapped out a whole alternate universe.

"The good news is, I was able to get hold of your file, and there are just a few things left to attend to before we get you guys married off!" I jumped right in, going down the list one item at a time and finalizing details both large and small. Fortunately, Stefan hadn't canceled every contract; I guess by the time he'd canceled the caterer, florist, and wedding cake, calling off the lighting guy and the party favors had seemed anticlimactic.

"I also wanted to go over the seating chart while I've got you here." I pulled an oversized printout from the folder. "It looks like you and Babs got a good start, but we should review it and make sure it still works." We went over the head table first, making sure it was in the classic boy-girl-boy-girl configuration. I tapped my fingernail on another table. "Which brings us to the parents' table. Everything here look good?"

She shrugged. "Yep, same old parents."

"Good. I look forward to meeting your stepmom." I checked the chart and then glanced up at Haley. "Yvonne, is it?"

"Yeah, we're supposed to go shopping together later this week. I think she wants to talk to me about something."

"Oh, yeah? What do you think it is?" I couldn't help but wonder if Yvonne knew about the affair.

"I don't know." Haley giggled. "But I sure hope it isn't the sex talk because, *ewww*!"

"So are she and your dad . . . doing okay?" I had wanted to say *still together,* but that seemed a little forward.

"Yeah, they're good. They're taking dance lessons so they can look good at the wedding."

"You didn't tell me there was going to be a dance-off." I smiled to cover my surprise. "Seriously, that's really sweet."

"They're great together. And it's nice to see him so happy."

"You guys seem like you're really close."

"Yeah, we are. Growing up without a mom was tough, but my dad always did the best he could. That's probably why I'm such a Daddy's girl."

"Have they been married a long time?"

"It'll be eight years this fall."

I stifled an urge to bring up the seven-year itch, and Farley started scratching his ear as if he could read my mind.

"It had always been him and me, but then Yvonne came along, and for the first time I could even remember, he seemed so happy." Haley stared out the window for a moment, lost in thought. "He told me once that the world had been black and white, but when Yvonne came along he was able to see in color again."

"Wow, that's . . . something." I couldn't imagine how devastated she'd be if she found out he'd gone out and bought an even bigger box of crayons.

It was pretty clear that Haley didn't know about the affair—and I certainly wasn't going to be the one to tell her. I decided to try one of the other topics on my hidden agenda.

"Speaking of your dad . . . did he get a chance to talk to Stefan about getting the deposits back?" I made my voice as neutral and just-casually-interested as possible.

"You know, I'm not sure if he did. I'll have to ask him."

"Oh." I tried not to sound disappointed.

"I mean, he had set up a meeting with him, but Stefan didn't show up."

"Oh?" This was news. "Do you know when they were supposed to meet?"

Haley shrugged. "No, sorry, I don't know. I think it was Thursday." *The same day I was supposed to meet him but found him in a wine cave instead.* Had Stefan really not showed, or was that just what Mr. Bennett was telling people?

"It seemed like your dad was pretty mad at Stefan when he found out about the contracts."

"Well, sure, we all were. It's hard finding out that someone you trusted could do something so awful." She looked pensive, but then her face brightened. "That's why we're so happy we have you! You've really helped save the day. It's so nice to be done with all that drama."

I forced a big smile for her, but I felt terrible. Whatever drama she thought she'd experienced was nothing compared to what would happen if any of this got out. If it turned out her dad had killed Babs, it would destroy her. Part of me didn't even want to know. I was ready to put my hands over my ears and sing "*la-la-la-la-la*" until we sent her and Christopher away on their honeymoon. But the other part of me had to know, and that part was a whole lot pushier.

I really hoped for her sake that her dad hadn't had anything to do with it, but I had one last piece of business that I had to cover: the keys I'd found on the floor of the wine cave. I'd asked Corey if they were Stefan's, but he'd told me all of Stefan's belongings were present and accounted for. Which meant there was a good chance that whoever they belonged to had been in the wine cave that day.

"Oh, hey, I've been meaning to ask you . . ." I pulled the keys from my desk drawer and dangled them from my index finger. "I found these keys after you guys were here last. They're not yours by any chance, are they?"

Haley studied them and shook her head.

"Or maybe Christopher's?" *Pause.* "Or your dad's?"

"I don't think so." She held out her hand. "Let me see?"

I tossed her the keys and she inspected them more closely, then pulled out her phone and snapped a picture. "I'll ask them tonight."

My mouth hung open for a second. I hadn't seen that one coming. If the keys belonged to her dad, he'd know exactly where I'd found them. And that was bad. I frantically tried to think of any excuse to ask Haley to delete the picture, but I couldn't come up with a single one.

Let's just hope they're not his.

CHAPTER 27

After Haley left, I spent the afternoon berating myself at regular intervals for handing the keys to Haley. No one knew I had them, they might be a clue in a murder investigation, and I really should have given them to the police in the first place.

Later that evening, Stanley Bennett e-mailed me to say he would drop by the next morning so we could get caught up on the budget. I'd know the minute I saw his face whether it truly was just a friendly visit or whether he'd recognized the keys in Haley's picture, but over e-mail I had no idea what to expect.

Under no circumstances did I want to be alone with him, so the next morning before work I called to make sure Laurel didn't have any other meetings and invited Brody to hang out with us until Mr. Bennett left. "C'mon, Brody," I said. "I'll even stop by that bakery on Fillmore and get those almond croissants you love so much." They required a special trip and parking would be a bear, but I was desperate.

"Um, that's great, except you're the one who's obsessed with those, so I can't help but doubt your motives."

"I thought those were your favorite breakfast treat!" I said indignantly.

"Nope, still you," he said, laughing. "Try to keep us straight."

In the interest of keeping the negotiations going, I resisted the obvious joke—that him being straight was a ship that had sailed long ago—and said, "Okay, fine, name your price. Venti mocha latte? Waffle on a stick? Green eggs and ham?"

"I don't need bribery, Sam I Am. I'll be there, but I'm only doing it to make sure you're safe."

I breathed a sigh of relief. "You're the best, Brody."

"It's true. So I'll see you in a bit?"

"Perfect. Oh, and Brody?" I said before he'd had a chance to hang up.

"Yeah?"

"You won't happen to be over by Fillmore, will you?"

"What? I can't hear you. You're breaking up. I'm about to go into a tunnel. Byeeeeee."

"Liar," I muttered. Even though he'd said he didn't need bribery, I couldn't help but feel like he would be disappointed if I didn't offer up some refreshments, so I stopped on the way into the office and loaded up.

A couple hours later, our stomachs full of almond croissants—which were delicious, as predicted—I paced my office while Brody and Laurel waited on standby as my impromptu security force, should the need arise.

When the doorbell rang, I went over to the top of the stairs, nodded to Brody, who was checking e-mails from his laptop in our front office, and buzzed our guest into the building.

Laurel stationed herself near the bookshelves outside my office, knitting her brows furiously as she searched for some imaginary missing tome.

"Don't overact," I whispered. "Less is more."

A few moments later, our front door opened and Stanley Bennett entered.

"Hello, Kelsey," he said, smiling. "Good to see you again."

"Mr. Bennett," I said, nodding politely. *So far so good.* If he'd seen the keys and recognized them, he wasn't letting on—but I wasn't going to let my guard down until he was gone, because that's how they get you.

"I brought my checkbook," he said, "and I wanted to go over a few things with the wedding. I want to plan a surprise for Haley and I was hoping you could help."

"Sure!" I said, plastering a fake smile on to my face and gesturing toward my office. "Can I get you some coffee? I have some lovely almond croissants."

"That would be great," he said. "If you don't mind, I'm going to go wash my hands. I took Muni to get here and there's just not enough hand sanitizer in the world."

"Down the hall, third door on the left." I pointed the way, then stepped into the kitchen, kicking myself for my eagerness to relinquish a pastry to a possible murderer. *Stop that,* I commanded myself as I pulled a plate from the cabinet. *He's not a murderer; he's a client.*

Then again, there was no reason he couldn't be both. I was just relieved that he didn't seem to know I'd been asking about him.

"You need help?" Laurel asked, appearing in the doorway to the kitchen.

"Sure. You wanna get the coffee?"

"Good call. Coffee's my specialty."

We buzzed around the kitchen nervously, and I peeked down the hall to make sure we were still alone. "Quick," I whispered. "Let's talk about something so it's not awkward."

"So . . ." Laurel paused, looking like a deer in headlights—one who'd just been handed a pop quiz. "Do you work out?"

I laughed and shook my head. "Yeah, that's not awkward at all."

Laurel shot me a slightly scowly look. "Well, you suggest something better, then."

"Hey, do you want to go on a site visit with me next month in Hawaii?" I asked.

"Do I?! Of course I do!" She lowered her voice. "Wait, is this for real?"

I nodded. "If I can work it into the budget. I think I'll need backup, if you're game."

Laurel was mid-squeal when an ashen-faced Mr. Bennett appeared in the door of the kitchen, breathing hard. His eyes darted wildly between me and Laurel. "What in the hell is going on here?"

"Hawaii?" Laurel said. "I've always wanted to go."

"Maui, to be exact," I said, as I desperately tried to figure out what he could have possibly overheard. In order, we'd talked about coffee, then working out, then Hawaii—none of which seemed particularly objectionable.

"So I'm a murder suspect now?" His eyes flashed in anger.

"Whoa, whoa, whoa. Did the police call you?" I was genuinely confused. We hadn't said anything out loud about that, and unless he'd just gotten a call from Haley while he was in the bathroom or he was able to read minds—

"I saw your little project down the hall."

The murder board!

"You did?" I blurted. "But how?"

"I opened the wrong door. I thought it was the bathroom. If you wanted to keep it a secret, you probably should keep it locked up." His fists clenched by his sides as he spoke.

"Probably the cleaning lady," Laurel said meekly. "We just hired a new service."

"Now Mr. Bennett," I said, frantically searching my mind for something super awesome to explain our actions that would make him laugh and say, *Well, of course when you put it that way!*

"How could you think I could have hurt Babs? What happened between us was none of your business! And to put up on that board that we'd had an affair? What if Haley had seen that?"

My mind scrambled to catch up. The Willows was new information and I hadn't added it yet. "But I didn't—"

Laurel's eyes turned big and she clapped her hand over her mouth. "Sorry, Kelsey," she whispered. "I updated it this morning."

Of course she had. She knew how much I appreciated it when she took initiative—*dammit.*

"Is there a problem here?" Brody asked from the hall behind Mr. Bennett.

"How dare you?" he said, ignoring Brody completely and glaring at me with a fierce intensity. "Do you really think I killed Babs?"

"Mr. Bennett, I'm genuinely sorry. Of course I don't think you killed anyone"—although if looks could kill, I wouldn't be alive long enough to continue my thought—"but as part of the process of figuring out who did, we had to look at everyone who had motive."

"How is this even any of your business at all?" Mr. Bennett asked.

"Fair question," I said, holding up my hands. "Stefan accused me of murdering Babs, and now he's in the hospital. I'm trying to clear my name, that's all."

"And so you think it's okay to go snooping into my private life?"

"Well, you were pretty angry when I told you about the contracts—"

"Can you blame me?" he sputtered.

"I'm truly sorry, Mr. Bennett. Of course I don't think you killed Babs." The jury was still out on that one, but placating him seemed like my best option while he was standing in front of me with an expression on his face that looked like a combination of a coronary incident and homicidal rage. "I was just using the board to think things through. I make lists. It's what I do."

"Well, put this on your list: I may have been sleeping with Babs, but I never would have hurt her."

"Then why did you fire her?" I blurted before I could stop myself.

Mr. Bennett seemed to deflate as he sank back against the doorframe. "Yvonne was starting to suspect. Too many late-night 'planning meetings,'" he said, using air quotes around the last two words. "She insisted that I fire Babs immediately if I wanted to save our marriage, and unfortunately, our prenup has a fidelity clause that was going to cost me a ton."

"So you just fired Babs? What about Haley and Christopher?"

"They don't know anything about this. I made sure Babs got a big fat check that was way less than my alimony payments would have been, and I figured the wedding would take care of itself. I mean, she'd planned everything already, right?"

"Well, I mean . . ." I bit my tongue to keep from explaining the wedding planner's role beyond the initial planning, as it seemed like the least of our worries in that moment. Maybe I'd send him a few links to some helpful articles from *The Knot* later.

"Anyway," he said, "that's the whole story. Babs and I parted on good terms."

It seemed reasonable. And yet . . . "What about Stefan?" I asked. Laurel and Brody exchanged uncomfortable glances as I delved further into the questioning that I had sworn I wasn't going to do. Of course, I hadn't planned on any of this, but I was emboldened by the fact that we outnumbered him.

Mr. Bennett's eyes narrowed to slits. "What about him?"

"The last time I saw you, you were furious with him, and now he's lying in a hospital bed. I'm sorry, I have to ask."

"If it was my fault?"

I gulped and nodded. "I mean, you did have plenty of motive to go after him."

Mr. Bennett leaned in until his face was close enough for me to smell his aftershave. "No more motive than you had."

"What's that supposed to mean?" I asked.

He stared at me intently. "I wasn't the only one who was upset that he canceled those contracts. You must have been really angry that he sabotaged a wedding you were working on."

"Oh, please," I said, my tone implying a little more eye roll than I'd intended.

"And then with your history . . ."

"What history?" I asked, my voice going into a higher octave.

"Word gets around, Miss McKenna. I heard that he very publicly accused you of murdering Babs Norton." He paused for a moment, sizing me up. "Of course I assumed it was all bluster, but now I have to ask myself—"

"No!" I said. "You don't have to ask yourself anything, because

I had nothing to do with it. What reason could I possibly have had?"

"Professional jealousy? Who knows? But now that Stefan's in the hospital, it certainly lends credence to his accusations. You'd better hope he makes it."

"Now wait a minute," Brody said, holding both arms up. "Kelsey didn't hurt anyone."

"How do you know?" Mr. Bennett asked.

"Because I know her," Brody said. "Now I'd appreciate it if you could take a step back." I was glad Brody had kept up his gym membership, because Mr. Bennett relinquished a little bit of my personal space back to me.

Bennett wasn't done, though. "When Stefan was found in the wine cave, I was in Toronto on business. Where were you, Kelsey?"

"I was working!" I put my hands on my hips in a show of defiance.

"Where? Oh, that's right! At the wine cave!" Spittle flew from his lips as he exaggerated his words for effect.

Wait, did he really think I'd had anything to do with what had happened to Babs and Stefan? I was going to have to turn this meeting around, and fast. I put on my most soothing tone, the one I use with hysterical brides when it's time for them to breathe into a paper bag. "Mr. Bennett, I promise you, I was only there doing my job. In fact, I was the one who found Stefan in the cave and called the ambulance. Now, look, I know we've all been under a lot of stress, so why don't we focus on the wedding?"

He crossed his arms in front of him and looked me up and down. "You know, I'm meeting with one of the detectives later, because they have some questions for me. Luckily, I have documentation that I was in another country, so it's just a formality. In fact, I was afraid I wouldn't be of much help to them, but now . . ."

Brody stepped between us, physically separating us this time. "Why don't we all take a deep breath and go sit in the front office where it's more comfortable?"

"There's no need," Mr. Bennett said, taking a check out of his pocket. He ripped it in half, then tore the remnants into several smaller pieces to make his point, tossing them in the air in an angry rain of confetti. "We're through here."

CHAPTER 28

The front door slammed.

"Coffee, anyone?" Laurel asked, holding out the latte she'd made for our departed guest. Despite her calm tone, her hands were shaking.

I shook my head. "I've got so much adrenaline pumping through my veins, I might not need any for days."

I knelt and picked up a couple of pieces of ripped-up paper, then decided to make it official and sank all the way down onto the hardwood floors. I leaned my head back against a cabinet door. "Well, our week just got a little less busy."

"Kelsey, I'm so sorry about the murder board," Laurel said. "I was thinking about it all night after you called and told me what happened, and I guess I was just excited to update it. But I swear I closed the door behind me."

"I'm sorry I even gave you the damn thing." Brody looked at me with concern. "You going to be okay?"

"I think so," I said as I finished picking the rest of the scraps of paper as well as myself up off the floor. "Mostly I feel really bad for Haley and Christopher being out a wedding planner—again."

Laurel nodded solemnly. "First Babs, now us."

"In the meantime, I'd better go call Lucas and tell him to expect an angry phone call." I tossed the ripped-up check into the trash. "Thanks for coming over."

"I'm glad I was here," Brody said. "I thought I was going to get to use all that kung fu training I got back in fifth grade."

I laughed at the image. "You have a bright future as a security guard if that whole photography thing doesn't work out."

"All right," he said. We walked back down the hall to the front office and he packed up his bag. "Call me if you need me."

"You know I will." We hugged goodbye, and he gently pulled the door shut behind him on his way out.

I dreaded telling Lucas that I'd been relieved of my duties on the Bennett-Riegert wedding. Should I try to explain or just keep my mouth shut? There was still the matter of the other weddings we said we'd help with, but I was worried that we'd suddenly find ourselves uninvited. Maybe "worried" wasn't the word for it; after all, we'd only agreed to do them as a favor. Besides, with Miles being one of the most prominent entries on my murder board, maybe it would be wise to walk away.

The only problem with that plan was that my professional pride wouldn't let me.

I dialed Lucas' number but didn't get an answer, so I quickly hung up before it went to voice mail rather than babbling some poorly thought-out soliloquy. Then I felt silly and dialed him back, leaving a short and sweet, "This is Kelsey. Call me back."

I just hoped I'd catch him before he talked to Mr. Bennett.

When Lucas finally did call me back, I was right at that point in the day between "I just had lunch" and "I need a nap." I'd stepped out to get some fresh air and found myself standing in line at Blue Bottle Coffee, because it was the kind of occasion when only coffee made by somebody else would do. The line was long, as usual, and I'd already been waiting seven or eight minutes when I felt the buzz from my back pocket.

We said our hellos and I jumped right in. "I just wanted to update you on, um . . ." I glanced around furtively to make sure the bearded dude in front of me and the girl in ironic knee socks behind me weren't listening.

"No need. I talked to Stanley already." Lucas's office chair squeaked loudly in the background, and I could picture him sitting at his desk.

Great. "So he told you . . . ?" I hated to use the word "fired," but it was apt.

"He did. In fact, he said you accused him of murdering Babs Norton."

I tried to keep my voice low as I abandoned my place in line and stepped outside. "No! It wasn't like that! He came into the office and he went to wash his hands and—"

"Kelsey, that's really serious." If his face matched his voice, he was furrowing his eyebrows into a disappointed expression.

I mentally counted to ten before I spoke. Okay, it was probably only five, but at least I paused. "I didn't accuse him; I just suspected him. And I had my reasons."

"Well, you can't just go around making outrageous statements like that. It's a bad reflection on all of us."

A bad reflection? *I* was a bad reflection? After Stanley Bennett and Babs had besmirched both the institution of marriage and the entire wedding-planning profession? I did my best to stay calm, but I wasn't going to take the fall for Mr. Bennett's behavior. "I didn't *say* anything to him."

"Then how did he know you suspected him?"

I didn't want to have to explain why I had a murder board in our spare office, so I steered the conversation in a different direction. "I don't suppose he mentioned that he and Babs were having an affair, did he?"

A pause. "No, but that doesn't seem like it should be any of your concern."

"It's not just that! He acted like he didn't know her! Then, after what happened to Stefan in the wine cave—"

"That was an accident." His abrupt tone signaled that I was crossing a line. I would have to proceed with caution.

"I'm sure it was. It's just, he was really angry with Stefan, and I thought—well, it seemed like maybe there was more to it."

Lucas didn't jump right in with assurances that he understood, but he did seem to soften his tone ever so slightly. "The only saving grace is that they brought you in on their own and we weren't the ones who recommended you. So as far as Mr. Bennett is concerned, you're just some nut his daughter hired."

"Gee, thanks."

"I'm not saying I agree. I'm just saying that as far as he's concerned, it's no reflection on us."

"That's good, I guess."

"But if you're going to be working here, I need to know that I can trust you in front of our clients."

I was tempted to say that as long as their clients weren't psycho, lying cheaters it wouldn't be a problem, but I didn't think that would be a good way to prove my trustworthiness.

"I'm sorry. You can trust me. This was a unique situation."

"Apology accepted," he said. "But in the future, it would be best if you focus on your work and leave the investigating up to the police."

I almost gave Lucas a rude gesture and told him he could *focus on this,* but I figured over the phone the message would get lost. Instead, I swallowed my pride and apologized again. After all, he was only looking out for the winery's best interests. And maybe I had overstepped a little bit.

After we hung up, I went back inside and took my place at the end of the line, trying not to grumble out loud about the fact that the girl with the knee socks was walking away from the counter with her coffee. I did grumble silently, though, about the call with Lucas.

I couldn't believe he wasn't more interested in finding out what happened. I mean, he'd lost his main wedding planner under suspicious circumstances, and then another one was injured on their property, which could open them up to a lawsuit. From where I was sitting, I was the least of their worries.

Twenty minutes later, I finally got my pour-over and pulled up a chair at one of the café tables outside. It was one of those rare spring days in San Francisco when the sky is blue and the temperature is just right, and it seemed a shame to be stuck indoors. There'd be plenty of time for that come summer when thick fog blanketed the city and you couldn't go outside without a jacket.

Poor Haley. What was she going to do? I knew what I needed to do, and that was call her and apologize. I pulled up her contact info and dialed her number.

"Hey, Kelsey," Haley said on the other end of the line. It wasn't going to be easy, but I had to let her know I was sorry for what had gone down with her dad.

"Hi there. I just wanted to call and—well, say I'm sorry, I guess."

There was a pause on the other end of the line. Would she accept my apology? Would she be mad that I'd put her dad on the murder board?

"Sorry," she said. "What for?"

I smacked my head in a perfectly executed facepalm. *She didn't know yet.* "Um, have you talked to your dad recently?"

"No, he left me a voice mail, but I haven't listened to it. I wish I could talk him into texting when he needs something. Why? What's up?"

I took a deep breath. "Your dad came by the office earlier, and there was a little misunderstanding, and well, he let us go."

"He *what*?!" She covered the phone and said something to someone on her end, then came back on the line. "Kelsey, what are you talking about?"

"I'm so sorry. I just assumed he would have—well, anyway, I won't be able to help you with your wedding."

"I'm sure it was just a misunderstanding. . . ." She tried to keep her tone light and breezy, but I could hear the desperation in her voice.

"No, he seemed pretty clear about it."

"Hold on a second, okay? I want to listen to his message. I'm sure it's not what you think."

Massaging my temples, I waited while she put me on hold. After a few moments, she was back. "So, yeah," she said, resignation heavy in her voice. Whatever her dad had said in the message, it seemed like my interpretation of his ripped-up check and storming out of our office was, in fact, accurate.

"But can I ask—what happened?"

My brain went through a quick slide show that included the murder board, the rose-strewn bathtubs at the Willows, and Mr. Bennett's face, livid with rage.

"Creative differences?"

"Come on, Kelsey, I know my dad, and I know he has a temper. First he fired Babs out of nowhere, and now you. What gives?"

I paused. There was no way to explain it that didn't make things worse. "Look, Haley, you're going to have to talk to your dad about it, okay?"

"All right," she said with a doleful voice that didn't sound very all right to me.

"And I'm really, really sorry. I really wanted to be there on your big day."

There was a pause. "Maybe I could get him to change his mind!" she said, her voice bright and hopeful.

"I don't think so," I said gently. "He didn't seem open to suggestions."

Haley sighed into the phone. "I can't believe he'd do this to me. Twice! I know we'll probably get through it okay, but this was supposed to be his present to us. A big, fancy wedding that we didn't even really want, just to impress all his friends, but it was okay, he said, because we wouldn't have to lift a finger. 'Just show up and enjoy!' he said. Well, fat chance of that happening now."

The despondent tone in her voice was killing me. "Look, I'll do whatever I can to help you. I can send you the names of a couple of wedding planners who might be able to help out!"

"It's too late to start over with someone new."

"Not necessarily. We'll find you someone who can pull it off, and I'll make sure they have everything they need so that it goes perfectly."

"I guess that would work," she said, a tremor in her voice.

"I'll *make* it work. I owe you that much."

"But if you change your mind . . ."

"I'm sorry," I said. "It's not my mind that needs changing." There was silence on the other end of the line. "Listen, I have to run. You hang in there, okay?"

"Okay. Thanks for everything. And I'm sorry about my—well, I'm just sorry, that's all."

Poor Haley and Christopher. This whole thing had gotten out of hand. Now I *really* wished I could go back in time and do it all over again. I wouldn't have been so quick to suspect Mr. Bennett. I would have minded my own business—although, to be fair, Stefan had *made* it my business. I wouldn't have been so worried about what Babs would think that I took her those damned pastries. Heck, I wouldn't have even said yes to doing this wedding in the first place, because now Haley and Christopher were no better off than they were before.

But I'd just had to be a helper, had to try to fix everything for everybody, and look where we'd ended up.

Haley was without a planner, Stefan was in the hospital, and I was a police suspect.

Oh, yeah, and there was still a murderer on the loose.

CHAPTER 29

The next morning, I arrived at work early—even though Haley's dad had abruptly taken my most urgent assignment off my plate. "The gift of time," as one of my former employers used to call it.

First stop? Erase the murder board before it could cause any more problems. As much as I love a good organizational tool, it was time to release it back into the wild—or at least into our meeting room, where it could go on to a productive second career as a seating-chart planner.

I grabbed a dry-erase marker and wiped the board clean. I was about to add a fresh new header at the top, something innocuous like "To-Do List," when my phone rang. Danielle Turpin's face was staring up at me from the caller ID display.

No wonder. I'd never returned her call and she was probably still dying to get the scoop on Stefan. I wasn't entirely in the mood to be grilled, but then again—she made it her business to keep her finger on the pulse of the wedding-planning community. Maybe she could prove to be useful.

I clicked on the screen to connect. "Hi, Danielle."

"Kelsey! I just got a call from that nice couple, Haley and Christopher. Thank you so much for sending them my way!"

Oh, *right*. She wasn't calling to gossip; she was calling about the list I'd had Laurel send to the couple. They must have called her right away.

"No problem! They're great, and I'm thrilled you're going to be able to help them." Although in this case it was bittersweet, I loved playing matchmaker and was happy to have one less thing to feel guilty about. "I'll send you over their files, or you can come by and get them if you want."

"Or if you have time, we could meet up for lunch. My treat?"

I checked my calendar and saw that my next appointment wasn't until two o'clock. "That would be great. We'd talked about having lunch anyway, so this gives us a good excuse."

"How about that sushi place over on Stockton? Say twelve-thirty?"

"That's perfect." I'd be able to assuage my guilt about not being there for Haley and Christopher, enjoy some spicy tuna rolls, and maybe even pick Danielle's brain a little bit. I love multitasking—especially when it's served with wasabi and pickled ginger.

Hama Sushi was starting to fill up, so I grabbed us a table by the window and took the liberty of ordering us some edamame. When Danielle arrived, her face lit up and she rushed over and greeted me with a hug. She took off her coat, draped it over the chair, and sat across from me, smoothing her long blond hair behind her ears.

The waiter arrived with a steaming pot of jasmine-scented green tea, and we placed our order.

"Oh, and one spider roll," Danielle said before he had a chance to escape.

"Hold the actual spiders," I said.

Danielle giggled and laid her hand on my arm. "Oh, Kelsey, you're so funny." She turned to the waiter. "Do you think we ordered enough?"

He shot her an incredulous look; after all, we'd ordered half the menu. "One origami roll, two spicy tunas, a rainbow roll, a dragon mega maki roll, and a spider roll? Should be more than enough."

"So," she began, after he grabbed our menus and darted away. "Thanks again for the referral. Lucas called me already and we set up a site visit so he can show me around. I haven't been up there in years, so I'm excited to see what they've done with the place. Anything I should know before I go?"

I pulled a flash drive and a folder from my bag and set them on the table. "Everything you need is in here. We've got most of it all set up, although you might have to follow up on a couple of rentals."

"Oh! I meant, is there anything I should know about the couple?"

"Not really. They're nice kids. You'll really like them."

"But?"

" 'But' what? They're nice. Should be a piece of cake."

"Then why are you passing them on? C'mon, give me the dirt."

Ahhh, *that*. I didn't know how much she knew, but I wasn't going to fall for her fishing expedition. "It's complicated."

"Come on," she said with a knowing smile. "I sense a story, and I won't rest until you tell me!"

"Really, Danielle, it's nothing. Nothing that I can talk about, anyway. Client confidentiality, you know." I shrugged as if to say, *Whatcha gonna do?*

She waggled her finger at me. "You and I both know that's not a thing, and besides, they're my clients now, so it would automatically transfer to me."

"Nope, you can bribe me with all the sashimi in the world, but I'm not spilling the beans—or the edamame, as the case may be."

"Okay, fine," she pouted. "At least tell me they're not crazy. Or horrible. Or total you-know-what holes."

I thought about Haley's dad. He did have a temper, but with Danielle's limited involvement, she was unlikely to press any of his buttons. I believed him when he said he wouldn't have hurt Babs, although I wasn't as sure he wouldn't have hurt Stefan. Still, he'd had an airtight alibi for the time period in question—so airtight, in fact, that he was taking it to the police—which as far as I was concerned meant that he was all spittle and no chomp.

I shook my head and smiled. "You're fine. It was just a weird thing that came up that won't affect you at all."

"If you say so. I do appreciate the job, so I'll drop it."

"Thank you, Danielle."

"But if you change your mind . . ." She held up her hand and made the universal mime signal for "call me."

The waiter returned, bearing a platter of sushi that would have made a sumo wrestler blush. As we dug in, I talked her through everything she'd find in the Bennett-Riegert dossier.

"Wow, thanks for being so organized," she said. "You're sure making it easy."

I plucked a bite of spider roll from my bamboo-green plate and dunked it into my soy sauce, thinking about how right she was and how lucky that made her. "A heck of a lot easier than Stefan made it for me," I muttered without really thinking about what I was saying.

"Oooh, tell me more."

I popped the spider roll into my mouth, then pointed at it as I chewed. That would buy me a few seconds of not speaking.

It was tempting to tell her everything Stefan had done and let her spread it around to whoever she wanted, but that seemed tantamount to standing on the table and screaming, *Hey, everybody, I had a motive to hurt Stefan!* Besides, the memory of him lying there in the hospital bed had softened my feelings toward him. Karma was a bitch, and I was pretty sure it had turned around and bitten him in the rear. With everything that had happened to him, I didn't much feel like piling on.

"Oh, nothing." I took a sip of tea to wash down the roll and set the tiny cup gently back on the table. "I visited him a couple of days ago, you know."

Danielle's face flickered with surprise. "Oh, how *is* he? Do you know if he got the flowers I sent him? I've been meaning to go for a visit."

"He's still out of it, but I'm sure he'll enjoy seeing some flowers when he wakes up."

"I hope so." She dabbed at her mouth with a napkin. "Such a shame what happened. I do hope Haley and Christopher aren't planning on using the wine cave, since it's *clearly* not safe."

Danielle seemed to be watching for my response. What was she getting at? "No need to worry. They're out on the terrace."

"I'm just saying . . ." Danielle picked at a piece of edamame, pressing one of the soybeans back and forth in its pod. "Don't you think it's weird that Stefan got hurt after what happened to Babs?"

"Well, sure, but . . ." Danielle fixed me with a stare as my sentence trailed off. The mood at the table had changed. Why did I have a feeling she was trying to trap me into saying something?

"Okay, I don't mean to be rude," Danielle said in a perfect imitation of people right before they say something rude, "but Stefan accused you of killing Babs and now he's unconscious." She waved her hand in the air, inviting me to draw my own conclusion.

"C'mon, Danielle, you know me better than that." What kind of sushi ambush was this?

Danielle reached across the table and took my hand in a conciliatory gesture. "I don't really think you'd do something like that, but I guess I need to hear it straight from your mouth."

"I promise you. Cross my heart and hope to—well, I promise."

Danielle nodded, apparently satisfied that I'd told the truth, and gave my hand a squeeze before releasing it. "Don't worry, Kelsey. I've always been in your corner. I tell everyone who asks that there's no way you had anything to do with Babs' death."

I felt my cheeks grow hot. "People are asking? Who's asking?"

"No one who matters, just people. Forget it; it's nothing."

Fuming, I mixed some more wasabi in with my soy sauce, then dunked a bite of spicy tuna roll in it. Who cared if the glob of spicy horseradish paste burned my sinuses? I popped the bite into my mouth and chewed. It's not sushi if it doesn't burn a little.

Danielle pushed her untouched glass of ice water across the table toward me with a concerned expression. "You're turning red. You might need this."

I swallowed and took a gulp of the cool water, then settled back in my chair. *Worth it.*

"Oh, Kelsey, I'm sorry. This must be really hard. I meant it when I said I didn't think you'd done anything to hurt Babs."

"But what about Stefan? Do you think I hurt him?"

"You said you didn't, and I believe you."

"Thanks, Danielle. I appreciate it. You wouldn't mind spreading that around, would you?"

We both burst out laughing, the tension broken.

"Besides," she said, "it's not like you were the only person he didn't get along with."

I sat up in my chair. "Oh, yeah?"

She leaned in conspiratorially. "You didn't hear this from me."

"Okay, I didn't hear it from you."

"No, I'm serious, Kelsey. I haven't told anyone this." I kind of doubted it, but I wasn't going to refuse the information on a technicality.

"I swear. Mum's the word."

"Stefan told me that he had some major dirt on Lucas Higgins."

My eyes grew wide. "Really. Tell me more."

"I don't know what it was. I begged him to tell me, but he wouldn't say. He just said that it was something really big and he was thinking about going public with it."

"I wonder what it could be!" Lucas had such a polished public image; I couldn't imagine him doing anything to jeopardize that.

"I don't know, word on the street was that he and Lucas Higgins were—how to put this delicately?—an *item*."

"What?! But Lucas is straight!"

"You'd think so, wouldn't you? He has to maintain a certain profile, though, so if it's true, he'd have to keep things on the down-low. After all, he gets a lot of mileage from charming wealthy older women right down to their pocketbooks."

Laurel would be devastated that her make-believe boyfriend was pretending to be straight. Oh, the fake betrayal!

"But what's the big deal? I mean, if Stefan outed him, either no one would believe him or no one would care."

"I don't think that was the big news he was threatening to tell. I'm just saying that if it's true, then Stefan would have access to Lucas' secrets. And maybe he really did learn something worth killing over." She dropped her napkin in her lap and held up her hands. "Now I'm not saying he did it, okay? I'm just saying that . . . well, there's no telling."

"Danielle, have you told the police this?" This definitely seemed like intel they should have.

"There's nothing to tell, really. It's all just gossip. I don't have any proof at all."

"But he got hurt on Higgins property! They might really be interested to hear all this."

Danielle chewed her lip as she considered the scenario. "Let me think about it, okay? I get that it's important, but it's nothing more than whispers. And in the meantime," she said, giving me an apologetic look, "I can't exactly go and mess things up with Higgins right before I do my first wedding there, especially if I'm not even sure he did it."

I sighed in resignation. "I guess you're right."

"If I hear anything else, I'll let you know. Thanks to you, I'm going to be spending quite a bit of time up there the next few days."

"Okay, but be careful, okay? If Lucas did have anything to do with all this—"

"Then I'll be perfectly fine, because he doesn't know that I know anything at all."

I suddenly pictured Miles' angry face when he'd found me in the cave. What kind of viper pit was I throwing her into? I hoped I wasn't putting her in danger. "There's one other thing."

"Oh, no. What?"

The waiter picked that moment to bus our dishes and drop

the check in a slim black folder, so I waited until he was gone, then lowered my voice even lower than the *sotto voce* we'd employed for most of the conversation. "You should also watch out for Miles."

"The slobby one? Why?"

I explained his whole history with wedding planners, giving Danielle just enough detail that she'd be cautious around him. "I just get a bad vibe, okay?"

"All right, thanks for the warning." She dropped a credit card into the folder and placed it on the edge of the table. "I'm just going to go in, do my job in an orderly fashion, and stay far, far away from the wine cave."

"I'm sure you'll do fine." I said, feeling much better about the situation. "Thanks for lunch."

"Don't mention it. It's the least I could do."

I laughed. "I'm glad you still think so."

We hugged goodbye, and I walked up the hill to my car. I still had a couple of appointments, but after that I planned to go home, take a bubble bath, and forget all about Higgins Estate for a while.

As I was unlocking my car, my cell rang from a number I didn't recognize, so I climbed into the front seat and shut the door behind me.

"Hello?"

"Kelsey? It's Corey." His voice sounded strange and it immediately put me on high alert.

"Is everything okay? Where are you?"

"I'm at the hospital. Stefan's awake. And he wants to talk to you."

CHAPTER 30

*C*orey, that's great!"

Not only was Stefan awake and alert, he wanted to talk. He'd be able to tell me what happened, and I'd be able to get on with my life.

"I'm in my car. I'll drive up right now." I turned the key in the ignition and put my seat belt on.

"Wait!" Corey said. "I don't think that's such a good idea."

"What? Why not? I'm *so* ready to put this behind me, and I was running out of ideas." My money was still on Miles, but luckily, I wouldn't have to worry about it much longer.

"Kelsey, Stefan doesn't really remember what happened, but he's convinced that you were there!"

"What?! I *was* there, but I'm the one who saved his stupid life!"

"I know, but he seems to have the timeline all mixed up. I told him he's got it all wrong, but he doesn't believe me."

I resisted the urge to bang my head repeatedly against the steering wheel in frustration. No need to give myself a concussion on top of everything else. "Didn't he see the peace plant I brought him? It's a peace plant, for cripes' sake."

"He gave it to one of the nurses and told her to take it to the parking lot and set it on fire."

"Oh, that's real mature. Everyone knows you can't burn a live plant."

"Not really the point here."

"You're right." I was so dazed, I turned the car back off and just stared out the front windshield. What I really wanted to do was drive up there and tell Stefan he was wrong, but if there's one thing I've learned, it's that you can't argue with crazy. "So . . . what now?"

"I don't know. He wanted to talk to you before he called the police."

"The *police*?"

"Yeah, he's ready to press charges—but don't worry, I'll stall him."

"How are you going to do that?" I really didn't want to have another visit from the SFPD or the Napa PD or any other PD for that matter. But if Stefan called the police on me again, I had a feeling this time neither of them was going to play good cop.

"I'll tell him you're out of town or something. That'll buy you some time."

"Some time for *what* exactly?"

"To prove that it wasn't you."

After we hung up, I sat behind the wheel of my car, pondering my next move. I had the irrational urge to just start driving. Just take off with nothing but my credit cards, my cell phone, and the clothes on my back and Thelma and Louise it across the

United States. Maybe I'd even grab my passport on the way out of town and just vanish. Later they'd find my abandoned car at the airport in Phoenix or something and I'd be sipping drinks on a beach on a Caribbean island and cranking out all-inclusive, cookie-cutter weddings for some upscale resort.

Nah, I sunburn too easily and I'd be bored in a week.

Instead of fleeing, I did the next best thing: I called an emergency meeting.

Laurel, Brody, and I made plans to meet at Brody's house an hour later—partly because the police were less likely to come looking for me there and also because he had better snacks.

After we assembled in his mid-century modern living room, I filled them in on everything Corey had told me. "Which means I *have* to figure out what happened before he talks to the police."

Laurel jumped in immediately to reassure me. "I'm sure they'll know you didn't do it."

I cut her off before she went any further. "I'm not so sure anymore. And I appreciate the fact that you're trying to make me feel better, but right now the only thing that's going to make me feel better is getting some answers."

"So what's the plan?" Brody asked. "It seems like we're running out of options."

I thought about it for a second. "I can't help but feel like Higgins Estate is the key. Babs and Stefan were both working there, and in Stefan's case, it was literally the scene of the crime."

"So you think Miles did it?" Brody said.

I thought back to what Danielle had told me. "Either Miles or Lucas."

Laurel's eyebrows shot up in surprise. "Lucas? What did he ever do to anybody? Besides be adorable."

"When I had lunch with Danielle, she seemed to think that Stefan was going to go public with some dirt on Lucas. I don't know if there's anything to it, though."

Laurel frowned. "I know this is going to sound biased, but Miles seems like the way more likely candidate."

"I'm with you. After all, Miles hated Stefan, and for all we know, he got into it with Babs, too."

"So why don't you go to the police?" Brody asked.

"I don't know. Without proof, I don't think they'll take me seriously."

"You've got the planner," Laurel said.

"And the keys you found in the cave," Brody said.

"Neither of which proves a thing, and both of which make me look even more guilty having them in my possession."

"Good point," Brody said.

"So obviously, the thing that makes the most sense is to go back up to Higgins one last time and see if there's anything we might have overlooked."

"Like what?" Laurel asked.

She had a point. We'd already searched the wine cave and Babs' old office, and it's not like I was going to single-handedly march in there and interrogate Miles. "I don't know. Maybe I can figure out who the keys belong to, and I can at least put Babs' planner back where I found it."

Brody looked at Laurel and then back at me. "I don't know, Kelsey. That sounds dangerous. If what you're saying is true . . ."

"I'm sure it's fine, as long as I lay low. After all, I told Lucas I'd drop off a copy of Haley and Christopher's files, so I do have a legitimate reason to be there."

"Okay, but you're not going without me," Brody said.

"Or me," Laurel added.

"Fine, we'll go tomorrow."

"Wait!" Brody said. "I can't go tomorrow. I'm driving down to Santa Cruz for a photo shoot and we've already had to reschedule twice. Can we go Thursday?"

I bit my lip while I considered it. "I don't know. I really want to get this over with."

"C'mon, Kelsey, you shouldn't go up there alone."

"It'll be fine. Besides, I won't be alone. I'll have Laurel with me."

"I'd feel a lot better if we all three went," Brody said. "Safety in numbers, right?"

"Okay, I guess you're right." I certainly didn't want him worrying about me. "We'll plan on Thursday."

"All right, good."

With that settled, Laurel and I said our good nights. Brody was right, it really would be safer for all three of us to go together, and as soon as we got downstairs I told Laurel I'd pick her up the next morning at nine.

"But Kelsey, you just told Brody we'd wait for him!"

"I know, but that's just so he wouldn't worry. Look, you don't have to come if you don't want, but I'm going. Now that Stefan's awake, he might tell someone to go there and get the agenda, and if it's not there . . ."

"It's going to look really bad," Laurel said.

"I don't think I can wait."

"I don't know, Kelsey. . . ."

"Look, it'll be fine. Seriously. I'll drop it off, we'll look around, and then we'll leave. In and out. Besides, it'll be broad daylight with tons of people around. How much trouble could we get into?"

As I drove through the gates of the winery the next day, the metal nameplate glinted in the sun: *Higgins Estate Winery.* A shiver ran down my spine. *Here goes nothing.*

After I pulled into a spot, we took a moment to formulate a plan—namely to stick together and not get ourselves killed—and then we walked up the path to the winery.

Lucas was sitting at a table outside, enjoying a glass of wine with someone who looked important. Bigwigs in suits seemed to be part of his core contingency.

Inside, we found Zara working the tasting room and she waved us over to the counter. "You here to keep me company? We seem to be having an afternoon lull."

I looked at Laurel and shrugged. Why not? Maybe Zara could tell us something new.

"Hey, Zara," I said. "Have you met Laurel?"

Laurel gave a little wave. "Nice to meet you."

"Same here," Zara said as she set two wineglasses on the counter. "What do you want to try?"

Going a whole day without getting in any trouble.

"White?" she said. "Red?"

Oh, right. The wine. "Maybe next time," I said. "We can't stay long, and I've gotta stay sharp."

"You can always spit it in the bucket," she said, gesturing to a pewter canister sitting on the counter.

"That doesn't bother you when people spit it out?" I asked. "I always think I'm being rude."

"No, some of the people who come in here are pros. They'd

be drunk if they swallowed everything they tasted." She shrugged. "It seems like a waste of perfectly good wine, but people do it all the time."

"All right, then, dealer's choice." I set my bag on the floor and leaned against the counter.

"You got it." She pulled the cork out of a bottle of Zin and poured us a tasting-sized portion, just a couple of ounces.

"So I never got a chance to hear how Miles took the news about what happened in the wine cave the other night," I said.

"He took it surprisingly well." Zara shrugged. "Go fig."

"Yeah?" I swirled the wine around in the glass and held it up to look at the deep-garnet color in the light.

"Yeah, I was shocked. I guess their insurance is going to cover the damage, but still, I had expected a full-on flip-out."

"Well, that's good." I took a sip of the wine, swirled it around my mouth, and then reluctantly spit it into the bucket.

"Yeah, he was more upset that the police came and questioned him about it. Did they contact you?"

My mind flashed back to Detective Blaszczyk's angry accusations. "They did. They came by my house and asked me some questions, I guess since I was the one to find him there."

"So were they able to figure out what happened?" Laurel asked, taking a tiny sip of her wine.

Zara shook her head. "Miles thought Stefan must have gotten himself locked in and hurt himself trying to escape."

"Lucas mentioned that to me, too. But is it really possible to lock yourself in? After all, Stefan knew the code. I mean, there was a keypad on the inside, wasn't there?"

"That's the digital security system, but there's also an exterior lock. Miles thought one of the workers must have locked it by accident not realizing Stefan was inside."

Likely story, I thought. "But why an exterior lock? Isn't the whole point to keep people out instead of in?"

"It's left over from when they were building the cave. It was their way to keep the critters out before the security system went in."

So Stefan *had* been locked in the cave.

Zara offered us another taste, but I put my hand over my glass in the universal signal for "I'm cutting myself off."

"Speaking of locks and stuff, you don't happen to recognize these, do you?" I retrieved the keys from my pocket and dangled them in the air for her to see. "I found them outside."

"No, sorry. You can drop them at lost and found."

I nodded. "I'll do that," I said, with no intention of doing that. At least not right away.

Laurel and I excused ourselves and went down the hall to Babs' office. While Laurel stood guard, I dug Babs' agenda from my bag, gave it a quick wipedown, and returned it to its former hiding place in the credenza. *Phew.* I was happy to have it out of my hands. I'd have to let the police take it from here.

"Okay," Laurel said. "Can we go? We promised Brody we'd be in and out."

I paused. "Just one more thing."

"Kelsey, we *promised.*"

"I know, but this might be our last chance to find out if those keys belong here."

Laurel put her hands on her hips and pursed her lips. "This is why Brody didn't want you coming up here without him. We're going to get in trouble."

"I won't tell him if you won't," I said diplomatically. "Besides, I'd do the same for you."

"What, you mean let me endanger my life to satisfy my curiosity?"

"I hear what you're saying, but no one's endangering anything here. People put keys into locks literally every single day with no adverse effects." She didn't look convinced. "It'll be fine."

I could see her resolve starting to crack.

"All right," she finally conceded, probably because she knew that every minute she tried to stop me was one more minute before we could leave. "But then can we get out of here?"

"I promise." I chewed my lip as I studied the key ring. "This small key looks like it's to a desk or a filing cabinet." I looked around the room and immediately zeroed in on the credenza where Babs' agenda was stored. I tried the small key, but it wasn't a match. Then I checked the desk. Also not a match. What about the big keys? I crept over and tried the door. Not only did none of them work, but one almost got stuck and I had to wrest it loose.

"You go make sure Lucas is still in his meeting," I said. "I'm going to try the other doors."

"Okay, but hurry," Laurel said, and then she scampered down the hall.

Trying to look casual, I strolled up and down the hall in search of doors with locks, but my efforts were fruitless—not to mention stressful. Every sound put me on high alert, and I perfected the art of checking my phone whenever I heard someone coming.

Laurel caught up to me and confirmed that Lucas was still out on the patio, and I told her to keep an eye on him while I checked upstairs.

"I thought we were supposed to stick together!" she protested.

"We'll get out of here quicker if we split up. Besides, it's the middle of the afternoon. What could possibly happen?"

"Okay," Laurel said dubiously as I headed for the stairs. "But Kelsey?"

"Yeah?"

"Be careful."

I crept partway up the stairs, then, realizing I didn't need to creep, bounded up the rest of the way. I quickly made my way down the hall, trying the doors that had locks one by one, but none of them were a match.

At the end of the hall loomed the door to Lucas' office. *Okay, this is my last chance.* I knew Lucas was outside, but I knocked anyway just in case. I waited a moment for a response, then held my breath and tried the keys.

Nothing.

I twisted the doorknob and discovered that it was unlocked. I glanced furtively behind me before swinging the door open.

Okay, I'll just check inside his office, and then I give up.

I slipped inside. I could feel my heart pounding as I quickly glanced around the room.

The office had several pieces of furniture with locks, so I snuck up on a credenza and tried the key. Not a match. Desk drawer? It was a long shot, but I didn't want to look back later and wish I'd been more thorough, so I crept around and pulled his office chair out a couple of inches.

Just as I was about to insert the key into his desk drawer lock, I heard a voice from the hall.

"Lucas!" It was Laurel, her voice uncharacteristically loud and slightly manic. "Hey, I'm so glad I bumped into you. I have a couple of questions."

Panicked, I looked around the room for an escape route.

This was my honk.

CHAPTER 31

I looked around the room, desperate for a place to hide. If this were an old movie, I'd tuck myself behind some heavy draperies, but since Lucas liked an expansive view, there wasn't a curtain in sight. Spotting another door in the corner of the room, I rushed over in the hopes it was an alternate exit or maybe a secret passageway, but just my luck, it was a closet. Quickly weighing the pros and cons of stuffing myself into a closet versus getting caught rummaging through Lucas' office, I chose the former and wedged myself into the tiny space next to a vacuum cleaner.

The door to the office opened, and Lucas entered the room. As quietly and slowly as possible, I cracked the door open and peeked out.

Laurel had followed him in and was chattering in the breezy way she does when she's nervous. "So we were thinking that you might want to consider investing in a speaker system, because every wedding needs one and that way your brides wouldn't have to rent them."

"I'll consider it," Lucas said. "It could also come in handy for some of our corporate events."

"Great," she said, looking around the room. "Hey, have you seen Kelsey?"

Lucas smiled handsomely. "I saw her earlier out in the garden, but she's not up here."

That's what you think. I focused all my brainpower on sending Laurel a psychic message: *Don't leave me here!* My psychic messages seldom did much good, but I was at a loss for a backup plan.

Laurel turned to leave, then spun back round. "Maybe I could even price some for you. Sound systems, that is. I have a pretty good idea what kind of setup you'd need."

"That sounds great, Lauren."

Her face fell. "Oh, it's Laurel."

"Sorry, Laurel, of course." He beamed his trademark smile, then slipped some papers he'd been carrying into his desk while Laurel stood there. "Was there anything else?"

"Um, well . . ."

Another smile. "I need to hop on a conference call right now, so maybe you could send me an e-mail."

I silently willed Laurel to ignore his not-so-subtle hints.

"Okay," Laurel said with a last look around. "I'll send you the information."

And then she left, despite all my psychic efforts.

A loud squeak from Lucas' desk chair told me that he was settling in. I hoped the call would be short; my glutes were starting to cramp.

Lucas punched in some numbers and waited.

"Hey, just wanted to update you on our situation," he said at last.

Business call, blah blah blah. I might as well make myself comfortable.

"He just left, and everything's looking like a go." He must have been taking about the man in the suit.

"Yeah, Miles signed, just like I predicted." A pause. "No, of course I didn't tell him. There's no way he would have agreed to it. But lucky for us, he can't be bothered to read the papers I put in front of him."

I stifled a giggle-snort—partly from the absurdity and stress of being stuck in a closet and partly from Lucas' characterization of his brother.

He leaned back in his chair and put his feet up on his desk. "No, he's going to be pissed, but it doesn't matter. We need the money for the expansion."

Expansion? This was getting interesting. I wondered what Lucas had planned that he wasn't letting Miles in on.

"He doesn't see it now, but someday he'll thank us for it. He'll get over it. He'll have to."

Miles didn't seem like the type to get over things, but maybe it was different when it came to Lucas.

"It's not like he's losing the whole vineyard, just a few rows of grapes. And after the pipeline's in, he can always replant over it."

Wait, a pipeline? That's what this is about?

"Yeah, it's for natural gas. Clean energy and all that, you know? Anyway, they're paying us a ton, and it's not like Miles has to stop making wine altogether."

I felt like all the air had suddenly been sucked out of the room—and considering the size of the room, there hadn't been much to start with. After what Zara had told me about how protective Miles was of his vineyards, I couldn't imagine that would go over well.

"Once the deal goes through," Lucas said, "there won't be anything Miles can do about it, short of chaining himself to the bulldozer. Not that I'd put it past him." Lucas let out a derisive laugh at his own joke. As uncomfortable as I was learning about Lucas' questionable business decisions, I was even more uncomfortable in the increasingly stuffy closet. I shifted my weight to inhale some of the fresh air creeping in through the cracked door.

"No, right now there's no chance of him finding out, unless one of us tells him, and I'm certainly not going to."

Wow, that was a pretty big secret. I wondered how long he was intending to keep it from his brother. I peeked out and saw Lucas listening intently to whoever was on the other end of the line.

"You mean the wedding planner?"

I clapped my hand over my mouth. The wedding planner? Which one? *Me?*

"Yeah, he almost blew it for us."

Stefan.

"No, that problem seems to have taken care of itself."

My heart started pounding, and I leaned against the wall to steady myself. I remembered what Danielle had told me. Stefan had known some secret, and he was threatening to tell.

"Let's just say blowing the lid on our deal has moved way down his list of priorities."

I couldn't believe what I was hearing. There were two scenarios floating through my mind. Either Lucas was the beneficiary of incredibly impeccable timing or he'd taken matters into his own hands.

"Yesterday."

A feeling of dread grew in my stomach.

"Uh-huh."

Had he done it himself, or had he gotten someone to take care of it for him?

"No, don't worry. The two of them were the only ones who knew."

Oh my God. The two of them—was he talking about Babs? My head was spinning. I had planned on waiting Lucas out, but I was starting to feel panicky. I grabbed the cell phone in my pocket, turned it to silent, then typed out a message to Laurel:

SOS! Get Lucas out of his office!

A second later she replied:

Where r u?

Was it my imagination, or was I running out of oxygen?

In the closet! Get up here!

A minute later there was a knock at the door.

"I've gotta run," he said into the phone. "I'll call you later."

He sat up and picked up a pen, then yelled, "Come in!" He made a show of perusing his desk calendar as Laurel breezed into the room. "I'm so sorry," she said. "I know you're about to get on a call."

He gave her a patient nod. "It's okay. It got canceled."

Liar, liar, pants on fire.

"Oh thank God," she said, urgency tingeing her voice, "because there's some sort of situation down in the tasting room and they need you right away."

"Thanks for letting me know. I'll be down in a couple of

minutes." Lucas didn't seem particularly motivated to leave his chair, but Laurel didn't back down. "Okay, but you'd better hurry. One of the guests is really drunk and Zara said he threatened her."

Lucas dropped his pen on his desk and stood. "Well, in that case."

He ushered Laurel from the room and I willed myself to stay still until he'd had enough time to get down the hall. I was about to emerge from my hiding spot when the door to the office burst open again and I jumped back so fast I almost sent the vacuum cleaner toppling to the floor, cleaning tools and all.

"Kelsey?" Laurel whispered frantically. "Where are you?"

I flung the closet door open. "Right here."

She offered me a hand and pulled me from my hiding place. "How in the world did you end up in there?"

"I'll tell you later. Right now, we have to get out of here." I closed the closet door and looked around to make sure I hadn't left any signs of myself behind, then pulled her toward the hall.

I peeked out to make sure the coast was clear, then motioned for her to follow me. Once we were safely outside, I told her the news. "I think I know who killed Stefan."

"Oh my God! Who?" she whispered as we hurried down the hall.

I jerked my thumb over my shoulder and down the hall behind us. "Your boyfriend."

"What?" Laurel stopped in the middle of the hall, but I grabbed her arm and pulled her after me.

"I'll tell you in the car." There was no time to stop and explain. Laurel and I scampered down the stairs and through the tasting room. Zara was at the counter pouring red wine for a middle-aged couple, and she gave us a curious look as we darted toward the front door. "Kelsey! Lucas was looking for you."

"Sorry!" I yelled over my shoulder. "Champagne fountain emergency. Gotta run!"

"Okay, what's going on?" said Laurel, once we were safely inside my car.

"I think it might have been Lucas," I said breathlessly as I threw my car into reverse and pulled out of the spot. "He's been keeping some pretty major secrets from his brother. I overheard him on the phone, and he's letting someone tear up the vineyard to put in some sort of pipeline."

"Wait, what?" Laurel asked. "What does a pipeline have to do with Babs and Stefan?"

"Danielle told me Stefan was planning on going public with some sort of secret, but she didn't know what it was. He and Babs must have found out and threatened to tell."

"So?" Laurel said. "Lucas wouldn't have killed them over that, would he?"

"I don't know, maybe. Maybe he was afraid they'd blow the deal. He said some pretty creepy stuff about the problem being taken care of, and the way he said it sounded kind of like the way they say it in mob movies."

"So what do we do now?" Laurel asked. "Go to the police?"

"Yeah, it's time. My Nancy Drew days are over. The police will have to take it from here." I peered up at the château. "Might as well get a good look now, because we're not coming back here anytime soon. They're just going to have to find another wedding planner."

"Wait a minute!" Laurel said. "Danielle! She's working on Haley and Christopher's wedding. Don't you think you'd better warn her?"

I thought about it for a second. On the one hand, the less she knew, the better. But, then again, it didn't feel right letting her walk into what could be a dangerous situation. "Yeah, you're probably right." I punched in Danielle's number as I pulled out of the parking lot and started driving down the hill. *Pick up, pick up, pick up.*

Relief flooded through me when the line connected and I heard Danielle's voice. "Hello?"

"Danielle, it's Kelsey. Listen, I really need to talk to you."

"Hi, Kelsey." Was it my imagination or did her voice sound strange?

"Hey, you don't happen to have any meetings scheduled at Higgins, do you?"

"I'm supposed to go up tomorrow so they can show me around. Why?"

"I want you to postpone it. It's a long story and I can't really talk right now, but promise me you'll stay away from there."

"But—"

"No buts. It's not safe for you there, for any of us. I did some digging and—well, I'll tell you the whole thing later, but right now I'm heading to the police station to talk to them."

There was a pause. "Is this about the letter?" Her voice sounded strained, almost panicky.

"A letter? No. What are you talking about?"

"I got a letter in the mail today." I could hear her breath change to something fast and shallow. "I thought you might have gotten one, too."

"What does it say?"

"It says: 'You're next.'"

CHAPTER 32

*A*s Laurel and I made the drive to Danielle's house, my stomach churned with guilt over having gotten her involved with Higgins Estate. Leave it to me to introduce the town busybody to someone who was trying to keep a secret. Did Lucas think she knew about the pipeline, too? Or was he just trying to scare her off to keep her from finding out? After all, she made it her business to know what was going on with pretty much everybody.

Either way, Laurel and I agreed that it would help to have Danielle with us when we went to the police, and Danielle had been eager to join us after we told her what we'd learned. Half an hour later, we arrived at the address she'd given us on the outskirts of Napa, a restored Victorian home with a wraparound porch. According to the sign out front, it was also home to a law office and was on the National Register of Historic Places.

"Nice," Laurel whispered while I texted Danielle to let her know we were downstairs. "We should get a place like this."

The sun was starting to set, and I could see a light on in one of the turret rooms. I pulled my cell phone out and dialed her number, but after a few rings it went to voice mail. "That's weird."

I waited a second longer, then tried again. Voice mail.

"Are you sure she wasn't going to meet us at the police station?" Laurel asked.

"I don't think so. Oh, no, wait. She gave us this address. Duh." A nervous knot was forming in my stomach. *Where was she?*

"Maybe she's on the phone," Laurel suggested.

"Maybe," I said. "Let's just go up and get her."

"Good idea," Laurel said, unbuckling her seat belt. "Besides, I want to see her office."

"Don't go getting any ideas," I said.

"Hey, yeah! You think she's hiring?" Laurel gave me mischievous smile as she crawled out of the front seat.

The lawn was surrounded by a dark wrought-iron fence, and the sidewalk was lined with purple hydrangea bushes that complemented the dark-purple color of the house. We climbed the front stairs and rang the doorbell next to Danielle's nameplate, and a moment later we heard a loud buzz that let us know the door was unlocked.

Danielle stood at the top of the stairs holding a phone to one ear. With the other hand, she waved us up as she mouthed the word *"sorry."*

The interior of her office was just as impressive as the outside of the building, with wood paneling, an elegant chandelier, and period furnishings galore. Laurel nodded in silent approval and I resisted the urge to take off my shoes and roll around on the plush carpeting, instead sitting on the edge of the chair and crossing my legs politely at the ankles.

"Sorry about that," Danielle said as she hung up the phone.

"I wouldn't have even taken it, but I've been waiting on a call from a new client and I thought it might be them."

"No worries." I was just relieved to be far away from Higgins Estate. "We should talk about what we're going to tell the police. You still have the letter?"

She reached behind her and picked up a folded piece of paper from the desk. She held it in her hands for a moment and took in a deep breath before passing it over to me.

Sure enough, printed in big block letters were the words exactly as she'd said them, no more, no less: *YOU'RE NEXT.*

A shiver ran down my spine. What had I gotten the three of us into?

"Who do you think could have sent it?" she said.

"I hope it's just someone trying to scare you." Not that someone wanting to scare her was anything to scoff at, but it was way better than the alternative.

"I've been a nervous wreck all day." She sat across from us in a tufted wingback chair, took a deep breath, then exhaled loudly. "Can I get you guys anything? Tea? Water?" Despite her attempt at hospitality, I could see that her face was lined with worry.

"Thanks, we're good."

Danielle gestured toward a glass of wine sitting on a side table. "I actually opened a really nice bottle of wine earlier if you'd care to join me." I started to decline, but she interrupted me. "C'mon. I insist. Like I said, it's been a day."

She got up and went to the kitchen and returned a moment later with two full glasses of red. Laurel and I each took a glass, and Danielle returned to her seat. "It's the Higgins Estate Zinfandel. Lucas had a couple of bottles sent over. Cheers," she said flatly.

Laurel and I both raised our glasses, but the thought of

anything related to Higgins Estate was more than I could stomach, so I set the glass aside.

Danielle leaned forward, took the letter, and folded it back up again. "I can hardly stand to look at it." She took a swig of wine. "Do you really think I'm in danger?"

"I hope not, but I do think we need to take it seriously, just in case." I looked at Laurel, not knowing what to say. "Danielle, you know how you said you thought Lucas might have been responsible for what happened to Stefan?"

Danielle nodded, her eyes wide.

"I think you might have been right. Lucas did have a secret all right, and Stefan found out about it."

"Oh my God, what was it?"

I told her about the natural gas pipeline and how Lucas had been signing agreements behind his brother's back.

She took another sip of wine and topped off her glass. "How did you learn this?"

"I was up there today and I overheard Lucas talking to someone on the phone."

"Oh, no," Danielle said. "And here I thought he was such an upstanding guy."

Laurel nodded sympathetically. "I thought so, too."

"I know," I said. "I'm so sorry I got you involved in this mess. I don't know if you're really in danger or not, but we have to show that letter to the police. If all three of us go in and tell them what we know, at least we might be able to get justice for Babs and Stefan."

Danielle's eyes teared up. "I just can't believe it. What a monster."

I opened my mouth to speak, but her phone rang again.

"Excuse me one moment." Danielle took the phone into the other room.

"Man," said Laurel, "this really is a great office. Check out the fireplace." She got up and walked over to inspect it more closely. "I bet you can actually burn wood in here."

In the meantime, my phone chimed to let me know I'd received a text. I reached into my bag to turn my ringer to silent and saw a text from Brody.

> What time are we heading up to Higgins tomorrow?

Oh, yeah, he still didn't know that we'd checked that little item off our list without him. I started to type a response, then paused as I decided what to say.

"Kelsey, look at this!" Laurel waved some papers in my general direction.

"What is that? And why are you snooping?"

"It looks like the layout for a brochure. But look what it says!"

On the top page was a picture of a smiling Danielle along with the words "Danielle Turpin. The Queen of Wine Country Weddings."

"Are you kidding me?" I looked up at Laurel and her shocked face mirrored my own. "Man, she didn't waste any time stealing Babs' tagline."

"That's so rude!" Laurel said. "I mean, right?"

Beneath the picture, a paragraph of flowery prose reiterated Danielle's credentials as the Queen of Wine Country Weddings and went on to explain why she was so deserving of the title.

I clenched my teeth in irritation.

On the next page was a picture of Danielle standing in front of the Higgins Estate château. The very one I'd been standing in front of earlier today. The one Danielle said she hadn't visited in years.

"Laurel," I whispered, "when I had lunch with Danielle yesterday, she claimed she hadn't been up to Higgins in a really long time."

"Well, that can't be right. Didn't you say they just put in those orange umbrellas that are in the background?"

"Yeah, like a week ago." *A week ago. When Stefan was locked in the wine cave.*

I quickly counted backwards to see how many days it had been, and my eyes landed on Danielle's antique desk.

Her antique desk!

On a hunch, I grabbed my bag and dug the keys I'd found in the wine cave out of the bottom. Laurel looked up at me questioningly and I laid my finger on my lips, then crept closer to the door Danielle had exited through to make sure she was still on the phone. I heard the low murmur of her voice from the other room and darted to the desk.

There, smack dab in the center of the middle drawer, was a tiny brass circle with a keyhole in the middle of it. Heart pounding, I selected the small key and slipped it into the hole.

It was a perfect match.

The lock turned with a click, and I tugged the drawer just enough to make sure it was unlocked. The drawer slid out effortlessly, and I closed it again quickly. "Oh my God," I whispered. I stared at the desk, momentarily frozen. The keys were Danielle's. It was officially time to freak out.

My mind was spinning as I quickly reviewed the facts. I'd found the keys at the crime scene. Ergo—and I didn't think this was too much of a stretch—Danielle had been at the crime scene. That didn't necessarily make her a killer, but it definitely made her a liar, and I wasn't prepared to stick around and find out exactly which charges she was guilty of. I quickly shut the drawer and yanked the key from the lock. "We have to get out of here."

"It fits?" Laurel whispered frantically as she grabbed her bag from the floor.

"Yep." I ran back to my chair and collected my own bag from underneath it.

"Where are you going?" Danielle said from the doorway. How long had she been standing there?

"Sorry, we have to go!" I blurted as we raced toward the door.

Danielle looked surprised by our hasty exit. "Aren't we going to the police?"

I gripped the doorknob and said, "Yeah, we're going to the police all right."

Which would have been a really dramatic exit line had the door not been locked.

In the split second it took me to slide the ancient dead bolt open—a little WD-40 would have come in really handy right about then—Danielle darted across the room to her desk drawer that I'd so helpfully left unlocked for her, and a moment later I heard a distinctive *click*.

I froze, my hand still on the doorknob.

"Let's sit and finish our wine, shall we?" Danielle gestured to the two chairs with the small revolver she'd retrieved from the drawer. Her voice was cool and steady, and if I didn't know any better I would have thought she just really didn't want our evening to end.

Laurel and I turned around slowly, our hands out in front of us, palms facing forward. The international signal for *you now officially have all the power.*

"Sit," she said, pointing the gun at us all willy-nilly. It was obvious that she hadn't brushed up on responsible gun ownership protocols.

Laurel and I returned to our chairs, but the newly self-crowned Queen of Wine Country Weddings stayed standing, the gun shaking unsteadily in her hand.

"Danielle, you don't want to do this," I said. "We're all friends here. Why don't you just put the gun down and we'll talk?"

"It's too late for that."

"It's not too late!" Laurel said, her voice anxious. "Maybe we can help you."

Danielle let out a bitter little laugh. "Is that what you came here for? To help me?"

"Well, *yeah.*" I reached over and picked up the threatening letter she'd received and held it aloft. "That's exactly why we came here."

"And you couldn't leave well enough alone, could you?"

"You were in trouble!" Laurel said. "And Kelsey felt guilty for putting you in danger."

Danielle crossed toward us and snatched the letter out of my hand. She wadded it up into a ball and tossed it over her shoulder. "I suppose you think I should be grateful? Well, *thanks.*"

I opened my mouth to speak but then thought better of it. Danielle was in a much better position to be sarcastic than I was, what with the gun and all.

Danielle held her hand out, palm first. "Now hand over the keys."

The keys cut into my palm as I gripped them tighter. She'd lied about being in the wine cave, and the keys were the only proof I had. Still, it's not like she was asking. Grudgingly, I released them into Danielle's outstretched hand.

"Where did you find them?" Danielle asked, her eyes steely.

"Lost and found," I said, hoping she'd believe me.

She kept her expression neutral. "Thanks for getting them back to me. I didn't like having them out there floating around."

"Of course not!" I said as breezily as I possibly could under the circumstances. "So you see? There's no problem here. You got your keys back, and now we'll be on our way."

"Oh, cut the crap," Danielle said. "You don't think I'm standing here holding a gun on you because I wanted my keys back?"

I was pretty sure the answer to that was *no,* but then again, who knew what this new version of Danielle was thinking?

"Look, Danielle," I said, my tone conciliatory. "I don't know what you've done, but it's not too late to fix it."

"Of course it's too late," she spat. "First I find out Stefan's still alive, and now here you are? I should have killed him while I had the chance. But believe me, I won't make that mistake twice."

CHAPTER 33

*E*ven though I'd pretty much figured it out at that point, Danielle's words were still a shock to me. Thanks to her impromptu confession, there was no more pretending Laurel and I didn't know anything.

I pointed at the crumpled-up piece of paper on the floor behind her. "So the letter . . . ?" I'm no handwriting expert, but it now seemed pretty obvious she'd hastily penned it herself after we'd gotten off the phone.

"It served its purpose," she sneered.

Laurel's mouth opened wide as the realization struck. "You mean it's not even real?"

"Of course it isn't," Danielle said. "You were going to the police and I needed to find out what you knew."

"Well, we didn't know *anything* until you made us come here!" My tone was just this side of *I mean, seriously, people!* but Danielle didn't seem to appreciate the irony.

Laurel squirmed in her chair. "I hate to bring this up right now, but I *really* need to use the little girls' room."

"It can wait," Danielle growled.

"But—"

"Quiet! I need a minute to *think*."

I didn't know what Danielle's plan was—but from the sounds of it, neither did she. I looked down at the floor where my purse was. If only I could reach my phone, maybe I could call 911 without her noticing. As slowly as possible, I inched my foot toward the strap hoping I could hook it and drag it closer. No luck. It was just out of reach.

Was there any chance I could reason with her? We'd been friends once. At least I thought we had—although the gun was a new facet of our relationship that I wasn't super fond of. "Danielle, why don't you tell us what happened? I'm sure you didn't mean to hurt him. Whatever it is, I'm sure it'll be fine."

"You're right about that. I never meant for Stefan to get hurt. Okay, maybe I meant for him to get hurt just a little bit. . . ."

"So you followed him to the wine cave?"

"I decided to drop by Higgins. You know, taste a little wine, drop off a business card, maybe even introduce myself. But when I arrived, I noticed Stefan's car pulling out of the parking lot. He went up the hill instead of down, so I followed him."

"Why?"

"I guess I wanted to give him a piece of my mind. He'd been spreading all sorts of rumors about me, and he was threatening to ruin my reputation." She turned and looked me in the eye. "You of all people should know how that feels."

I nodded. *All too well.*

"He drove up to the wine cave and went inside. I noticed that he'd left the door open behind him, and I thought, 'Well, there you go! If I'm ever going to confront him, this is my chance, when there's no one around.' After all, you know how he likes a public spectacle."

I flinched as I remembered the scene he'd caused at Margot's house.

"So I followed him in," Danielle said. "I found him in that dining room, the one with all the lights on the ceiling, and I let him have it. We ended up getting in a huge fight, of course. He's such a *jerk*." Danielle paused. She chewed her lip for a moment as if she were weighing her words.

"It's okay, Danielle. I know how nasty he can be."

"He got right up in my face. It was getting out of control and he was acting so crazy that I was afraid of him. So I grabbed a bottle of wine off the table and hit him in the head with it. He fell to the ground, and I figured I'd better get out of there *fast*. That must have been when I dropped those," she said, pointing at the keys.

"So you just left him there?" I asked. "You could have killed him!"

"I thought I had! I turned off all the lights and locked the doors, hoping that no one would find him for a few days."

I stared at her in shock. "But *why*?"

"Oh, come on, now. Would it really have been such a big loss?" she asked. "He'd been badmouthing me, just like he bad-mouths *everybody*. And I guess I just snapped."

I wasn't buying it. As big of a gossip as Danielle was, surely she could have waged an effective countercampaign against Stefan. "It had to be more than that. What did he do to you?"

Danielle shook her head. "Nothing. It doesn't matter."

What? She was going to pass up a chance to be the star of her own story? That didn't sound like the Danielle I knew. Maybe I could use it to my advantage.

"Ohhhhh." I nodded knowingly. "Lucas Higgins must have signed a contract with him to be Higgins Estate's full-time planner. I'd heard that was happening."

"What?!" Danielle said, shooting me an annoyed look. "No, that wasn't it at all."

Laurel glanced over at me, and I could tell by the look in her eyes that she totally got what I was doing. "Oh, you know, Kelsey, I bet he sabotaged one of her weddings. Was that it, Danielle?"

Danielle's face was turning redder by the second and she shook her head adamantly.

"It's okay, Danielle," I said. "He did the same thing to me. I can see why you'd be pissed."

"Higgins wasn't going to hire him!" Danielle grabbed her glass of wine from the table near her chair and gulped down the contents. "That job was mine. Or at least it would have been."

"Then why'd you lock him in the cave?" I dropped my voice to a lower pitch. "Were you in love with him? I'm so sorry. Honey, it wasn't your fault he didn't love you back."

Danielle had held it in for as long as she could. "No, no, no! *God* no!"

"Then what was it?"

"He made me kill Babs Norton! There, are you happy?"

Danielle clapped her hand over her mouth, looking as stunned by her sudden confession as I was. In a movie, this would be the scene where the detective says, *Of course! It all makes sense now!* Except this wasn't a movie and it didn't make any sense at all.

"He *made* you kill Babs?" I asked. "How exactly did he do that?"

"It was all his fault. I wouldn't have even *been* in that office if it weren't for him." Danielle sank down into the chair, suddenly looking exhausted.

"Danielle?" Laurel said gently. "What happened?"

Danielle stared at the ceiling for a moment, then shook her head. "I'd lost several bids to Weddings by Babs. Then I heard around town that Stefan had been intentionally going after my clients." She waved the gun in the air. "You know how people talk."

I nodded, feigning sympathy. "Of course."

"I wanted to find out if it was true, so I broke into their office."

"As one does." What can I say? I wanted to keep her talking.

"I wanted to find out if Babs had known about it, and I guess to be honest, I wanted to get even. So I went to her computer and I was snooping around and deleting some files. It was just a harmless prank. I wanted her and Stefan to know they couldn't mess with me and get away with it."

It sure didn't sound like a "harmless prank" to me. Danielle was clearly delusional. I wondered if she would say holding us at gunpoint had just been a harmless prank.

"Anyway, I was sitting at Babs' desk when she walked in on me. I thought everyone was gone for the evening, but I guess she came back for something."

"What did you do?" Laurel asked. She stifled a yawn, and I looked over at her wineglass. How much had she had to drink? *C'mon, Laurel, I need you to stay alert!*

"I made up some excuse as to why I was in her office and then I ran for the door. She stepped in my way—I guess she was trying to stop me from leaving." Danielle's eyes welled up.

"So you pushed her out of the way and she fell?"

"No, I grabbed a paperweight from her desk and hit her on the head with it."

I'd like to think I had a passable poker face, but my expression must have given away my horrified reaction, because Danielle made a face back at me. "What? I didn't think it would kill her."

The room was silent for a moment as I pondered everything Danielle had just told us.

Laurel was the one who finally broke the silence.

"Danielle, I really, really have to go to the bathroom. It can't wait."

"I said no."

"C'mon, Danielle, I can't hold it anymore."

Danielle thought for a second. "Okay, but give me your phone first. And no funny business. Remember that I have a gun on your partner here."

Laurel stood and stretched as she let out a big yawn, causing me to reflexively yawn in response. "Sorry, I can't seem to stay awake." No sooner had the words left her mouth than she clutched at a nearby table.

"Are you okay?" Laurel couldn't possibly be drunk off the half glass of wine she'd had.

By way of response, Laurel slumped to the floor.

"Laurel!" I cried, jumping up to help her.

Danielle spun around and trained the gun on me, a fierce intensity in her eyes. "You! Stay right where you are!" She went over to Laurel and nudged her with her foot, but Laurel was out cold.

Come to think of it, Danielle didn't seem particularly surprised. In fact, she looked rather pleased with herself.

Laurel's half-empty glass sat next to her chair. Had Danielle added something to our wine, like a sedative? My heart started racing. *Or was it something even worse? Please dear God, don't let it be lethal.*

"Danielle, you don't want to do this," I said, the panic rising in my voice.

"You've left me no choice. You shouldn't have even brought her here."

"Did you put something in her drink? We need to call an ambulance."

"Now why would I go and do that? Kind of defeats the purpose, doesn't it?"

"C'mon, Danielle, Babs' death—that was an accident. You don't want to go down this path."

"I don't want to go to jail, either. The police might have believed me that Babs was an accident, but two accidents? No way."

"And when they discover our bodies in your office, then what are you going to do?"

"Oh, don't be such a worrywart. It's not going to kill you. You'll just have a nice long nap. Now, be a good girl and drink your wine. You don't want to seem like an ungrateful guest, do you?"

I quickly weighed my options—and they weren't looking good. If I was going to help Laurel, I'd have to stay awake. I crossed my arms in front of me and shook my head. "I'm not drinking it."

"It's either *that,* or this," she said, holding her gun up. "Doesn't a nice glass of wine sound like the better of the two options?"

Well, sure, of the two . . .

"Besides," she said, "guns are just so *messy,* don't you think?"

She had me there. I lifted the glass to my lips but kept them firmly closed to keep from ingesting any of the wine. Then I swallowed as convincingly as possible.

"More," Danielle demanded, pointing the gun at me. "You hardly drank any at all."

Laurel was still on the floor passed out cold, and my mind raced as I tried to decide what to do. I wasn't willing to roll the dice that Danielle was just trying to escape and not to destroy the evidence—the "evidence" being me and Laurel.

I quickly calculated which course of action would be the bigger risk.

"No, I drank most of it." I held the glass out for her inspection. "See?"

Danielle scowled and took a step toward me. "No you didn't! You just pretended."

Right when she leaned forward to inspect my still-full glass, I flung the wine in her face and dropped to the floor as a shot rang out from right above my head. I scrambled under the desk and popped out the other side, ready to make a run for it and hoping like crazy that Danielle wasn't actually prepared to shoot someone in her own office.

"Stand up," Danielle demanded from across the desk. Her hands were shaking, and the way the whites of her eyes were showing made her look more than a little unhinged.

"Danielle, think about this." My heart pounded in my throat. "If you shoot me, there's no way you'll be able to cover it up. You won't even be able to claim it was an accident."

"I won't have to!" she said. "I'm going to call 911 right now and tell them I think I hear an intruder downstairs. I'll beg them to hurry. After all, someone's been killing off wedding planners— probably you—so if I shoot you in self-defense, who could blame me?"

She kept both her eyes and her gun trained on me as she pulled her phone from her back pocket, then glanced down to punch in the three digits. "Yes, I'd like to report an intruder," she began. "I'm at 831 West Bellevue and—" Before she could finish, there was a sudden movement from the floor as Laurel sprang up out of nowhere. She ran toward Danielle and body-slammed her as hard as she could, knocking them both to the floor.

Scrambling around the desk, I jumped on top of Danielle, holding her down while she thrashed around on the floor. Laurel tried to wrest the gun from her hand, and it went off again, shattering a Tiffany floor lamp. Danielle fought like a cat at bath time, limbs flying in all directions.

"You get her legs!" I yelled. I grabbed Danielle's right arm and slammed it repeatedly against the hardwood floor until she was forced to release the gun. Danielle and I both lunged for the discarded weapon, but I got there first since I didn't have Laurel grabbing on to my feet. Relief flooded my body as I grabbed the gun and turned it on Danielle.

"Laurel! You're alive!"

She got up from the floor and dusted herself off. "Yep! I'm not even sleepy."

"You were playing possum?" I asked, impressed by my friend's acting ability.

"I knew that wine didn't taste right, and then she kept watching to see if we were drinking it. So I poured half of it into that ficus tree over there when she wasn't looking."

The sounds of police sirens blared in the distance, and Danielle jumped to her feet with a panicked look in her eyes. "The police are here. If you let me go, you can escape out the back before they get here."

I crinkled my forehead at her. "What are you talking about? We're not going anywhere. You just confessed to killing Babs Norton."

"Or another way to look at it is you broke in here and now

you're holding a gun on me," she said. "I guess we'll see which one of us they believe. Especially since you're already a suspect."

I couldn't wait for the cops to arrive, if for no other reason than to shut her up. "You're not going anywhere."

Laurel ran over to the window to look for the squad cars, whose sirens were growing louder and louder.

An expression of calm crossed Danielle's face as she walked over and removed her coat from the coatrack. "Actually, come to think of it, *ladies,* I think this is my cue to leave."

"Stop right there!" I yelled.

"Oh, come on, you're not going to shoot me. If you do, they'll arrest you immediately for my murder—and you'll never recover from that."

There was no denying that it would look pretty bad if they came in and found me hovered over Danielle's dead body.

"Ah, go ahead and shoot her," Laurel said.

Danielle and I both turned to Laurel in shock. "I don't know, Laurel, I think she might be right."

"Nah, I called 911 back when I hit the floor and they've been listening ever since." She smiled proudly as she held up the phone display for us to see.

Danielle dropped the coat and sagged against the door frame. "Oh my God, what have I done?" She sank to the floor and put her head on her knees.

Tires screeched to a halt outside, and flashing red and blue lights danced on the curtains. The front doorbell chimed loudly and Laurel buzzed them up from a keypad by the door.

I turned to Laurel and smiled as heavy footsteps clambered up the stairs. "I take back what I said."

"What's that?" Laurel asked.

"You make an excellent lookout."

CHAPTER 34

*B*y the time we went downstairs, a crowd of neighbors and passersby had gathered on the sidewalk. For their efforts, they got the special honor of seeing Danielle Turpin being escorted to a squad car in handcuffs, a royal perp walk for the short-lived Queen of Wine Country Weddings.

Members of the crowd whispered and pointed, and some of the younger ones took videos with their phones. Danielle scowled at them, but seeing as how she would have been texting everyone in the tri-county region if she were a bystander, she didn't really have any room to judge.

When the police took our statements, I was tempted to ask them if they could call my BFFs at the SFPD and let them know they could scratch me off their suspect list, but I figured they'd find out soon enough. It felt good knowing that I wouldn't have to endure any more questions from Detective Blaszczyk and his sidekick, Ryan—unless the question was, *Would you like to go to dinner?* to which my answer would be, *Sure, but not with you.*

On the drive home, we called Brody and gave him the highlights, instructing him to have ice cream waiting for us back at his apartment if he wanted the full story.

He greeted us at the door with a hug, then quickly ushered us into the kitchen, where he'd set out a buffet of Ben & Jerry's ice cream. Four cartons were lined up along his granite counter-tops, lids off and spoons at the ready.

"I know what flavor you eat when you're happy, and which one you eat when you're on a diet—which seems self-defeating, but we can talk about that another time—but I wasn't sure what flavor you prefer when you've been held at gunpoint."

"All of the above," I said, scanning the selection. I grabbed a carton of Chunky Monkey, just because I had to start somewhere. "And thank you."

We settled in on the couch, and while I recounted the evening's events we polished off a quantity of ice cream that was probably more than what would be considered therapeutic.

Brody listened intently, occasionally interrupting to clarify important facts. "So, wait, you were going to let Kelsey drink the poisoned wine?"

"It wasn't poisoned," insisted Laurel. "Just drugged."

"Still, you were going to let her drink it?"

"Right?! That's what I said!" I was grateful for Laurel's quick thinking, but things could have gone very differently if her plan had backfired.

"Kelsey never drinks when she's on duty, and I knew she wasn't going to start now."

"I guess you know me better than I thought." I scraped the last drops of Peanut Butter Cup from the bottom of the carton. "Still, a heads-up would have been nice."

"That's cool," Laurel said. "I just saved our lives and all. No need to thank me."

I grabbed the Vanilla Toffee Bar Crunch and held it up in a toast. "Here's to your quick thinking and superior acting skills."

"Hear, hear!" Brody said as we all clicked spoons.

"Does this mean I can take tomorrow off?" she asked.

"Definitely. We're closed tomorrow. The wedding world can wait."

By the next morning, Danielle's arrest was all over the news. By noon, I'd gotten so many calls, texts, and e-mails that I decided to turn my ringer to silent just to get a break. Not that I didn't love being able to clear my name, but the sheer volume of calls was starting to overwhelm me.

As I went to switch the phone off, I saw Haley Bennett's name on the caller ID. Oh, jeez, she was out a wedding planner. *Again.*

I took a deep breath before answering. "Hello?"

"Kelsey, it's Haley! I just heard Danielle got arrested!"

So the word was out. "Yeah, it's been quite a week."

There was a pause on the other end of the line. "Did she really do all those things they're saying she did?"

"Yeah, I'm afraid so." Suddenly I felt embarrassed, like Danielle's behavior was a bad reflection on me. "I'm so sorry. If I'd had any idea, I would never have recommended her."

"Of course," Haley said. "I know you wouldn't. She had us all fooled."

The memory of her dad standing in my office right after seeing his name on the murder board flashed through my mind and I winced. He may have been guilty of having an affair, but he hadn't been a killer, and I knew firsthand how bad it felt to be a suspect. "Will you do me a favor and tell your dad that I'm really sorry for thinking he had anything to do with it?"

"I will. Although he's got bigger things on his mind right now.

My stepmom found out about the affair with Babs, so he's in pretty hot water."

"Yikes." I was dying to ask her more about that, but I decided this was one time when I would just mind my own business. "So other than that, how are you doing?"

"I don't know. This whole thing has gotten so out of hand. Dad wanted to give me the wedding of my dreams, but the whole thing's turned out to be a nightmare."

"I'm so sorry. I can give you the name of another planner if you want. There's not usually this much drama. I swear!"

Haley laughed. "Oh, I know." She paused. "Any chance I could talk *you* into helping us out?"

"Oh, Haley, I don't know. . . ."

"I know things got kind of weird with my dad, but he'll be fine. He's on his best behavior right now."

I rubbed one temple as I thought back to our last meeting. "Yeah, it's just . . . I kind of accused him of murdering someone." In other words, *awkward.*

"Would it make you feel any better if I told you he thought you did it?"

A loud laugh burst from my lips before I had a chance to stop it. "Not really."

"Well, now he knows you didn't. Can't we just call it even?"

"I don't know, Haley. I want to help, I really do, but I really don't want to be involved with any weddings at Higgins Estate." Maybe it wasn't entirely rational—after all, neither Lucas nor Miles had actually killed anyone—but so far, that place had caused nothing but regret.

"I get it, especially after everything that's happened." She sounded a little wistful. "Dad wanted us to do it there to impress his friends, the bigger the better, you know? But it doesn't even feel like my wedding anymore. If I had my way, I'd just have it out under the trees somewhere."

A lightbulb went off in my head. "What are you doing right now?"

"Nothing," she said, her voice curious. "Why?"

"Let's go for a ride."

A week later, I was standing with Haley and her bridesmaids at the top of the path leading down to the old barn behind Jake's tasting room. The live oak tree was strung with all the twinkle lights Laurel and I could find on short notice, creating a glow that lit up the entire area. Underneath the tree, Christopher waited beneath an archway of flowers, a huge smile lighting up his handsome face. Farley sat nearby, wagging his tail enthusiastically while dutifully obeying the command to "stay."

Of course, Jake and Brody had been more than happy to pitch in to get everything done in time. After all, Brody's staged photo shoot was now a real photo shoot, and Prentice Vineyard was hosting their first official wedding.

"Kelsey, I can't thank you enough," Haley said. "I can't even imagine how you made all this happen."

I smiled and wiggled my fingers at her. "I'm magic."

Haley laughed. "I really think you are!"

Despite what I'd told Haley about not wanting to go back to Higgins Estate, I had made one more trip through their grand front gates. During a meeting with Lucas, I'd explained that not only would he need to find a different wedding planner to work with, but that Haley and Christopher wanted out of their contract.

When he declined—which, to be fair, I assumed he would—I offered him a little extra incentive. Namely, I would let him be the one to tell Miles about the pipeline agreement and, as a special added bonus, I wouldn't go to the press.

It was no surprise that Lucas had agreed to my terms, and I told him if he ever needed someone to plan another wedding at Higgins he should be sure to call anyone but me.

All in all, it had been a productive meeting. And now Haley and I were both enjoying the wedding of our dreams.

Laurel and I sat in the back row as the couple said "I do" underneath the giant oak tree.

"Wait," Laurel said as the ceremony was coming to a close. She pulled out a tissue and handed it to me. "You're leaking."

"Damn allergies," I said as I patted gently under each eye.

After the officiant was done pronouncing them husband and wife, we rolled open the doors to the barn and invited everyone inside for the reception. Vintage chandeliers hung from the wide beams, candles flickered on every table, and loose arrangements of roses and hydrangeas in pinks, ivories, and greens cascaded from every surface.

The crowd murmured appreciatively, and I could tell from the oohs and aahs that we'd achieved the desired effect.

After dinner, Laurel and I watched while Haley and Christopher shared their first dance. Jake had called in a favor from a great swing band he knew, and they were more than happy to help inaugurate the space. Afterward, the rest of the guests crowded onto the dance floor to join them, and even Mr. Bennett and his wife, Yvonne, seemed to be having a good time. I couldn't help but think what a different scene it would have been if the evening's festivities had been at Higgins Estate.

During a break in the music, Christopher jumped up on the

stage and borrowed the mic. "Haley and I wanted to thank every-body for coming. It means so much to us to have you all here." A few cheers rippled through the crowd along with a congratula-tory whistle. "We also wanted to thank our wedding planners, Kelsey and Laurel. I don't know how they did it, but they pulled off the impossible, and we can't imagine having a better wedding day than this."

As everyone burst into applause, I turned several shades of pink. I mean, sure, we'd pulled off an awesome wedding while si-multaneously fighting crime, but I wasn't doing it for the attention.

Not content to let me enjoy the moment anonymously, Laurel pushed me out of the shadows, then pointed at me just to make sure everyone knew who I was. I smiled and waved to the crowd, then took a few steps back. "You are so fired," I said as the band started up the next song and everyone resumed dancing.

"Yeah, right. What would you do without me?"

I laughed. "Okay, fine. You're the wind beneath my wings."

"That's more like it."

"Hey," said a voice behind me. I turned around to see Jake, who had crept up beside me.

"Hey yourself," I said, my heart fluttering—and not just because he'd startled me. It was the first time I'd seen him in person since our picnic with Brody—we'd talked a couple of times, but in all the excitement we hadn't had a chance to go on our date—and I'd forgotten just how dreamy his dreaminess could be.

"Wanna dance?" he asked, gesturing toward the floor.

"I'm on duty," I said, blushing.

"C'mon, I paid a lot for that floor. The least you could do is help me enjoy it."

"It is a pretty nice floor."

Jake led me to the dance floor, and as the music slowed he pulled me in close. "I wanted to thank you again for everything you did."

"Oh, don't mention it," I said, secretly pleased that he had mentioned it.

"This is going to be great for the winery." He pointed to a woman across the way. "That lady over there asked me if I have any dates open in October."

"You'd better get used to it. You're going to be booked solid before you know it."

"And it's all thanks to you."

I looked over at Haley and Christopher, who were enjoying a slow dance and whispering in each other's ears, smiles plastered on their newlywed faces. "I'd say it worked out pretty well all around."

"Maybe we could collaborate on something else," he said.

I looked up into his blue eyes. "Like what?"

"Like this." He leaned in and kissed me on the lips, right there in front of everybody.

"Oh, um . . ." I glanced around to see if anyone was watching. All eyes were on the bride and groom, as they should be, so I turned my attention back to Jake. "I'd like that."

After one more song, I excused myself to check on the cake. It didn't really need checking on; I just needed to take a break before I got too distracted. After all, it was Haley and Christopher's night.

I took a sweep around the room to make sure everything was running like it should, then planted myself off to the side. It wouldn't be long until it was time to hand out sparklers and send them off on their honeymoon, but for now I had a moment to relax and enjoy.

Brody sidled up next to me. "So, you and Jake Schmake, huh?"

"We're going to have to come up with a better nickname than that."

"Why? You don't want to be Mrs. Schmake?"

Jake was across the room talking to some guests, and he smiled when he caught us looking at him. "If you ever tell him I called him that, I'm going to kill you."

"We'll see." Brody snapped a picture right as I lifted my glass of champagne toward Jake and smiled. "And also? You're welcome."

A moment later, Laurel joined us, and we watched Christopher twirl Haley around and dip her before planting a big kiss on her mouth. Laurel sighed contentedly. "Look how happy they are. This was such a good call."

I nodded in agreement, a feeling of pride swelling in my chest. "Yeah, funny how things work out."

Although it wasn't the wedding Babs would have planned, I couldn't help but think she would have approved.